WHO

THE BANQUO LEGACY
ANDY LANE & JUSTIN RICHARDS

BBC

Published by BBC Worldwide Ltd,
Woodlands, 80 Wood Lane
London W12 0TT

First published 2000
Copyright © Andy Lane & Justin Richards 2000
The moral right of the author has been asserted

Original series broadcast on the BBC
Format © BBC 1963
Dr Who and TARDIS are trademarks of the BBC

ISBN 0 563 53808 2
Imaging by Black Sheep, copyright © BBC 2000

Printed and bound in Great Britain by Mackays of Chatham
Cover printed by Belmont Press Ltd, Northampton

Dedications

Andy:

To Deborah Powell, in the unlikely event that you ever
read this, for persuading me to remove the line 'my heart
leaped within me like a salmon' and thus rendering the
book readable at least.

And to Justin Richards, Craig Hinton, Andrew Martin and
Mike Nicholson – friends then and friends now.

Justin:

For Alison, Julian and Christian, as and for ever.
And to friends then and now: Andy (of course), Andrew,
Craig, Dave, David, Gary, both Peters, other Andrew, and the
rest of the DumbleCon crowd. And Steve.

Front Matter

Beginnings: 1798

Even the kitchen windows had bars, despite being set so high up the solid walls. Quite ridiculous, mused Thomas Jeffries out of habit rather than insight as he lifted the tray of plates and set off on his last journey down the long cold corridor. Only one more tray, then he could get home.

Home. Warm and dry, his own supper waiting and Jane sitting by the fire nursing William. Only the echo of his nailed boots on the hard floor prevented Thomas from slipping completely into reverie. Not long now, if he could only survive the storm outside.

Perhaps, he thought, Pamela would want to talk. She often did. He enjoyed listening to her, despite her childlike nature. She would tell him how beautiful the storm was and how she was not in the least frightened by it. And he would tell her about what was happening in the village, all the local gossip. How her cousin was up at the Manor, and what they were saying this week about her dead grandmother. Pamela would tell him how silly they all were and how they ought to be looked after properly. And Thomas would laugh and leave her to eat her bread, hoping the storm would soon abate.

A piercing scream rebounded along the corridor. Thomas absently kicked at the door it came from as he passed. He was wondering again why William was such a sickly child. Best not to worry, Doctor Merrick had said.

Pamela too had been a sickly child when Thomas had first seen her four years ago – was it really that long? Now she was fit and healthy. A healthy body if not a healthy mind.

'Why is she here?' he had asked. And they had told him. He still found it hard to believe. She was a good girl. Slow and childlike even now, her attitude lagging behind her nineteen years. But she meant well. Everything she said and did she believed in her heart was for the best. So few worries. For Thomas, even the small cut on the neck from shaving remained an annoyance as it rubbed against his starched collar.

He balanced the tray on one hand as he pushed the key into the lock with the other. A metallic scrape, a staccato click, and the heavy door swung slowly open.

She noticed at once. 'What have you done?' Pamela's eyes were wide with worry.

'It's only a scratch. From my razor.' He put down the tray, fingers grazing at the thin red line.

'But, doesn't it hurt, Thomas?'

He laughed at her concern. 'It's just a little blood. That's all.'

She looked at him for a moment, thoughtful. 'I must kiss it well again for you,' she said at last.

He laughed at her serious manner. 'All right.' He wished he had a daughter like her, to help nurse his sick son.

She stepped closer, her eyes fixed on the scratch at his neck. He smiled as she reached up and put her arms round his head. Her lips closed warmly on the thin red scratch as she closed her eyes.

He felt strangely tense, despite her closeness and the moisture of her mouth sucking slightly at his neck. Thomas closed his arms around her, protecting her, and felt the heat from her body as he embraced it.

'*She killed a cat.*'

He heard the voice drifting out of the dead years, and then his own voice answering. 'That hardly seems enough.'

An invisible chuckle. And then: '*She drank its blood,*' came the cold reply as she buried her teeth in his soft throat.

For a second his frame went rigid. Then he relaxed, his weight falling on her receiving body as his warmth and life throbbed into her. She held him upright, pressed hard against her hot breast, her mouth wide open.

After a while she opened her eyes, relaxed. She listened to the moon-red rain spattering against the flagstones outside and the blood dripping to the floor. She felt warm and vital. Ready to go out. Ready to play.

Robert Dodds – *the* Robert Dodds – tied his dressing gown cord with a flourish. Hands lightly but firmly in the pockets, he looked around the chamber.

'Get thee to bed,' he said hugely to a chair by the window, then turned smartly towards the door. He removed a cigar from the box on the dressing table and held it cradled in his hands in front of him. He glared at it furiously, eyebrows knitted in concentration as from the base of his stomach he declaimed: 'Is this –'

He broke off, concentration suddenly snapped, and glanced around. Nothing seemed amiss. So why was he suddenly so nervous? He felt a chill, as if a door had been opened and the storm outside was working its way in towards him. He knew that some actors were deeply superstitious, especially when dealing with 'the Scottish Play'. But Dodds was not one of them – *Macbeth* held no fears for him.

'Is this', he repeated, 'a dagger which I see before me, The handle toward my –' He broke off again. He was sure it was the handle, but what was it 'toward'? With theatrical disdain Dodds raised the cigar to his mouth. Banquo was a far better part, anyway. One that only a true genius (such as, for example, himself) could fully bring to life. A fitting memorial for his late, beloved aunt. His late, beloved, rich aunt.

Dodds looked around his bed chamber again, satisfying himself that the legacy was intact. Property – a sound investment. But already the house made strange noises. He could swear that earlier he had heard someone moving downstairs. But he knew the house to be empty.

Smiling at his own foolish fancies, Dodds placed the cigar precisely on his desk, between blotter and hourglass, and prepared (right hand over heart) to deliver his finale. Banquo Manor would once again re-echo to the words of Shakespeare, the words of his master creation: Banquo himself.

He cleared his throat into a silk-red handkerchief. Then, pushing the kerchief back into a pocket, he raised a hand and bellowed, 'Hold, take my sword.'

A creak from the landing. The house seemed to appreciate the immaculate performance.

'There's husbandry in Heaven...'

The gas lamp looked on, with cold indifference as the candles on the bed sputtered nervously...

'Their candles are all out.'

...and went out, as if caught in a draught.

'Take thee that too.' Dodds held out his imaginary dagger. He was defenceless now. 'A heavy summons lies like lead upon me, and yet I would not sleep.'

The creaking seemed closer now – as if approaching down the ill-lit corridor outside. And from further away there was another creaking – a rhythmic, mechanical grating.

'Merciful powers.' His voice had gained all the frightened nuances of reality, as if the creaking of the floorboards was gesturing to him, hastening him to the end of his performance. He tried to regain a grip on his shaking emotions. 'Restrain in me the cursed thoughts...'

Was that shadow in the doorway somehow deeper now than it had been?

'...that nature gives way to in repose.'

No, surely it was his imagination. An unreal shadow, as in a bad dream. Yet still it seemed to be gaining form and substance.

'Give me my sword.' Dodds was sure now: there was someone outside in the corridor. His hand closed on nothing, and he realised at last that there was no sword. 'Who's there?' he stammered.

'A friend.' The voice was light and honeyed, a young woman. It seemed to cloy.

Dodds felt suddenly sick. And the formless shadow in the doorway stepped forward into the light.

He had seen only her a few times, and then to ease his aunt's – her grandmother's – conscience rather than his own. But he recognised her at once. Instinctively.

At first he thought that she had fallen down in the grounds, that she was wet from the rain and mud. But as she stepped further into the diffuse light he realised his mistake, and backed away.

Her long hair was soaked, plastered to her head and then falling in thick bunches across her shoulders. Several stray strands had blown forward and down over the material that clung wetly to her bosom. Against the dirty white of the shift he could see that she was drenched red. Her bare feet were muddy, and about her ankles were splashes of dried blood. Some were from the cuts and scratches on her feet and legs from the long walk. But not all. The shift itself was still near white at the top, but lower down, while just as wet, clinging to her body as if she had bathed in it, the material became progressively darker.

His first thought was that she had met with an accident, but then he saw the red light in her eyes and the dried blood that caked her mouth and chin, which had dripped and streaked down her body. And he saw a dagger before him, its point towards his heart.

In the same moment he felt his back meet the wall and begin to prickle as the perspiration sought out a space to run down from his pores.

There was a flash like lightning behind his eyes as the knife – from his own kitchen, though he scarcely had time to remark it – was driven up past his ribs and into his heart. He felt his sweat freeze and saw his blood splash over her. His arm lashed out unbidden across the table, catching the hourglass, knocking it on its side and shattering the lower bowl.

'Our time –' he gasped. But he could not finish the line. Already he could feel the blood as it rose in his throat and she pushed the knife back into his chest. He felt a sudden final impulse to catch the grains of sand as they trickled over the edge of the table to the floor. But they fell dryly through his fingers and he felt the floor smash into his falling shoulder.

For a split second he saw her standing beautiful over him, the knife dripping like her gory locks as she raised it again. Then the image glazed and the crimson of her mouth and hair blurred until everything was scarlet and silent.

She let the knife slip to the floor and knelt down over him, pulling the stained dressing gown away from his ripped torso. She held her face close against his chest and let the blood bubble and gush into her mouth and nose and eyes. Laughing into it. She felt clean at last, rubbing handfuls of the liquid over her hair and face, into her cold stomach and wet breasts, bathing in his death.

The still, gaunt figure in the doorway watched impassively. 'It seems I'm just in time,' it murmured.

Arrival: 1898

'What the hell's going on?' Fitz shouted above the maelstrom of noise. It was the third time he had shouted the same question. It was the third time he got no answer.

The light was a blood-red strobe that scythed back and forth through the blackness of the console room. Compassion's cries were quieter now, but the anguish, the hurt, was every bit as intense. They mixed in with the roar and scrape of materialisation.

The Doctor was clinging to the console with one hand; the fingers of his other hand rattled over the controls and he peered at readouts, snatching information from the flashes of illumination as the light passed.

Fitz was sprawled across a chair, afraid to move in case he was tipped out and flung around the bucking floor. 'Will someone please –' he shouted again.

'Power drain.' The Doctor did not seem to be shouting, but nonetheless his voice was clearly audible as he cut across Fitz. 'Ninety per cent loss of Artron energy.'

'Artron what?' Fitz gave him five seconds before adding. 'Sorry, I expect you're busy with… stuff.'

'See if I can stabilise the systems. Hang on, Compassion!' The Doctor's hands were a blur of stop-motion in the flashing light, seeming simultaneously to be poised in three different positions.

'What about emergency backup power things?'

'They use Artron energy too.'

'Can I help?' Fitz asked, making no effort to move. His stomach lurched with the floor. 'Or shall I just keep quiet for a bit then?'

'That would actually be a help.'

He said nothing. Was it his imagination or was the noise diminishing now? He strained to hear the sound of Compassion's engines, her materialisation noise, above her shrieks of pain. It was not pleasant, and he ached for her more than he would have thought. She was sarcastic and caustic, indifferent and aloof, emotionless and unfeeling. But for all that there was a bond between them. He liked to think that somewhere, under that cool heartless exterior was... well, something at least. Listening to anyone crying in pain was difficult. But when it was a friend, someone you –

The crying stopped. The floor straightened itself out. The light settled into a dull blood-red glow rather than a hysterical searchlight.

'Well done, Doctor.' Fitz leaped out of his chair and joined the Doctor at the console.

'I did nothing,' the Doctor confessed.

Fitz shrugged. 'Well done anyway. Whatever.'

'How are you?' the Doctor asked. There was concern on his face, his eyes were glistening.

Fitz was touched. 'Oh, I'm fine, actually.'

'Not you,' the Doctor told him.

'Dying.' Compassion's answer was from all around them. But it was weak, difficult, broken: 'I – am – dying, Doctor.' A pause, the sound of a faint sigh. Then: 'What is happening to me?'

The Doctor was shaking his head. 'I don't know. An almost total loss of Artron energy.' His face was grey, lined, as he looked at Fitz. 'I feel it myself.'

'It's what you run on?' Fitz asked in surprise.

'In a manner of speaking. It's a... well, a source of energy.'

'Like sugar?'

'Like oxygen.'

Fitz stared. Gaped. '*You're* dying?' His voice was a whisper.

The Doctor shook his head. 'Oh no. Well, not yet. But I couldn't regenerate, which is something of a worry.'

'Tell me about it,' Fitz muttered. 'And Compassion?' he asked more loudly.

8

The Doctor was edging round the console, checking controls and stabbing ineffectively at buttons. 'It's everything to her. There's some sort of inhibitor in operation nearby. Locked on to us as we started to materialise.'

'The – Time – Lords,' Compassion's voice gasped.

'Is it?'

The Doctor tapped his chin. 'Could be. Could be,' he conceded. 'I don't know how they could have found us, could have predicted we would be here, wherever *here* is. But it's a deliberate attack, I'm sure.'

'Help me, Doctor.' Above them, Compassion's face washed hazily into view on the scanner, distorted by the weakness of the image. And by pain. 'There is a transtemporal emission. I'm blocking it.' Every word was an effort now.

'What's that in human-speak?'

'The Time Lords,' the Doctor said. His fist slammed down on the console. 'Or some agent of theirs. Sending a message to Gallifrey, telling them where and when we are.'

'But if Compassion is blocking it...'

'For the moment. She's getting weaker by the second.'

'Stabilised now.' Her voice was still drained. 'But won't last. Blocking the signal for as long as I can.'

'While we find the inhibitor,' the Doctor said. His frown deepened suddenly. 'How did you manage that?' His hands flew over the controls and a stream of text and symbols spewed across Compassion's face above them. 'I see. Very clever.' There was pride as well as admiration in his voice, as if he reckoned he deserved some of the credit.

Well, Fitz thought, he probably did. Whatever it was for. 'And for the hard of deciphering?' he prompted.

'We were plucked out of the vortex and materialised in midair. Thrown across the sky like a comet.' Sudden levity now as the Doctor considered. 'Probably very spectacular.'

'Yes, I felt that bit,' Fitz agreed.

'But Compassion has managed to latch on to a local host for her outer plasmic shell. Something approximating her natural appearance that can provide a surrogate shell until we disable the inhibitor. Gives her stability and us time.'

'Neat,' Fitz said. 'I assume.'

The Doctor was nodding in appreciation. 'Oh yes, very neat. Now we need to get out of here before we're trapped inside. As she loses more power, Compassion will lose her ability to create a portal through the shell.'

Fitz thought about this as the Doctor buttoned his coat. 'So,' he said slowly, 'given the choice, we're going to get ourselves trapped outside instead of inside. Right?'

'Right,' the Doctor agreed. 'In the snow.'

'In the snow.' Fitz considered this. 'With a Time Lord agent.'

'Very probably.'

'Who has immense powers and is waiting for us out there in the cold.'

The Doctor sucked in his cheeks, then blew out a long breath. 'I don't think he'll be that powerful,' he said at last. 'After all, his own Artron energy will be inhibited too. It's an all-or-nothing deal.' He frowned. 'I imagine.'

Fitz rubbed his eyes. It didn't really help. 'And we are, where? When?'

'Earth,' Compassion said. But her voice was not her own. It was softer, gentler somehow. 'England. Late nineteenth century.'

The Doctor rubbed his hands together in a gleeful gesture that was belied by his sombre expression. 'Quite my favourite time and place,' he said. 'Given the choice, if I had to be trapped in one time and place –'

'Then I'd choose about a hundred years from now,' Fitz interrupted. 'What', he continued, 'has happened to Compassion's voice?'

'Come on, don't dawdle, we haven't much time,' the Doctor said. 'And in answer to your question,' he continued as the doors swung slowly, almost painfully open, 'I imagine it's already taking on the properties of the new outer shell. Of the host.'

As he followed the Doctor through the doors, the implications began to dawn on Fitz.

The Doctor's voice was faint, muffled, distant as it floated back to him. 'Unless I'm much mistaken, personality erosion will follow as Compassion's energy drains away. We can't let her slip away too far or even her primary focus of blocking the transmission will fail. And after that her systems will shut down completely as she drains the energies of the host entity as well. They're an organic gestalt. Inevitably there will be some confusion of identities. And if one of them dies…'

But Fitz was still working it out as he tumbled headlong out of Compassion. He was cold, he was wet, he was struggling to his feet in a moonlit sea of snow. 'You're telling me,' he spluttered, 'that this *host*, which is the closest match Compassion could find to what you call "her natural appearance", is –' He stopped short as he caught sight of the figure standing there, watching them.

'Obviously,' the figure that was and was not Compassion said.

Fitz jumped as a hand tapped him on the shoulder. He swung round quickly. Behind him the Doctor was smiling. 'So far so good.'

'The house is this way,' she said. 'Did you get lost?'

Fitz and the Doctor both turned slowly to stare at her.

'You must be exhausted after your long journey. Let me show you the way.'

'Confusion of identities?' Fitz asked. He was having trouble tearing his eyes away from her. 'Stunning gestalt, by the way,' he said, to the woman's evident confusion.

'You know,' the Doctor replied quietly, 'I think it's going to be one of those days.'

Finale: 1968

It was a room for the dying. Everyone knew that, including the frail figure lying in the bed. What light there was struggled through the faded thin curtains and was absorbed by dusty surfaces. The sounds of the home were muffled by the door and the plasterboard-thin walls. Outside a Ford Corsair stuttered into uneasy, throaty life. A dog barked.

The door opened, old and cracked. Its creak mingled with the high-pitched nasal sigh of the breathing from the bed. A rectangle of yellow light was broken by the figure that shuffled into the room. A broken, angled silhouette. The figure in the bed twisted slightly to see, waved a weak and wrinkled hand.

'Is it time for tea already?' The old woman's voice was as reedy and hesitant as her breathing and her hand. 'I don't know where the time goes.' She gave up the struggle to lift her head and let it sink back into the crushed hollow of the pillow. 'Time.' She rattled a coughing laugh. 'I can hardly see any more, but I know what Time looks like. And I do know where it goes.'

'Time,' the dark figure repeated as it reached the bed. The door clicked shut behind it; the light faded back to a dusty gloom that shadowed the figure's face. 'It has taken me a long time to find you.'

The woman twisted, trying to crane her neck sideways so as to see who was standing beside the bed. 'Do I know you?' she murmured.

'We have met. A long time ago.'

'I'm sorry, I can't quite place your voice. I have met so many people, you see. And my eyes are not what they were.'

The dry rasping sound might have been a laugh. 'It took me over fifty years to recover,' the croaky voice said. 'Another twenty or more to find you.'

12

'So many people,' she repeated as if she had not heard. 'I have known so very many in my –'

'Time?' Again, the rasping laugh.

She struggled again to sit up, working her elbows into the mattress and shifting her weight. 'Are you sure we have met?'

'Very sure.'

She gave up and sank back again. 'They will bring the tea soon.'

'I don't think so.'

'Oh they always do, you know.'

'I know. But not today.'

'Oh.' She accepted that. No comment. No curiosity. If she screwed up her eyes, tried to focus, she could just make out the pinprick glint of another pair of eyes looking at her. It was blurred, it looked as if there were two sets of eyes. Shimmering, moving, scratching.

Scratching? She could hear scratching. His nails perhaps. A nervous gesture. She had known someone once who… But that was almost a lifetime ago.

'Did you come to talk?' she asked. 'About old times?'

'I came to read. About old times.'

'Then you are blessed with eyes that are better than mine.'

'Or cursed.' Her whining breaths mixed with his stertorous rasps. 'Where do you keep them? The manuscripts.'

'I don't know what you mean,' she lied, even as she felt her blood run cold.

'Where are they?'

'What manuscripts?'

'The account written by your late husband.'

'Ah.'

'And the one written by your former lover.'

She breathed heavily for a few moments, summoning up the breath to answer. 'You know of them?'

Another pause, as if he was considering his reply. Then: 'Obviously.'

That caught her. She felt it. And she knew that it was indeed time… 'They are in the middle drawer of the cabinet. I like to keep them close.' Her wrinkled hand described an arc towards the cabinet by the bed. Towards the drawer he had already opened.

He swept the tumbler and the small vase of dying flowers from the top with a gesture, and put the two sets of papers in their place. One was held together with rusted paperclips. They had left brown marks etched into the mottled paper. The other was bound with a faded, brittle ribbon. He snapped it, then reached into his jacket pocket.

'You know, I only read them the once,' she said. The scratching sound was louder now. A staccato tapping, at once rhythmic yet random. She peered through the gloom to see what he had placed beside the papers. There was something by each pile. He was turning the leaves of both manuscripts at once. She could see the blurred motion of the pages. And beside each, glinting, scratching shuffling was… She stretched slightly closer as she spoke. 'They brought back such memories.'

'I can listen as well as read,' he said softly. 'Tell me your memories. Everything. Somewhere in here, or here. Or in your mind.'

'Is what?'

'The answer. The information I need.'

'I remember…' she began. But then a breeze lifted the curtain slightly, allowed a little light to spill into the room.

And she caught sight of his face. His eyes. She gasped and sank back into the bed. 'How – how can you read?'

'I can't,' he told her. 'But I have friends who can.'

And in the same flutter of the curtain of time she remembered. And she saw what he had placed beside the papers on the cabinet. And the horror and the terror merely sharpened her memories.

Body

THE ACCOUNT OF JOHN HOPKINSON (1)

I knew that the snow would hamper my progress from the small railway station at Three Sisters to the Manor. But I needed to clear the fog from my mind and so, despite the additional inconvenience, I walked. The winter of 1898 was unusually cold in that part of South-East England, I recall. As the trees thinned out around the path, I found myself looking at Banquo Manor. Somehow, seeing it so suddenly, and noting the carriage drawing away down the drive having delivered my luggage, made me feel the more uneasy. There was no going back now.

I realised with a frown that I had stopped in my tracks, and mentally shook myself to wake up. I was, after all, only meant to be here for a few days, and if staying with an old friend also counted as work then so much the better. The presence of Richard Harries was something that I could well have done without, but since it was his experiment that I was here to witness this was scarcely feasible. What exactly it *was* that I was to witness I had no idea, but there had to be a solicitor present. And an observer from the Society for the Propagation of the Forensic Sciences; and probably Her Majesty as well, knowing Harries's penchant for the melodramatic, especially where his work was concerned.

Looking up at the Manor House it seemed the ideal setting for a strange, secret experiment – shrouded in snow yet with the bright sunlight flashing on its windows. Taken as a piece of architecture the house is a puzzle. Look at it straight and it is simply a house, about a hundred years old, stone-fronted, large and unremarkable. But look away, and there is always something that jars in the corner of the eye, some feature that is suddenly 'wrong'. Looking back it is impossible to see what is so wrong about it, and some other facet catches the attention. As I looked up at Banquo Manor from the edge of the frosty woods that afternoon I was overwhelmed that this sense of 'wrongness'. Suddenly it seemed that the geometry of the entire house was askew, and the window eyes laughed back at me in the sunlight. Each corner and line was perfect, yet as a whole the frontage seemed to add up to more than the sum of its angles, as if the straight lines were somehow curved, and the corners made up from edges that did not in fact meet. To claim that in that moment, paused on the snow-clad path, I felt some foreboding or premonition would be to read too much into my feelings. It was not odd that I was fascinated by the house in such a way – I always was, and seeing it again in the crisp clarity of the winter sunshine after being away from it for so long combined with my emotional confusion to emphasise the singular character of the place. As a 'legal man' I like to be able to explain and define everything in terms of exact precision, and Banquo Manor has always defied me in this. For this reason alone (and God knows there are sufficient others) it haunts me.

I reached the door to discover Simpson struggling gamely to manoeuvre my largest suitcase through it. His hair was perhaps showing just a shade more grey in the brown than it had on my last visit, but his face was the same solemn mask behind which no man could discern a thing. I suspected that he was really a comic player underneath. Every time I met Simpson I remembered some of his first words to me; I had gone out into the hallway in answer to the doorbell (I forget who was calling), but Simpson beat me to the hall and as he passed me he paused to report: 'I'm just going to the door, sir. To open it.' This explanatory habit coupled with the strange way in which he seemed unable not to peer down his nose at everybody, and the fact that his Christian name was, I had recently discovered, 'Cuthbert', was enough to endear him to me.

Simpson looked up as my shadow fell across his efforts to

manipulate my case: 'I'm just taking in your luggage, sir.'

I smiled, again trying to place his accent – it was either cynical and very correct or dragged up from the gutter by its bootlaces, but which I could never quite decide.

At last he managed to wrench my case lengthways through the broad opening, and disappeared suddenly from sight, leaving me alone on the doorstep with my small suitcase.

'It's all right, Simpson,' I called, 'I'll bring this one.' And I followed him into the hall.

Inside Sir George Wallace was waiting, watching as Simpson dragged my large case across to the stairs.

'John,' he exclaimed, and his grey eyes lit up as he offered his hand affectionately. I transferred the case and took his hand, feeling my own face brighten.

'Hello, George, old chap. You look well.'

'Oh, not so bad now.' He looked past me, down the hallway. 'Gordon not travelling with you?'

'No,' I said quickly. 'No, he's not. How's Elizabeth?'

'Fit as ever, thank you. Don't know how she manages it, and that's a fact.'

I laughed. 'You manage very well yourself.'

Sir George smiled and let go my hand at last. 'Well,' he said, 'get settled in and then come down for à glass. Be lunch before long I expect.'

He glanced up at Simpson, who had paused for breath at the half-landing.

'In about an hour, I gather, sir.'

Wallace nodded, and Simpson renewed his attack on the luggage.

'I'll just show Mr Hopkinson to his room, sir.'

Did he smile slightly as he said it, I wondered as I followed his struggling form up the stairs? As ever, I could not say for certain. I transferred my attention to wondering what I had in the case that could possibly be so heavy.

I unpacked my small suitcase first, and then washed the journey from my face and hands. They had given me the same room as always, off to the left of the corridor from the stairs. From it I had a good view from above and beside the front door, out over the grounds and my footprints walking backwards to the woods. I turned from the window and made an effort to heft my large suitcase up on to the bed, so as to be able to open and unpack it. In fact it came up so easily that I nearly fell over backwards. I surveyed its bulky shape on the bed and pictured Simpson's apparently desperate struggle to shift the comparatively light weight, and shook my head in amused disbelief. As I began to sort out some clothes to wear for lunch, my mind drifted back to less pleasant things – such as the strange purpose of my visit. And Richard Harries.

It was a quiet meal – not least because Harries did not attend. He took all his meals, I was informed by Wallace, in his 'laboratory' – or the conservatory, as it had been until Harries descended upon it. Quite why George tolerated Harries's presence I had never been quite sure, but the business of the last few days had raised one possibility in my mind.

'Still,' said Wallace, picking at the salad, 'not to worry. Soon be free of him, you know. Once he's performed this miracle for us tonight he'll be away showing it to all and sundry I expect.'

'What exactly is this "miracle", as you call it?' I enquired.

'Better ask him that. Damned nuisance, though.' Wallace pulled apart his piece of chicken and peered ruefully at it. 'Can't abide cold food,' he whispered confidentially, and his wife concealed a smile. Elizabeth missed very little.

'Richard has insisted that we send away the servants for the week,' she explained. 'Cook, both kitchen maids, the scullery maid, the gardener –'

'Why on earth should he do that?' I interrupted before she could enumerate the entire staff.

'Doesn't want any tongue-waggers. Getting worked up over nothing in my opinion,' scowled George. 'No cook, so no cooking.' He poked at a lettuce leaf with his fork.

'George managed to persuade him that we couldn't cope without Simpson,' Elizabeth continued. 'And he also let us keep on one of the others. George opted for Beryl rather than Cook. Didn't you, dear?'

George peered more closely at his chicken and said nothing. Beryl, waiting at the table, reddened slightly and moved back to the sideboard. She was a pretty young girl of about eighteen, with blonde hair, a small nose and a mouth that seemed slightly too wide. She had been with the Wallaces for about three years and lived with her parents in the village. Ever since I had known her, she had looked as though she was short of a few hours' sleep, but she was energetic enough in her usual work as a chambermaid.

At that moment Simpson returned, having taken a tray in to Harries, and refilled our glasses.

'I'll just refill your glass, sir,' he said quietly, reaching over my shoulder. 'Careful now, sir,' he added as I almost choked on a pickle. He straightened up, task completed. 'Professor Harries says would you care to join him in the conservatory sometime this afternoon, sir?'

I suspected that Professor Harries had in fact referred to the room as his 'laboratory', but Simpson liked to stick to the 'proper' terms for everything. Knowing Harries, I imagined that an answer was not required – only my presence.

'Does he?' I murmured in reply.

'Yes, sir,' said Simpson patiently, in a tone of voice that implied that I was accusing him of having invented the message.

'I should see him pretty early, if I were you, John,' Elizabeth Wallace said, allowing Beryl to remove her empty plate.

'Yes,' agreed her husband, 'I imagine Gordon will be here

soon. And Dr Friedlander, looking forward to finally meeting him, you know. Then Catherine arrives at three. You know what they're like when they get together, no stopping them.'

Dr Friedlander I had not heard of. But I knew Catherine, Richard's twin sister, who seemed his opposite physically just as she was similar psychologically. They were close. Very close.

'And Susan,' Elizabeth added.

'Who?' I asked.

'Susan Seymour. Richard's fiancée,' George told me.

'His what?' That was the first time I had ever heard of Susan Seymour. It was also the last until she arrived with Miss Harries later that afternoon; for, although I went to see Harries immediately after luncheon, he never once mentioned her.

THE REPORT OF INSPECTOR IAN STRATFORD (1)

Humankind cannot bear too much reality. We shy away from it, inventing excuses, reasons, justifications; anything, in fact, that stops us from confronting the truth. I was unaware of this simple fact for many years. Unaware and happy that way. That state of blissful ignorance persisted until the day that I met John Hopkinson and Dr Friedlander, and came face to face with…

But I am getting ahead of myself. Best that this story be told in order. Best that the conventions of proper form be observed.

Looking back on it now I find it strange that I was not involved with Banquo Manor from the start. I came into things at a slant, in such a way that I did not realise the full scope of the affair until it was too late to stop it. Far too late. In fact it was in the winter of 1898 at Mortarhouse College in Oxford that I took the first few steps towards the terrible legacy of Banquo Manor: a legacy that was to lead me through fields of horror before finally allowing me to find hope, and love.

It was winter, and bitterly cold with it. The grass of the front quad covered in snow; only the corners were visible, revealed by the careless footsteps of students in too much of a hurry to stick to the path. I stood at the bottom of some steps leading up to what I had been told was the hall by a passing student whom I had stopped. I had been there for ten minutes or more, staring at the period architecture and slowly freezing to death.

'Inspector Stratford?' came a voice from the top. I turned carefully, trying to keep my footing on the ice. 'One of the students told me you wanted to see me.'

The man was small and dapper, with a beard that clung like fungus to his cheeks, and discoloured teeth that were revealed when he smiled in greeting. 'Professor Sowerden?' I asked, my words frosting the air.

He nodded. 'Indeed I am, Inspector. Pleased to, ah, make your acquaintance.' The professor descended the steps and extended a polite hand. He was a lot smaller than I was, and rocked back on his heels as he looked up. 'What can I do for you?'

'I wanted to ask you a few questions about an ex-student of yours.'

The yellow teeth flashed again. 'In any trouble, is he? How terrible.'

'You could say that, sir.' I paused for effect. 'He's dead.'

Sowerden instantly looked contrite. 'Good Lord, who is it – *was* it, rather?'

'Gordon Seavers. I do not know if you remember him. It would have been about ten or eleven years ago.'

'Poor old Seavers,' muttered Sowerden, rocking back absently on his heels. 'Yes, I remember him. Quite distinctly.' He looked up at me. 'Look, ah, my scout is in my room at the moment. Perhaps we could walk…'

'Scout?'

'Oh, ah, cleaner. You know.'

'Yes, of course,' I replied with a cold smile. Little in-jokes, private languages, all the things I had noticed in my superiors at the Yard, the Commissioners and such like, this was where it all started. Almost as though they were a race apart.

'Not an Oxonian by any chance, Inspector?' said Sowerden, almost as though he had read my mind.

'No, sir.'

'Ah. Cambridge.'

'No, sir,' I said firmly as we moved off around the square. 'Perhaps you could tell me something about Gordon Seavers?'

'Yes, yes of course. Seavers was in my tutorial group for, ah, two years I think.'

'And you teach?'

'Oh – natural science. Yes, I've been here for donkeys' years.'

We turned right at the side of the quad, beside an imposing chapel. Two young men ran past in long black robes and mortar boards. One of them was still doing up a white bow tie.

'*Sub fusc,*' said Sowerden cryptically. 'They've all got to wear *sub fusc* during their exams. You, ah, didn't say how young Seavers died, Inspector. Murder, I assume.'

'No, sir, suicide.' We turned right again by an ivy-covered wall.

'Suicide?' his voice was faint. I turned to find he had turned off towards a doorway on the left.

'Yes, suicide,' I said following him. The doorway led through to a smaller quadrangle, with an irregular wall on the right.

'Fellows' Garden,' said Sowerden. He pointed towards a green-domed tower looking above the square. 'That's the Sheldonian Theatre,' he observed. 'Designed by Wren, you know. That's Christopher Wren, the architect.'

'I had realised, sir,' I hissed. The damned man was taking every opportunity to patronise me now that he had discovered I wasn't Oxbridge.

'What can you tell me about Gordon Seavers?' I asked, keeping my feelings to myself.

'Ah, morning, Rector,' said Sowerden as we passed a stout gentleman walking in the opposite direction. His reply was carried away by the morning breeze.

'Professor?'

'Sorry, Inspector?'

'Gordon Seavers. Could you tell me something about him?'

'Of course, of course. He was an average student. Not particularly bright, but a hard worker. Ah, seemed to get on pretty well with his peers, no problems settling in. He was a member of the college cricket team, I recall. Good all-rounder, proud to have him there. Ah, what else? Oh yes, he was engaged to a girl in St Anne's.'

'You have women here?' I was surprised.

'Oh yes. Four colleges of the dears. The fourth only opened this year.'

'Was there ever any gossip about Seavers, any rumours or suchlike?'

'No, ah, nothing like that. He was quite unremarkable.'

I stopped walking suddenly. It was time to get the interview back under my control again. 'If Gordon Seavers was so unremarkable, then how do you come to remember him so well?'

Sowerden merely flashed his teeth at me enigmatically. 'Oh, I have a comprehensive memory, Inspector. Quite comprehensive.' He sat down at a nearby bench and gestured for me to join him.

'Why did young Seavers kill himself, Inspector?' he asked.

'I was hoping you would shed some light on that, Professor.'

'So you don't know?'

'We are pursuing lines of enquiry. This happens to be just one of them. There is a chance that something in his past might have triggered him off.'

'As I thought. You don't know.'

'Not as yet, Professor.' Time to try another tactic. Sowerden was proving an elusive subject. 'Professor, correct me if I'm wrong, but you implied that Gordon Seavers was not a particularly bright student.'

'Quite true. Yes, quite true.'

'And that, although he was a hard worker, he failed really to shine at the subject.'

'You're generalising now, Inspector, but you are still correct. No, he didn't really "shine", as you so quaintly put it.'

'Then perhaps you could explain how Gordon Seavers became one of the top men in his field before his untimely death? He was a well-respected scientist held in great esteem by his contemporaries. All this from someone who failed to show any great aptitude for science?'

Sowerden was avoiding my eyes. 'Really, Inspector, I, ah, cannot be held responsible for the conduct of my students after they leave our hallowed halls. My opinion is just that: an opinion. For all I know he might have hidden his light under a bushel while he was here. It happens, you know. The atmosphere in Oxford can sometimes be a little… oppressive, shall we say? The presence of so many other talents can sometimes be off-putting. No, I'm afraid that I can't be of any further help to you. I've told you everything I know about the fellow. I'm sorry, Inspector, but the burden of finding a reason for his death rests on your shoulders. Ah, good luck. Now I'm afraid I shall be late for a class if I don't leave.'

He rose and extended a hand. 'Thank you so much for coming.'

'Thank you for your help,' I said grudgingly as he turned to walk away. After a few steps I remembered something.

'Oh, Professor?'

He turned unwillingly, 'Yes, Inspector?'

'Did you know a contemporary of Seavers? A man named Hopkinson. John Hopkinson.'

He paused for thought. 'Studied law, I believe. Here at Mortarhouse as well. Oh yes, he injured his ankle playing cricket in the college team; had to retire from the sport. Why?'

'No matter.'

As I left the college grounds I reflected on the interview. I got the impression that Sowerden was hiding something, but I didn't know what. Or why.

I left the spires to their dreams and returned to London.

THE ACCOUNT OF JOHN HOPKINSON (2)

I had not visited the house since Harries had moved in, and upon entering the conservatory I was surprised at the extent of the change. Most of the glass was blocked out, and tables and chests were adorned with haphazard pages of scrawled handwriting and weird collections of scientific equipment – bowls and tubes and beakers all linked together in extraordinary and disharmonious patterns. The centre of the room was all but filled with a long trestle table, with a few upholstered chairs (looted, I noticed, from a couple of the smaller bedrooms) scattered incongruously around it.

In one of the chairs, pen in one hand and a sheaf of notes in the other, sat the young figure of Richard Harries, like a worker ant in a cluttered nest deserted by its fellows. He was facing towards the concealed windows, so that I saw him side-on as I entered, silhouetted against one of the few unhindered panes of glass. His chin jutted forward slightly as he sifted through the papers, discarding some and holding on to others to reread, so that he appeared to possess a vaguely simian profile, which belied the expression of intense thought that wrinkled his brow. The tray of salad that Simpson had brought him lay untouched on the table.

After standing a moment taking in the changed decor, and noting appreciatively that the wall to one side of the door now boasted a large – and full – bookcase, I decided that Harries was not going to remark me of his own free will and coughed as loudly as I dared, oddly fearful of breaking the silence. Harries started, and looked up.

'Ah, Hopkinson – there you are. Good.'

He went back to his notes, leaving me feeling embarrassed and alone on the other side of the untidy room. 'Wait just a moment, and I'll be with you,' he continued at last.

Feeling for some reason that my presence was now

legitimate, I turned my attentions to the bookcase and looked along the titles. They seemed for the most part to be scientific journals and books, not by any means of uniform shape, size or age, but apparently meticulously ordered.

Glancing down one shelf I noticed such names as Burdon-Sanderson, Darwin and Ferrier, but the book I was most attracted to had nothing to do, as far as I could tell, with physiology, evolution or the brain. I noticed it most, despite its being on the shelf above the one I was looking at, because the script on its spine ran counter to the others in the bookcase, thus making it harder to read. Added to this, the single word was not a title or, possibly, author's name with which I was familiar. It said, in faded gold lettering up the old brown leather, *Necronomicon*. My curiosity enlivened, I pulled the book from between its shelf-fellows and opened it, only to find that it was not as I had suspected one of those annoying volumes that have the title stamped wrong side up along their backs, but had merely been replaced on the shelf upside down. I smiled and turned the book over, surprised at how free from dust it was compared with its companions.

A further surprise was that the text was in Latin. The language held no secrets from me of course, but I had not imagined Harries to be fluent in the tongue. Evidence perhaps of how I underestimated his abilities even at that late stage. I flicked through a few pages, then began to read a passage, translating it to myself as I went. While the style was odd to say the least, the content was by far stranger:

> *That is not dead which can eternal lie,*
> *And with the passing of strange aeons even death may die.*
> *Fhtagn mglw, nafn*
> *R'lyeh wgah nagh fhtagn.*

I was still puzzling over the last few words, how they should be pronounced and in what language they could be, murmuring them as accurately as I could, when the book suddenly leaped from my grasp. I made to catch it before it fell, but looking up I saw that Harries had crossed the room and was now holding the *Necronomicon*, having snatched it from me. His eyes were burning in their sockets, and for a moment I was afraid he was about to strike me. Then the fire dimmed a little as he blinked it away.

'Please do not disturb my books,' he half whispered, and I could hear the anger choked back in his voice. Anger and also, unaccountably, fear. He closed the book carefully. 'I have spent a long time in ordering these shelves,' he continued somewhat more calmly, 'and everything must be replaced exactly as it was.'

So saying, he slid the thick leather-bound volume back into place. My surprise had now abated somewhat, and my eyes met Harries's with little difficulty.

'When I removed it,' I pointed out, hoping to undermine something of his officious manner, 'that book was the other way up.'

Harries had started to turn away to move back to his chair, but as I spoke he froze, as if captured in a painting. 'Impossible,' he said; but his voice was so faint that I barely heard it.

'I am not in the habit of lying, sir,' I said, perhaps a little forcefully, and he turned back to face me.

The change in him was remarkable. I fancied that he had again given way to anger, but after a moment I saw that it was fear. His lips had drawn back over the teeth and his cheeks had paled and sunk. His skin seemed stretched far too tight about his black-rimmed eyes. It was like staring at the mirthless smile of a skull. The effect endured for only a second and then his face seemed to sag, to fill out again into some semblance of life. His reddened eyes dulled and he stared at the bookshelves for a moment.

'I apologise,' he muttered. 'I have been working very hard, and it must have been I who replaced the book upside down.'

I made to answer, but he continued, his voice vibrant and husky. 'After all, who else could it have been?'

As Harries walked slowly and stiffly back to the cluttered table in the centre of the room I could see the fear in his gait, as I had tasted it on his breath. It took him several minutes to recover his composure and for his features to regain their boyish set. The act of explaining something of his work to me seemed excellent therapy, however, and soon he was well into his stride.

'I will give you a small-scale but practical demonstration of the effect I will want you and the others to witness tonight,' he said suddenly as I leafed through an incomprehensible – not to say illegible – bundle of notes which Harries had thrust into my hand. I looked up, partly glad to be able to cease pretending that I understood anything of his scribbles, and partly surprised that he was so forthcoming and enthusiastic towards someone he could scarcely count as a friend. The excitement of his work seemed to take hold, no matter to whom he explained it.

'I cannot overemphasise the importance of what you will see,' he went on. He never once looked at me as he prepared. 'Sir George is a man of repute and –' he paused as if in amusement – 'respectability. Gordon Seavers brings scientific integrity.' Again I fancied there was a hint of amusement in his voice. 'Dr Friedlander has considerable expertise in the new science of forensics. He is, I am reliably informed, the foremost practitioner and most experienced of his discipline in Europe.' Now he did look at me, as he said, 'And I also need an unbiased observer who has no preconceptions but is of unimpeachable integrity within a respected professional field. In short, yourself.'

He returned immediately to his work before I could comment, clearing a wide space on the table. This he achieved in the main by sweeping piles of paper and several books on to a nearby chair. Then he lifted a large wooden contraption into the clear area.

I thought at first that it was merely a shallow box, but looking inside I could see that there were walls within it too, and an opening at one side about four inches across. He had, I realised, built a miniature maze. Of what use it could possibly be, I could not fathom. Until he produced the rats.

He had two of them in a wooden cage on one of the packed windowsills, jammed between a collection of wires and metal pins and a pile of notes. I had not noticed it earlier, but as Harries picked his way over to the window I saw the brown blur of movement from within. He brought the cage to the table, seeming not to notice the papers following in its wake. Before he opened the cage he again turned his attention to the maze, flicking hinged sections of the long walls across the corridors inside until the geography of the course from the centre to the opening at the side near the cage was completely altered. Then he opened the lid of the cage and reached inside.

The two rats looked identical in size, colour and markings. As I watched Harries lift out the nearer of the two, I wondered why people felt so nervous and revolted by the small creatures, which seemed after all only large mice. Its companion watched silently from the cage, its small eyes glinting between the slats. But as Harries placed the first rat in the open area of the square heart of the maze, a long segmented tail unwound into my view as if with a venomous life of its own And when the rat paced the inside of its prison, exploring the several passages leading off, it was as if the tail was a separate animal pushing the furry body ahead of itself as it coiled and snaked in the rat's shadow. I swallowed dryly, and wondered no longer.

Harries seemed unaffected by the animal, and watched closely as it scuttled into corners and retraced its steps, becoming more and more frantic as it found its way blocked. He spoke the whole time, his voice racing like the rat's feet, his eyes darting like its tail. I did not hear all of what he said for the rat held me fascinated with its movements, and what I understood of what I heard seemed unconnected with what I saw.

'A hundred years ago Galvani stimulated living tissue with electric current. We now know that a potential difference exists between the cut ends of muscle fibre and the intact external surface bathed in saline solution... Nernst explains this as the positive and negative ions in the solution moving towards equilibrium. Somewhat simplistic perhaps, but he is right.'

The rat scratched at a hinge for a moment, than gave up and retraced its steps, discovering a new turning and darting into it, tail lingering for a moment cautiously before following.

'I submit that this biopotential in living tissue is due to variations in the potassium ion concentration of the cell membrane. Thus nervous impulses, and even the workings of the brain itself, are electrical in nature... I have found that there are four types of brainwave, distinguished by their pulse frequency...'

I lost him for a while as he explained, more to himself than to me, about how each brainwave signified or indicated a different level of brain activity, from deep sleep to anxiety or great mental disturbance.

'You are satisfied that this rat is unable to escape my maze?' Harries said, and it took me a moment to realise that he was not still talking about brains, and inducing a 'smoothly fluctuating magnetic field about the cerebellum by means of a driving current applied to electrodes on the skull', to which he had moved on. Before I could reply, he had removed the rat from the maze and replaced it in the cage, pulling out its fellow as he did so. 'Let us see how your brother fares,' he murmured and set the second rat down in the central space. As it too struggled to escape, Harries continued from where he had left off:

'The field is started at a frequency of ten cycles per second, then reduced slowly to one. When the change in modulated brain waves from the cerebellum is detected, the amplitude of the driving waves is increased to cause resonance inside the brain cavity. Positive wave reinforcement causes the output to rise sharply to an easily detectable level.'

He paused, eyes still following the rat, and I seized the opportunity to say something, if only to prove that I existed.

'Like soldiers marching, do you mean?' I hazarded.

Harries looked up, startled, and I saw that he had indeed forgotten that I was there. 'Yes, exactly,' he replied after a moment. 'If they fail to break step on a bridge, the reinforcement of the vibrations could cause it to fall down.'

'Could the brain fall down too, like the walls of Jericho?'

Harries ignored this; or perhaps he did not hear it. 'The output from the brain is then overlaid on to a basic sine carrier wave of one cycle per second applied to a second brain. Thus the modulations corresponding to the thoughts of one can be induced in the other.'

'And what does that mean?'

Harries reached into the maze and shied the rat away from one turning and towards another. 'I'll show you,' he said and lifted the rat back to its starting point. Then he guided it through, pushing it from one doorway to another and encouraging it along the passageways until he had brought it to the opening. He picked it up and held it for a moment.

'Of course,' he spoke as if to the rat, 'the brains have to be biologically similar to begin with.'

He took the first rat from the cage again and replaced it with the one he had guided through the puzzle. 'These rats are from the same litter,' he said, returning the first to its prison in the centre of the maze.

At first I thought it was by chance that the rat made straight for the right opening off the square, but as it continued along the path towards the way out – the path that the same rat had just now failed to find despite several minutes' exploration – scrambling ever faster and making not a single wrong turn, all without hesitation, I knew as surely as it did that chance was not a factor here. It was as if this rat had been guided through also, and remembered the route exactly.

I looked up and saw that Harries's eyes were fixed on me now; he knew what the rat was doing.

'Thought transference,' he whispered, and without looking caught the rat as it hurtled out of the maze. He returned it to its companion and there was a knock at the door.

It was Simpson.

'Miss Harries and Miss Seymour have arrived, sir,' he told us. 'I thought you should be informed.'

'Thank you,' said Harries abruptly and strode from the room, brushing past Simpson as the butler moved to retrieve the lunch Harries had ignored.

'I'll just remove this, sir,' said Simpson as he carried the tray out, but I barely heard him.

I was staring at the rats, sitting quietly now in their cage. *From the same litter*, I reminded myself; and as Harries greeted his sister I had my first intimation of what he intended...

THE REPORT OF INSPECTOR IAN STRATFORD (2)

It was lunchtime when I finally arrived at a snowbound Scotland Yard. I spent a few minutes writing up my fruitless interview, but broke off when I felt someone standing behind me. I turned. It was Chief Inspector Driscoll.

'You've an aunt in Three Sisters, haven't you, Stratford?' he snapped. I paused, wondering why he was asking.

'Well?' he demanded, his tiny moustache twitching impatiently.

I nodded, then hastily added, 'Yes, sir, I occasionally stay with her when I'm on a walking holiday.'

'Thought so,' he said with a brief triumphant smile. Driscoll prided himself on knowing everything about his men down to the last insignificant detail. He took pleasure in parading his collection of trivia, recalling things that might have been mentioned over a year before, and then only in passing. I had noticed that it was usually the things one did not want remembered that he retained. A white lie, an embarrassing error, a social gaffe: it would all be filed for later use. It was the nicer things, like praise for a job well done or recommendation for promotion, that somehow slipped his mind. The only reason that he remembered my aunt was that he disapproved of my love of walking.

'You are going down to visit her,' he informed me. 'That is where Hopkinson has gone, according to his statement. It is my opinion that you might get some local insight into his character from your aunt. Besides, it will save putting someone up at the local inn overnight.'

His moustache twitched again, probably in disapproval. Driscoll wasn't against drinking as such, but he was against both beer and public houses. He was a port man himself and felt that ale played on a man's emotion to the detriment of civilised behaviour.

A sudden thought struck me. 'But if you want me to stay the night…'

'That means your train leaves this afternoon,' he finished. 'We want this Seavers thing cleared up quickly. You've got nearly an hour until the train leaves, plenty of time to pack.' He thrust a thin folder into my hand and strode back to his office.

Within five minutes I was in Great Scotland Yard hailing a cab. It took a good half-hour to reach my lodgings in Notting Hill, and the first thing I did when I entered my rooms was to check the tattered Bradshaw that usually propped up a short leg on the hatstand by the door. Driscoll had underestimated the time and I found that I still had an hour before the four o'clock train departed Paddington for Three Sisters. I allowed myself a cup of tea and threw a change of clothes and some other essentials into a bag. I let my landlady know that I would be away and set out on the short walk to the station.

It felt strange, beginning the familiar ritual of the journey knowing that it was business rather than pleasure that motivated me. I often visited my aunt on the spur of the moment. I found long ago that the strain of police work could be cleared by long walks in the countryside, and I used her house as a base. She and I were the only surviving members of our branch of the family. She had never married, and my parents had died some years before.

I arrived at Paddington with ten minutes to spare, settled into a comfortable compartment and finally began to read the file that had sent me on my way. In the main it detailed the case I had been involved in: the suicide of Gordon Seavers. Inspector Hetton was handling the case, but I had been roped in to go to Oxford when he was detained elsewhere. He had given me an informal briefing over a pie and a pint in a public house near Scotland Yard, but this was the first time I had actually seen the file. Hetton was a conscientious worker; the report was crammed full of detail and fact but contained precious little emotion.

Despite his academic record at Oxford, Gordon Seavers had, in the space of a few short years, gained a large measure of respectability. He was a member of several prominent government committees and was regularly quoted in the newspapers on matters of scientific import. As far as was known (and Hetton had talked to Seavers's entire domestic staff, as well as a number of his colleagues) his life was lived respectably and openly. He was a man without secrets.

And there lay the rub. When he failed to respond to a call for breakfast one morning, his wife attempted to gain access to his study. The door was locked, and there was no response from within. A guest of Gordon Seavers – one John Hopkinson – had eventually broken the door down, fearing, quite sensibly, that Gordon Seavers had suffered some form of seizure or heart attack. In a sense, he had been correct. Gordon Seavers's heart had indeed been attacked – by a letter opener. The door was locked, the windows were locked and his fingers were curled around the handle of the knife.

I looked up from the closely typed report and glanced out on to the snow-clad landscape flowing past the window. Already the flat farmlands of the Home Counties had been replaced by gently varying hills and hollows. The snow obscured the shades of the countryside, replacing them with a uniform white shadowed only by the low evening light. I remembered an artist's sketch of Mary Seavers at the inquest from one of the dailies, her paper-white face thinned by misery and her eyes shadowed in anguish. She had no idea why her husband should kill himself, but she would blame herself for the rest of her life.

I turned back to the report. The crimson light of approaching sunset made it difficult to read, and I angled it towards the window.

Had anyone else been conducting the investigation things would have rested with the suicide verdict, but not Hetton. He was a big, bluff man whom I had worked beside in K Division when we were mere sergeants. He was promoted to inspector long before I was but had remained there because of the injuries he had received in the Scotland Yard bombing several years earlier. He had been left with seven fingers, a scar on one cheek and a deep fear of alarm clocks. Nonetheless, he was a good detective. Too good to pension off.

A minor inconsistency in Mrs Seavers's statement had alerted Hetton to something amiss. She told him that her husband had entered his study to open the post, minutes before his death. Checking a list of the contents of the study, Hetton found that an empty envelope had been found addressed to Seavers. The postmark was obscured by blood because the envelope had been found beneath Seavers's body. Of the letter there was no sign. The first person in the study had been John Hopkinson: if anyone had removed that letter, then it was he. He had informed Hetton that he would be at his London lodgings for a few days more and thereafter could be contacted at Three Sisters. He and the deceased Gordon Seavers had been invited to stay with a certain Sir George Wallace for a few days.

Banquo Manor. It stood gaunt and alone about a mile from the village and the same from the station, forming the third point of a rough equilateral triangle. I had occasionally seen it in my rambles around the area, glimpsed through the trees where I had not expected to see it, although on reflection it was in the right place, and I was the one who was lost. I had never met the owner. The house itself was... unusual. There was something about the design that made one want to grit one's teeth and look away. I do not know what it was – it may even have been a psychological effect due to the local gossip. According to my aunt, a particularly grisly murder had taken place there a century before. The then owner of the house had been butchered and drained of his blood by a lunatic cousin freshly escaped from a nearby asylum. They never found her. Whatever the reason, I didn't like Banquo Manor. The opportunity of finally meeting the residents did nothing to quell my unease. Nothing at all.

I shivered, and looked out of the window again. The sun was setting over a snow-capped copse of trees, layering the clouds in scarlet and orange. I stared so hard at the fading rays of sunset that Three Sisters caught me unawares. As the train slowed majestically to a halt I started in surprise, then grabbed my case, shoved the report into a side pocket and made for the door. Within a few minutes I was walking down the well-remembered but now snowbound road to the village of Three Sisters.

Although the sky had been crystal clear throughout the journey, the first traces of a ground mist began to swirl through the trees and about my legs as I trudged along. The snow was only an inch or so thick, but the weather remained cold enough to keep it on the ground. There seemed to be little or no danger of an immediate repeat but I hoped we would not be in for an encore of the previous year. That winter had been disastrous, the worst in living memory.

It was some minutes before I noticed the ground mist was now thick enough to blot out all but the few nearest trees along the side of the road. I had never seen mist over snow before; the effect was strange and not altogether pleasant. I was sure my aunt would have some country rhyme to explain it. She usually did.

I soon passed the offshoot of road that led to the gates of the Manor. It wasn't signposted, but at least one person had managed to find his way, judging from the footsteps that veered from my path and headed into the mist. Hopkinson perhaps? The footsteps were set between the tracks of a cart, presumably the one they had sent for his luggage. Then why didn't he use the cart as well? There was no real point in speculating about the idiosyncrasies of John Hopkinson, but without facts to deal with I often found my police-trained mind grinding away like a millstone without any corn.

Leaving the route to Banquo Manor behind me, I continued on towards the village. My useless speculations were broken by a strong gust from the previously unnoticed wind. It twisted the mist into odd shapes which closed in upon me until my vision was restricted to a circle of a few feet. I was walking alone and cocooned, and the soft sound of the wind in the leaves surrounded me like a continuous conversation.

Someone whispered my name.

I stopped. I was sure I had heard something croon 'Ian' long and low through the darkness. I listened intently, but there was nothing. A spot between my shoulder blades began to prickle and I turned around more quickly than pride would normally have allowed.

Nothing. Just the darkness and the mist.

I turned back and started walking. Almost as if it had been waiting for me to relax, something ahead of me whispered, 'Ian…'

The wind was blowing cold on my skin as I paused and peered uncertainly ahead. There was something standing there, something twisted and bent waiting for me, half hidden by the mist.

'Ian…' it whispered, and as my heart began to pound the wind pushed the tendrils of mist away from its bent limbs.

It was a tree, set prominently where there was a slight bend in the road. I had been confused by the mist and the wind, and my own imagination had provided phantoms to frighten me. My heart was still beating fast and, cursing myself, I increased my speed towards the warmth and life of the village. I began to shiver, but it was only the cold.

Within a few minutes I passed the first houses on the outskirts of the village. The mist was beginning to disperse now, revealing patches of brightly starred sky. As I looked up a shooting star crossed one of the gaps and vanished within a second, leaving a pale-green afterimage etched across the darkness for a handful of seconds. I hoped I would see more during my stay. My favourite childhood memories concerned staying with my aunt and sneaking out in the dead of night to watch for shooting stars.

It was thus, smiling foolishly at childhood memories, that I entered the village of Three Sisters.

THE ACCOUNT OF JOHN HOPKINSON (3)

It was perhaps hardly surprising that I could bear to greet Catherine Harries and Miss Seymour about as much as I could bear to stay with the rats. What I wanted was a drink – not, as sometimes now, to choke back the memories that still rush in upon me in unguarded moments, but because the realisation had dried my throat so that even my breath seemed to scrape it. I could hear Harries and his sister in the drawing room, and I was reasonably certain that the carafe in my room was empty, so I made my way through the dining room to the area under the stairs that was Simpson's domain.

The door was all but concealed within the panelling of the corridor down to the kitchen area, and as usual it was closed. In fact, I don't recall ever seeing it left open. Certainly I had never been inside the butler's pantry before that day, though I had seen Simpson emerging from its gloomy interior on rare occasions. I tapped on the door, inclining my head towards it in order to hear if Simpson was within. I heard nothing, no response, and pushed open the door.

As I surveyed the dimly lit room within, it did not occur to me that I might be trespassing, that Simpson might resent my unauthorised entry into his world. I just stood there, looking in surprise at the long narrow room that was concealed beneath the main staircase. It was difficult to credit that there was so much space available.

What light there was came from an electric lamp on the sloping wall to the right of the room, the wall that abutted the rising stairs. Beneath this light were two lead sinks with folding covers, and beside them a fireproof safe that, I presumed, held George's valuable plate between dinners. Along the other wall, where the ceiling was higher and afforded more space, there was a long table. It was in fact hardly more than a wide shelf. Upon it was a row of empty decanters and an assortment of bottles and corkscrews, trays and salvers, plates and cutlery. The implements and accoutrements of a well-equipped butler.

It took me but a moment to spot a dusty, dark bottle of port in amongst the sherries and the whisky. I crossed the room and lifted it gently from where it nestled in with several implements the function of which I could not fathom. It was heavy, obviously full. Yet the cork was half out of the bottle.

By now my throat was so dry that I was tempted simply to extract the cork and drink from the bottle itself. But, as I gripped the end of the cork, I looked round for a glass. I think it was the dust that had put me off the idea.

I must have flinched visibly at the cough from behind me. It was a deliberate 'polite' cough, though it was obviously not intended to sound polite at all. I swung round, fingers still gripping the cork, to see Simpson framed in the narrow doorway.

'Can I help you, sir?' he asked levelly. There was a harshness to his voice that I had not remarked before, and at that moment – in that instant – I realised that I was trespassing within his territory.

'I'm sorry,' I all but stammered. 'I was after a drink.'

In a moment he was beside me. 'Of course you were, sir.' He lifted the bottle from my hands and replaced it carefully exactly where it had been. 'Crusted, sir,' he murmured.

'I beg your pardon?'

'Best to decant it first,' he explained. His eyes met mine, and he seemed to have recovered his usual demeanour. 'I'd suggest you look in the kitchen for some ready-decanted port, sir,' he said. His eyes did not blink or waver.

'Of course.' I nodded. 'I was just passing. I thought –'

He made no comment, but turned to the table and busied himself rearranging the bits and pieces on it. Had I known him less well, I would have assumed it was an unhappy accident that he made it seem as if he were checking that nothing had gone astray or disappeared.

'I'll see myself out, thank you, Simpson,' I said in an attempt at a joke. Again, I got no response. I almost tiptoed out of his sanctuary, and closed the door quietly behind me. He had made no explicit comment, offered no admonition for my behaviour, yet I knew that I had overstepped an unspoken mark. I knew that I would not venture into Simpson's world unbidden again. At least, not lightly.

I arrived in the kitchen at the same time as Beryl. She had apparently been home, or at least back in the village, for the afternoon. As I entered the kitchen from the house, she came in through the outside door, closing it on the darkness and the snow. She seemed quite surprised to see me, but I told her what I was after and she offered to find me a glass.

'Please don't worry,' I assured her. 'Warm yourself first.'

She smiled a thank-you and came over to the stove, holding her wet hands out over it.

'Is it raining? It wasn't earlier.'

'No.' She seemed uncertain for a moment. 'I fell over in the snow.'

She smiled, and I smiled back.

'Very slippery I expect. Especially in the dark,' I murmured and she seemed pleased that I left it at that.

She stayed a minute longer before fetching out a glass and I watched her as she stood by the warmth, drying her hands. Her long hair was soaked, plastered to her head and then falling in thick bunches across her shoulders. Several stray strands had blown forward and down over the material that clung wetly to her bosom, dark against the white of her dress. If she had fallen down in the snow, she had been in no great hurry to get up again. It seemed odd that she, soaked to the skin, should hand me a glass of water, especially as she was evidently still uncertain of what I was thinking. She watched me drink, her fingers nervously playing along the handle of one of the kitchen knives lying on the table. My mood had improved somewhat when I joined the gathering in the drawing room, and before long I had forgotten the damp on my forehead and the dryness in my throat.

The drawing room of Banquo Manor is of a fairly standard design – large and square with a heavy fireplace backed on to the wall shared with the study, French windows which open into the grounds, and (mercifully, as it later transpired) a thick, strong door. Wallace had it furnished in a conventional manner – several coffee tables, a chaise longue, couch, armchairs towards the centre of the room, upright Chippendales against the walls. One of the coffee tables sported a selection of decanters and a tray of glasses, while a pair of ornate, but functional, oil lamps stood one at either end of the marble mantelpiece. The lamps were of course unlit, for the room had several newly installed electrical wall lights burning. Above the mantel was a brass plaque engraved with a quotation from Macbeth – part of an early speech of Banquo's:

> If you can look into the seeds of time
> And say which grain will grow and which will not
> Speak then to me who neither beg nor fear
> Your favours nor your hate.

Opposite the plaque, dominating the right-hand wall, hung a picture of a man in his late forties. He had black hair and moustache, a thin face and a nose which almost compensated for what his blue eyes lacked in character. He seemed pale, especially in contrast to his hair and the dark background, and his gaze, while fixed, was unfocused.

I nodded to Wallace and his wife as I entered. George poured me a sherry while I shook hands with Catherine

Harries. Harries himself was seated away from the others, who were standing, as though they had just entered, around the drinks table. However, it was neither Harries nor his handsome sister who held my attention, and Wallace had to nudge my arm to break my stare and hand me my sherry. He then introduced me, since Harries showed no such inclination, to Miss Susan Seymour.

I have seen several women whom I could describe as beautiful and it would be to exaggerate to suggest that Miss Seymour surpassed them all. But she certainly came close to it, holding my gaze even beside Catherine's fair-haired good looks. She was tall, about five feet seven, and seemed even taller being so slim, with her high-necked, pale-green dress trimmed with white lace. Her hair was fine and long, but done up behind her head. It was a deep black, but with a hint of red as it caught the light. Her eyes were deep and emerald while her cheekbones were high but not too prominent. As she smiled her perfect lips drew back just enough to reveal a set of equally perfect teeth. The smile lit her whole face and reached her eyes, which also betrayed her humour at my interest.

Then they broke away from mine and her eyes flicked over towards the door as Simpson entered, carrying a fresh decanter of brandy. When she looked back at me I saw a trace of humour in her gaze. And I realised somewhat foolishly that I was still holding Miss Seymour's hand in greeting. I released it and pretended not to notice her amused expression.

As she let go of my hand, Miss Seymour looked round the room. 'And Mr Seavers?' she asked. 'Is he here?'

'He hasn't arrived yet, Susan,' Harries explained.

'I did telephone earlier,' George went on, 'but there was no answer, so I would assume he's on his way.'

'Probably,' agreed Harries, 'but Gordon is usually so very punctual.'

Elizabeth Wallace smiled and changed the subject easily –

for which I silently thanked her. 'You know that we are always delighted to see Gordon, whatever the time. Just so long', she continued good-naturedly, 'as he does not talk about your science and supernature too much. The way that Richard and George have been going on the last few weeks it was an enormous relief when John arrived.' She smiled at me. 'He seems to know even less about science than I,' she added.

'You do me an injustice,' I laughed back. 'I've almost grasped what this experiment tonight is all about and I only arrived today. I'll wager even George needed a few moments to get the gist of it.'

'Yes, yes – well, just a few maybe,' chuckled Wallace. 'But to be fair, Richard wasn't altogether lucid you know.'

Harries of course had failed to grasp the humour of our conversation, although his sister and fiancée had both been quick to smile.

'I was as clear as I could be under the circumstances,' he protested, 'but given the nature of the experiment –'

He got no further as Elizabeth broke in.

'Here they go again,' she said loudly to me and Susan. 'John, Susan dear, can you please bring some sort of order into our household – at least until dinner?' Harries slumped back into his chair, apparently in a sulk.

Susan's mouth pursed in amusement as she looked at Harries. 'We shall see what can be done,' she said, sparing me a quick glance.

'Or,' I added, 'if this opaque language continues, we shall all adjourn for a long evening walk around the grounds.'

'There's a full moon tonight,' George said, actually greeting the prospect with enthusiasm. He rubbed his hands together in anticipation. 'A little light exercise would do us all the world of good. And I can show you the gardens by moonlight – including the new grotto.'

Elizabeth sighed. 'You're incorrigible,' she laughed. 'I promise we shall all come and admire the addition to the gardens. But in daylight if you don't mind.'

I had passed within sight of the new 'grotto' on my walk from the station. It was – or rather, was going to be – part of a hillside just off the main path in the woods. I left it to George to enlighten Miss Seymour and the others.

'Well,' he mused, 'it's not much of a grotto yet, I'm afraid. Be better next week when the chap's been to blow a hole in the rock.'

I decided that I might as well throw in my penny's worth. 'At the moment, there's just a small wooden shed full of tools and so on. I saw it from the path on my way up earlier. But if the plans are anything to go by, then George will have a very picturesque little cave to hide in when it's finished, overlooking most of the grounds.'

'The gardener isn't altogether sure about it yet, though,' said Elizabeth, and we all laughed. She led Catherine and Susan off to another part of the room. Harries was apparently in a world of his own, staring at his half-empty glass. This left Wallace and me together with the decanters. George refilled his glass, and then topped up mine before I could protest.

'Well, John – now you've met Miss Seymour what do you think of her?' he asked when sure that his wife had manoeuvred the ladies out of earshot.

'She's not exactly what I expected,' I said slowly, wondering how I could turn the conversation towards the topics I wished to broach with George. Harries, for example, and Gordon. Now that he had been mentioned I felt that I ought to say something to George, not for my own sake so much as for his. This was the first opportunity I had had to speak to George alone and I was loath to waste it. On the other hand, I had hoped to wait, to sort out my own feelings and position first. 'Also she's not so...' I struggled for the right word. 'I don't know – intense, I suppose. Not like Harries.'

'Yes, Richard does get a bit carried away at times, doesn't he?'
I agreed. 'Miss Seymour seems a very pleasant young lady all in all. From what little I've seen of her.'

Wallace laughed. 'Another difference from her fiancé, then.'

This was what I had hoped for. 'George,' I said quietly, 'why do you put up with him?'

I could tell from his eyes that George had heard, but he hesitated, looking over towards Harries, now talking to his sister, and then towards Susan Seymour and Elizabeth.

'I suppose Simpson and Beryl can manage dinner for all of us,' he said uneasily, as though the thought had just struck him. 'I'll go and check with Elizabeth.'

He walked stiffly over to join them, leaving me alone and puzzled. There was one explanation for his strange behaviour, but I could hardly credit it.

I needed to think; suddenly the room seemed full of people all breathing too little air, stifling me. I glanced quickly around to see that no one was watching me, then put down my glass and slipped behind the heavy curtains, opened the French windows and went out into the garden. I quietly closed the windows behind me and leaned against them for a moment, taking a deep breath of the cold night air.

The mist seemed to have ended and the night was of that crystal quality that one sees only in the winter when the very cold of the air itself seems to sharpen the edges of the trees against the moon and bring the clouds so close that one wants to reach out and pluck them from the sky. The stars sparkled like ice and the snow sang clearly with the breeze that drew away my steamlike breath.

I stood for a while, wondering whether the moon – or I – would ever tire of the images that flowed before it, and the constantly changing shadows that danced across the lawn like patterns thrown up by a magic lantern. It was while I was thus preoccupied that I saw the shooting star.

In a moment it was gone, but I could still see its pale-green trail across my retina for a while, until finally it succumbed to my blinking. My first idea was to run for all I was worth and see where it had fallen, for it had seemed so close that it must surely have landed in the Manor grounds. But while I still stood, entranced, the oblivious laughter from the drawing room reached me and the spell was broken. I crossed myself for the luck I wanted, shivered, and slipped inside the house.

THE REPORT OF INSPECTOR IAN STRATFORD (3)

It was just short of eight o'clock when I tapped on the door of the police station. My aunt went to bed early every night, and so I decided to check in quickly with the local constabulary before I arrived on her doorstep. A muffled reply from within invited me to open the door. Sergeant Baker sat behind a desk at the far side of a plain and purely functional room, separated from me by a waist-high bench. Although we had never met, my aunt had pointed him out before. He was a short, tubby man with more hair in his handlebar moustache than on his head. His hair was ginger and contrasted disconcertingly with his sea-green eyes. He had always put me in mind of the archetypal rural bobby, but he was highly respected in the village.

'Sergeant Baker?' I asked, more to start the conversation than anything else.

'Evening, sir,' he said. 'Well, night almost. What brings you here at this time?'

'Inspector Stratford,' I said by way of introduction, expecting him to straighten up respectfully. He merely smiled.

'Visiting your aunt, sir?'

'I am in fact down here on duty.'

'I know, sir,' Baker admitted. 'Your Chief Inspector Driscoll telephoned me this morning to tell me the situation.'

He gestured towards a telephone on the desk, but I was too busy contemplating Driscoll's unpleasantness to notice. Not only had he known about the necessity for my trip a good few hours before he told me, but he had also pulled the rug from under my feet by telling some country bumpkin police sergeant first. I had the dubious consolation of knowing that I was not special. He treated everyone that way.

I mustered all my reserves of calmness. 'Well,' I said, 'that saves me the trouble of explaining the situation. What is your estimation?'

'Well, sir –' he paused and looked thoughtful – 'if you ask me, there's something odd going on up at the Manor. You see, Sir George Wallace, who owns the Manor, has sent all the servants away bar the butler and the maid. Now, what with himself and his wife, Mr Hopkinson, Professor Harries and the ladies, that's a powerful lot of work for just two servants.'

'I take the point. Who's Harries?'

'Ah, Professor Harries is a *scientist,* sir.' He pronounced the term with some emphasis, as if it took on a different connotation when it was applied to Harries. 'He's been staying with Sir George Wallace for almost a year now, if my memory serves.'

'What's he like?'

'We don't rightly know, sir. It's a rare day when we see him in the village.'

'And the ladies?'

'Professor Harries's sister and his fiancée, I understand, sir. Don't know much more about them than that.'

'Hmm, quite a gathering.' I made as if to stand up. 'Well, if you'll allow me a few moments to see my aunt, we can be off to the Manor. I want to get this questioning over with as soon as possible.'

'I took the liberty of informing your aunt of your arrival this afternoon, sir,' said Baker blandly. 'And they'll be having their dinner up at the Manor now. It's only a twenty-minute walk, sir. Perhaps we've got time for a coffee before we go? It'll help to keep out the cold at any rate.'

'Baker,' I said, 'you are wasted here.' And as I sank back in my chair he opened a drawer in the desk and produced two mugs and a bottle of whisky. He rose to his feet and walked towards a stove in one corner, glancing at me to check my reaction. He obviously was not sure whether he had read me correctly or not. I was getting to quite like him, so I provided a helping hand.

'I was right,' I said. 'You *are* wasted here.'

We sat drinking coffee liberally laced with Baker's whisky (a gift, he informed me, from a local widow who had designs upon him) and chatted about the village and its inhabitants. Behind his reserve I found Baker to be a perceptive and likable man, and I could see why he was so highly regarded in the village. I was just about to quiz him further on the Manor when the telephone rang.

'Three Sisters police station,' said Baker gingerly, and I guessed the apparatus was a recent addition. 'Sir George! We were… Yes, sir… in fact… Professor Harries? Yes, sir… keep calm, please, sir, I'll take the particulars as soon as I arrive… About a quarter of an hour, sir… Right, sir, goodbye.'

'Sir George Wallace?' I asked

'Sir George Wallace,' confirmed Baker. 'There's been a death up at the Manor.'

'We'd better get up there.' I led the way through the gap in the bench and out into the cold night air. There I waited for Baker to tell me which way to turn.

THE ACCOUNT OF JOHN HOPKINSON (4)

I closed the French windows softly behind me as I came back into the drawing room. There was someone just the other side – the room side of the curtains from me. More than one person in fact, for I could hear the immediate hum of conversation above the general social noises from further into the room. I suppose I could have just stepped back through the curtains and allowed whoever it was to draw their own conclusions if they noticed me. But instead I froze between window and curtain, listening. Well, more than listening actually. I was straining to hear as much as I could. The voice I could make out more of was Miss Seymour's, and it was raised just higher in pitch than her companion's in anger, helping to carry some of her words to me.

'A choice?' Amazement mixed with anger. 'They didn't expect you to come along and –' She was interrupted, but I could not tell by whom any more than I could hear what was said to her.

'No!' Her voice was even closer now – either she was speaking much louder or, as the continued background buzz seemed to confirm, she had moved even closer to the curtain. I shrank back slightly, pressing against the panes of glass, feeling guilty and intrigued.

'Of your opportunism,' she continued, evidently contradicting her interlocutor. 'They live their own lives, or so they thought.'

I heard the answer this time, though it was still not clear. What was now clear was with whom she was talking, although it was hardly the conversation one would expect to overhear between a couple engaged to be married. In contrast to Miss Seymour, Harries seemed almost dismissive.

'If I thought you'd be so upset, I'd have –'

She interrupted him this time. 'You'd have done nothing,

Richard. I know you. It's not just because of this that I have decided not to marry you.'

So the young lady had as much sense as I had unconsciously credited her with after all.

'You know,' she continued, brushing aside Harries's muffled protest – for it seemed that this was as much news to him as it was to me – 'the more I come to understand you, Richard, the less I like you.'

Harries's reply was lost in an ironic guffaw of laughter from the other side of the room. I recognised George's gruff good humour. As his merriment subsided, I caught Susan Seymour's words: 'I'm not going to discuss it here,' she was saying. 'Or now.' There was a pause, the curtain twitched close to me and I sidled away from the movement. 'I'm going to get some air.' The curtain moved again, drawn back from the door. I could see Miss Seymour's dress in the exposed gap.

'That's right, a walk,' she was saying as I recovered my senses and pushed back as far as I could into the space between the curtains and the wall, away from the door. 'Alone,' she added forcefully, her hand and arm snaking behind the curtains in search of the handle of the French window.

Then in a moment she was gone. The door closed again behind her and the curtain blew slightly in the draught. She had stepped straight out into the night. She had not looked behind the curtain or she would have seen my shrinking form pressed away from her.

As the curtain flapped open again for a moment, I caught sight of the group of people in the room beyond. They seemed to be busily talking amongst themselves, oblivious of the conversation by the curtain (and, I hoped, to my extended absence). Richard Harries was staring after his former fiancée – surprise, anger and concern all caught on his face in that split second. He did not see me in my dark hiding space.

I gave him a few seconds to move away, then sidled along to the far edge of the curtain and stepped confidently out into the corner of the room. I paused to straighten the curtain, as if I had just noticed it askew, then picked up the empty glass I had left on a nearby table and walked over to the fire, conscious of the fact that my hand was shaking slightly – both from the cold and from having been so nearly discovered eavesdropping, albeit unintentionally. I was looking up at the plaque above the mantel when George came over to join me. My mind was elsewhere, wandering over the last few minutes, unable to snap away.

'There used to be one in the study as well,' he said.

For a moment I was thrown, then I realised that he was referring to the inscribed plaque.

'It was a different passage, but still Banquo,' he continued.

'How odd,' I replied, not quite sure what else to say. Had George noticed my absence, or seen me re-emerge from behind the curtains? Apparently not, for he continued without any hint of it.

'Not really. This is Banquo Manor, remember.'

Somehow, despite the inscription, I had always assumed that Banquo had been the builder or architect rather than the Shakespearean character. The plaque I had considered to be a light-hearted afterthought, although the choice of speech did seem to somewhat undermine the humour.

'There was a sixteenth-century architect called Roland Banquo or something, I believe,' George said when I displayed my ignorance. 'But he had nothing to do with this house. He died considerably before it was built.'

'Then why the name?'

George had obviously told the story many times before, although never to me, and settled easily into his narrative.

'Well, in 1793 Robert Dodds inherited a substantial amount

of money from his aunt and commissioned the Adam brothers to build him a house. This house. That's Dodds up there.' Wallace interrupted his polished flow and pointed up at the portrait opposite. The dead eyes stared back at us implacably. Were they amused or frightened? There was something, deep behind them.

'Having got the house, Dodds had to find a name for it.'

'Yes, but why "Banquo"?' I asked, glancing furtively back at the pale face on the canvass. It was fear, I was sure. 'Did he see a ghost or something?'

'No,' replied George slowly. 'But it's odd that you should say that.'

'Oh?'

'The villagers say that Dodds murdered his aunt for the legacy, then built the house as a sort of penance. Like Macbeth, his conscience got the better of him.'

'Seems a funny way to go about it.'

I ran my fingers over the words cut into the brass; somehow they did now seem appropriate. Dodds had fallen down through not foreseeing what would happen. However, George's next words dispelled any sense of justification.

'There's absolutely no truth in it of course,' he chuckled, taking a sip of his drink. 'His aunt died of old age really, in her sleep. She was eighty, so she lasted quite well. Dodds was abroad – in Italy, actually – at the time.'

'Not quite so exciting. And it still doesn't explain the name,' I reminded him.

'Oh that's no problem – though a little dull after the villagers' story.'

'Really?'

'Yes. Dodds fancied himself as an actor, do you see? His best role – or so he always maintained, although I gather he was not actually much good at any of them – was in *Macbeth*.'

I began to understand. 'Banquo?'

George nodded and pointed to the plaque. 'That was his favourite speech. According to some critics, it's also the only one he could ever remember.'

I laughed with him, and the portrait glared back across the room, unamused.

'So what became of Dodds?' I wondered.

'Ah, well that is a little more interesting.' George was back with a story he enjoyed. 'His aunt's granddaughter was in an asylum. I'm not sure how she came to be there, but she was evidently in the right place. Somehow she heard about the rumours in the village about her grandmother's death. She escaped one night, came here, and stabbed her cousin to death in revenge.'

A shiver played down my spine and the firelight flickered as the door was closed, but I did not turn to see who had come into the room. For a moment I was convinced that if I did I would be confronted with Dodds's cousin, spattered with blood, the knife still wet in her hand. The impression continued only a second, and George continued, oblivious.

'It's said that his last words were, "Our time doth call upon us." He drained his glass and reached past me. I turned and realised that Beryl was standing behind us with a tray of empty glasses. I placed mine alongside Wallace's and Beryl smiled up at me.

'Dry now?' I asked, baffling George. Neither Beryl nor I cared to explain.

'Yes, thank you, sir,' she replied, a little shyly I thought, and turned to leave brushing so closely against me as she did so that I wondered if she had done it deliberately. George watched her cross to the door, and neither amusement nor fear showed in his eyes.

'Which room did she do it in?' I asked, feeling that I should say something. Wallace looked confused and startled for a moment. 'The killing,' I prompted and the redness passed from his face.

'Oh, er – the master bedroom, as it was then. Harries has it now.'

I smiled, thinking how appropriate that was. 'There was another plaque in the study, you say?'

'Yes, although I'm not sure what it said,' George answered quickly. 'Father had it removed. Said it distracted him. Something about armed girls and a baby rhinoceros, I think.'

I was sure that could not be correct, but before I could say so Simpson was at our side.

'Dinner will be served in about fifteen minutes, sir,' he told George. 'If that is convenient,' he added as if as an afterthought.

'Ah, thank you, Simpson. Yes, that will be fine.'

'Very good, sir.' Simpson began to move off. 'I'll just inform the others, sir,' he explained, managing not to catch my eye. A few moments later we were joined by Harries, who wanted George to help him check over the equipment before dinner. George seemed less keen, and pointed out that it had been checked by them both only an hour earlier. Harries, chastened, capitulated and he and Wallace followed the others out to the hall, leaving me to contemplate the plaque with Robert Dodds.

'It's a pity Gordon isn't here to witness your great triumph, Professor Harries,' I called after him, and Harries paused at the door, my sarcasm wasted on him.

'A great pity,' he replied. 'Perhaps he will join us later, Mr Hopkinson.'

'I was rather hoping that you would join him,' I murmured as Harries left the room. I paused a moment to look again at the portrait, and this time it seemed to me that it was amusement that Robert Dodds harboured. Was he looking into the seeds of time? I wondered. But he did not speak to me, so I followed the others through to prepare for dinner.

The doorbell rang as I was on my way to the dining room. Simpson was standing by the open dining-room door as the bell jangled distantly in the servants' corridor. He was holding a salver on which I noticed was an opened envelope – a telegram addressed to Sir George Wallace. I pitied the poor boy who had doubtless struggled through the snow to deliver it and wondered if the bell signalled his return to beg for shelter from the worsening weather.

'I should just answer that if I were you, Simpson,' I said as seriously as I could manage.

'I shall, sir,' replied Simpson peering down at me as if I should be ashamed of making such an obvious suggestion. I smiled as faintly as I was able, and went through to the dining room while Simpson made his way to the front door – to open it.

I seemed to be the last to arrive at dinner save for Miss Seymour. Perhaps, I considered, she was still cooling off in the grounds. Cooling off in more senses than one, for I had noted from my bedroom window that the snow was falling lightly again now. A few stray flakes, nothing more. But enough to make me shiver as I watched.

I was saved from either having to admit I knew where Miss Seymour was, or from lying by her arrival. Simpson reappeared in the doorway as I helped myself to a plate from the end of the long table and was reaching for the serving spoon in the first dish. I froze at the sight of Simpson, and behind him Miss Seymour and two people I did not know.

'Who was at the door, Simpson?' George asked. From where he sat he could not see the trio of people behind the gaunt figure of the butler.

'Miss Seymour, sir.' Simpson stepped aside to allow Miss Seymour into the dining room.

She paused in the doorway, then stepped hesitantly, almost shyly, forward. 'I was...' She stopped, looking round as if suddenly unsure of herself – a distinct contrast to her earlier confident demeanour. 'I was taking the air.' She blinked several times in rapid succession. Perhaps her eyes were stinging from the cold outside, I thought. 'And I met...' Once again she broke off, turning back towards the door, as if unsure whom she had met.

It was Simpson who introduced the two newcomers to us. 'Dr Friedlander and his assistant,' he said, an edge almost of contempt audible in his tone, 'Herr Kreiner.'

With that, Simpson hinted at a deferential bow and withdrew, allowing the gentlemen behind him to step across the threshold and into the light.

'Friedlander?' George was on his feet at once, dropping his napkin on to the table. 'But I just this minute got your telegram. I understood you were unavoidably delayed by the inclement weather.'

'Really? Well, it was a rather hazardous journey, I'll admit.' Friedlander took a step into the room. 'But here we are, safe and sound. As you can see.'

We could indeed. And I have to admit that Dr Friedlander was not what I had expected. From the silence round the table, I don't think he was what any of us expected. Judging by the esteem with which Harries had told me he was held in the forensic community, I had expected someone older. I had a mental image of a crusty old man with a lined face and a mane of long, white, straggly hair receding from a lined forehead above a wizened face. I could not have been further from the truth.

I was vaguely aware that, his confusion having passed, George was making the introductions as I looked over the doctor. He seemed somehow to be both overdressed and shabby. He wore a paisley waistcoat beneath a velvet frock coat. A large cravat was fastened askew at his neck by a single gold pin. His trousers were damp from the snow, some of which still clung to his battered shoes. It was as if he had dressed for a formal occasion ten years ago and never bothered to change.

But, while his clothing seemed eccentric, it was his face that held my attention. A mass of brown hair framed his youthful visage. His mouth was set into a half smile, as if he were at once both amused and bemused by what he saw. His face was long, unlined but somehow giving an impression of age nonetheless. And his eyes were deep wells of experience that darted back and forth taking in everything as he spoke.

'Hello, everyone,' he said lightly in response to George's introductions. He gave a small wave and bobbed his head politely. 'If you just call me "Doctor" that will do very nicely, thank you.' His smile widened, and I tried to decide whether his expression was ingenuous or calculated. I was left with the overall impression of cross between a down-at-heel aristocrat and a cardsharp trying to con his way into an exclusive gentleman's club.

As the Doctor seated himself beside Miss Seymour at the table, smiling round at each of us in turn and finishing with a lingering, almost sad, glance at his neighbour, there was a polite cough from the doorway.

'I'm so sorry,' the Doctor said without looking. 'This is my assistant, Herr Kreiner. Say hello, Fitz.' His hand turned in the air, approximating another wave.

Herr Kreiner sat on the other side of the Doctor. The table was now full and it took me several seconds to realise that this must mean that an extra space had been laid. So far as I was aware, Herr Kreiner had not been expected. And, looking at his sullen expression, I decided that probably he had not wanted to come at all.

Kreiner was at that indeterminate age somewhere between

the late twenties and mid-thirties. On the cusp of middle age, when illusions fly from you and reality begins to crowd in just a little too close for comfort. He met my stare without apparent embarrassment or worry and deliberately fixed a monocle into his left eye as he gazed back. The impression of disdain was only slightly mitigated by the fact that, as he raised an eyebrow at me, the monocle slipped from its position and fell back on its string.

There was an edge, a tension in the room. But typically, Elizabeth Wallace dispelled it at once. 'I trust your journey has been pleasant.' she enquired as she passed a plate to Dr Friedlander.

The Doctor smiled in reply. 'Not without its upsets and mishaps, I have to confess,' he said.

'Ach,' said Kreiner, 'always ve haff mishaps. Again and again. Time after time.' He had fixed his monocle back in position as he spoke. His Germanic accent was so pronounced that my first inclination was that he was affecting it for some reason. He gave a sharp nod of his head as he accepted a plate from Elizabeth. And his monocle shot out of his eye and clattered on the china. He stared at it for a moment as if in disbelief before blinking furiously and stuffing it into his waistcoat pocket, fingers fumbling in the process.

The conversation progressed as we helped ourselves from the various dishes in the centre of the table. But I heard little of it at first. It had just occurred to me why there was an extra place at table. It was intended for Gordon Seavers. Only I knew that he would not be coming, and a combination of guilt at not sharing my knowledge with George and the sadness that this realisation brought kept me silent and introspective for much of the meal.

'What news of the Society for the Propagation of the Forensic Sciences?' George asked Dr Friedlander, cutting in on my reverie at last.

For a moment, Friedlander looked blank. He blinked, and turned to look at Miss Seymour. She met his gaze levelly, and he turned back to George. 'Oh,' he said vaguely, 'you know how it is.'

This struck me as a rather strange response, since if George had known he would not have asked. But I kept my observation to myself.

'Keeps us very busy, doesn't it, Doctor?' Herr Kreiner said. He grinned round with an easy nonchalance, apparently unaware that his accent had evaporated.

'Careful, Fitz,' the Doctor said with a smile, 'your persona is slipping.'

'What?'

Miss Seymour sighed loudly. 'Your accent,' she said. 'Obviously.' Her voice was laced with a mixture of sarcasm and boredom which seemed quite out of place and unexpected. Even Harries spared her a worried glance across the table.

Herr Kreiner shrugged. 'Oh,' he said. 'That.' His voice sounded more London suburb than continental Europe now. 'That's just for, you know, professional purposes,' he said. 'But we're all chums here, aren't we?'

'Are we?' I asked. 'I thought it was for your professional opinion that you had been invited.'

Dr Friedlander intervened before Kreiner could respond. 'Indeed,' he said. 'And we are grateful for the opportunity to give you the benefit of that opinion, aren't we, Fitz?' He was smiling that ingenuous smile again. And again I was aware of a depth, an underlying seriousness. 'So, why don't you remind us of what's involved?' the Doctor went on as he attacked his food. 'We have, as I said, had rather a long and eventful journey.' He was looking at Miss Seymour again now. 'Haven't we?' I hoped that my own admiration for her physical attributes was not as apparent as Dr Friedlander's.

But before Miss Seymour could respond, Harries spoke. I think it was the first time he had deigned to join in our conversation and we were by now in the final stages of the meal – apple pie (cold of course) followed by cheese.

'An excellent suggestion, my dear Doctor,' he said. And without waiting for further invitation or to hear whether anyone else had anything to say, Harries outlined his intentions.

Much of what he said I had either heard before of failed completely to understand. But it was evidently news to the Doctor and his assistant. I wondered just what Harries had told them to entice them into travelling across Europe in the middle of winter. George listened politely, while Catherine Harries and Elizabeth busied themselves with clearing plates to the sideboard, from where Simpson and Beryl removed them to the kitchen. Miss Seymour listened attentively, as if the information were new to her too, and I was surprised at her apparent interest.

'The basic motive behind this experiment,' Harries concluded, having described his progress with the rats, 'is to ascertain whether it is possible to induce artificial telepathy of a similar nature between two people by means of a mild electric shock.'

'Which two people?' asked Friedlander, a hint of trepidation in his voice.

'Myself and my brother,' Catherine smiled at him. 'We are after all the best suited.'

The conversation meandered for a while as Harries explained the reasoning behind this, none of which made much sense to me. Then he went on to talk about his early experiments with rats, which I was more able to follow. As he spoke, the Doctor's expression seemed to harden, like stone.

'I soon realised that the more subjects that did each puzzle, the easier that puzzle became for each successive rat.'

'How modest,' I mused; but Harries ignored me.

'Even if the rats were well apart, this was the case. I tested fifty in one maze in London, and when I tested a further ten rats here the results were unambiguous. The last rat solved the maze in eighty per cent of the time taken by the first.'

'Could have been a lucky rat,' Herr Kreiner pointed out.

'Or a clever one,' added Susan Seymour.

'If that were the case the results would not have been so conclusive. I used more than one test on many batches of rats.'

'And what conclusions did you draw?' the Doctor asked him. Wallace, I noticed, was silent, and I assumed that he had heard all this before. Probably several times.

'I hypothesised a form of collective memory.'

'A what?' Elizabeth was struggling as much as I was.

'A shared memory, if you like. All rats have a subconscious access to it. One rat gains new knowledge, so that knowledge becomes available, albeit below his conscious threshold, to all rats.'

'So,' said Dr Friedlander, 'the more rats that solve each puzzle, the more accessible the solution becomes to the other rats. Is that your conclusion?'

'And the quicker and easier it becomes for them to solve it as well. Exactly,' concluded Harries.

The Doctor raised an eyebrow. 'Not that far removed from Sheldrake's theories,' he murmured.

'I beg your pardon?' Harries asked. 'You are aware of some other published research in this area?'

'No,' the Doctor said quickly. He gave a short laugh. 'No, indeed. Well, not yet anyway. I think you're well clear of the field.'

'And from that point you moved on to experiments into telepathy?' Miss Seymour enquired. Harries nodded, but he was frowning too. Did he expect her to know this already? Or was he, like me, surprised at her interest

'You are not, I suppose, telepathic in any way already? Either of you?' The Doctor glanced from Harries to his sister.

'No, Doctor,' Catherine told him. 'But we do think in very much the same way, except of course when it comes to science. I remember that as children we always laughed together.'

The thought of Harries as a child, let alone a laughing and humorous one, left me cold.

'So you think that this experiment of yours will work?' the Doctor was asking. His tone suggested that he was far from convinced.

'Yes, Doctor, I think it has an excellent chance of success.'

'Just purely out of interest,' I mused, 'what good will it do anyone if it does?'

'If we can prove that it works for twins, it may be possible for any two people to be telepathically linked in the same way.'

Harries had missed my point.

But the Doctor had not. 'That might make the telephone obsolete shortly after its invention, I suppose,' he said. 'But there are other implications that you might want to consider.'

'Like what happens if we don't want other people eavesdropping on our thoughts?' I suggested. Harries frowned. 'Our minds are private property, Professor Harries,' I pressed. 'Or at least, they should be.'

I watched for any reaction from him, vaguely aware that the Doctor was also watching Harries intently, while Herr Kreiner and Wallace both shifted uneasily on their chairs, sensing the tension.

'I am not concerned with the moral implication, Mr Hopkinson,' came the level reply.

'Somehow I didn't think that you would be.'

'No, I can leave those to the Church. But if we are able to understand our brains – ourselves – better because of my work, then I think it is of some use. It can further our knowledge.'

'Has it no practical implications?' asked Wallace. He was

obviously trying to help, but Harries rounded on him sharply.

'Of course it has. Imagine, for instance, how effective an army could be if each soldier knew instantly what each other was doing; if the general had only to think of an order for it to be carried out.'

The Doctor was still watching him closely. 'So this thing can help humans to kill each other more efficiently, is that what you are saying, Professor Harries?'

'It was only an example. I could have suggested similar efficiency in a factory, or it could be used to help save lives – in firefighting, for example.'

'Or by the police?' I suggested. For a moment Harries was silent, and George quickly interceded.

'Er, well – I suggest that we move through to the conservatory, or laboratory rather, since we all seem to have finished eating.' He stood up and held his wife's chair for her. 'After you then, Elizabeth.' And we filed out into the hall, following Elizabeth Wallace through to the conservatory.

It was locked. George looked around for Harries, but he did not appear to have arrived yet.

'I'll see where he's got to,' I said, deciding that it was hardly worth going around the house to the outside door.

'I'll join you, I think, Mr Hopkinson.' The Doctor was at my shoulder.

'There's no need,' I said. But he just smiled in reply and together we made our way back to the dining room.

Harries was still in the dining room with Susan Seymour. The door was open, and I caught sight of them an instant before they noticed me. Harries was holding one of Susan's hands, but she avoided his gaze. Her eyes were moist and I suddenly felt terribly embarrassed. But she had seen me and I sensed a plea for help behind the moisture.

The Doctor seemed to have no qualms about interrupting them. Possibly, he had no idea of the situation, I reminded myself. I could not recall if George had introduced Miss Seymour as Harries's fiancée, and only I knew that the relationship was foundering.

'Ah, there you both are,' the Doctor said loudly, striding into the room. He removed Miss Seymour's hand deftly from Harries's and patted it gently. 'Coming?' he asked.

She turned to look at him, and I could see the tears plainly on her cheek. 'Doctor?' she asked, her voice betraying confusion as well as emotion. 'You're the Doctor,' she said after a moment, frowning.

'Ye-es,' he said slowly. 'Hold on to that thought, won't you?' It seemed to me that he was attaching more significance to his words than was warranted, but I said nothing. I merely watched as Miss Seymour nodded, biting her lower lip. Then she turned and walked briskly from the room, barely sparing me a glance as she passed.

I turned to follow. And as I turned I heard Harries's voice. I kept going, but I paused in the corridor, just out of sight of the door. The irony that I was myself eavesdropping – again – so soon after admonishing Harries about the morality of such an activity was not lost on me. But I remained frozen and intrigued as I listened to them.

'I met a Dr Friedlander in Wittgenstein several years ago,' Harries was saying.

'It wasn't me,' Friedlander responded. 'I've not been to Wittgenstein for several – for a very long time indeed.'

'I know it wasn't you,' Harries countered. 'But he was a professor of forensic science. Something of a coincidence, wouldn't you say?'

I strained to hear the Doctor's reply. 'Rather a noncoincidence, surely. Since we are not the same person.'

'But a relative perhaps?'

'Perhaps,' the Doctor agreed. 'Relatives are so hard to keep track of, aren't they?'

I could hear the tread of his feet on the polished wooden floor, and I hastened along the corridor. Like Harries, I believed that there was coincidence at work here. Or something more sinister.

The equipment that dominated the table appeared at first haphazard – a collection of wires and valves seemingly thrown together with no order to it. After a moment I began to recognise odd features – dials, meters, a transformer – in the midst of the confusion. Elizabeth was seated to my left, and on my right, at the end of the table, was Catherine. Harries was attaching a wire frame to her head, tightening it at the temples. The Doctor, Herr Kreiner and Susan sat on the opposite side of the table, and Harries moved to take his place at the head. George helped him to adjust a system of wires identical to Catherine's on his own head, and then took his seat between his wife and me. George was closest to the apparatus, and it struck me how ordered the seating arrangements had become, despite the spontaneity.

'All right, Richard; ready when you are.'

George reached for a switch set between the two dials.

'Very well.' Harries's smile was like a knife slash across his face. His sister returned a somewhat more genuine, if nervous, smile.

'What will you do if it doesn't work?' I asked as Wallace depressed the switch.

'It will,' he insisted, but nothing was happening.

'The power will take a few moments to build up,' murmured Wallace, and the Doctor leaned forward with evident interest, studying the mass of equipment. Elizabeth still seemed bewildered; Susan was biting her lower lip. Kreiner was lounging back in his chair as if bored with the whole business. Catherine gripped the wooden arms of the yoke-backed chair and watched for any reaction from her brother. There was none.

The low hum that had started when George pressed the switch was rising steadily in pitch and volume. But still nothing happened. The white of Catherine's knuckles became more pronounced and George looked to Harries.

'It's taking too long,' the Doctor said suddenly. His face was grave.

'Yes,' agreed Harries reluctantly, 'something's wrong.'

The equipment was vibrating now and the noise growing still louder. Elizabeth clasped her hands over her ears and Kreiner leaned back as if trying to escape the sound. Harries began to stand up. The Doctor was on his feet, reaching out.

'Switch it off, man,' the Doctor said loudly, but Wallace was close to the machine and its noise blotted out his words.

'Wallace – switch off!' he shouted across the table, and Catherine relaxed slightly as Wallace reached for the switch. Harries had risen to his feet and was also calling for George to shut off the power. He sat down again, breathing heavily.

But George Wallace's finger never reached its destination. As it approached, the valves burned even brighter, and the noise rose. Then the switch exploded. George whipped his hand back with a cry and Elizabeth screamed. Sparks were erupting throughout the apparatus, throwing cascades of fire into the air and out on to the table. Blue lightning flickered like St Elmo's fire over Catherine's headset, and I wrenched it from her temples – burning my fingers despite my speed as the wires spewed flame towards me.

Harries was struggling to remove his own headset as Catherine slumped back in her chair in a faint. Susan bit into her forefinger, her hand pressed hard to her face in horror and the Doctor pushed past her to help Harries, Kreiner close behind. They were a second too late.

George looked on in disbelief as all but one of the valves in front of him exploded in rapid succession like flares. I was still holding Catherine to prevent her from slipping from her chair on to the burning table. Elizabeth screamed again and Susan covered her eyes and turned away as the Doctor leaped back from Harries. Kreiner stood stock-still, mouth open in an astonished gape. Harries was staring forward, his eyes wide, his headset illuminated by blue flame and his temples blackening where the bare wire met them.

As he fell forward Harries seemed to lunge down the length of the table towards me, his hand groping out into the fire. His mouth was wide open as if in amazement as well as agony and the skin on his temples was burning back from the red-hot wires, and from his skull. His hair was scorched to the roots and his eyes rolled awkwardly in the visible bone of their sockets as red and black scars traced across his face, blistering and tearing the flesh.

After what seemed an eternity his clenched hand dropped open and he collapsed face first into the fire, sending up a shower of sparks and debris.

It was nearly a minute before we were able to drag his body from the flames, and even his sister – had she been conscious – would have been hard pressed to recognise what was left of it.

If not for the macabre situation, my journey to Banquo Manor would have been more pleasant than my previous walk to the village. The mist had dispersed and the snow crunched crisply underfoot as we retraced my footsteps down the narrow, tree-lined road. The presence of Baker did much to reassure me as we walked and there was no recurrence of the panic I had experienced before. I could not help but wonder what awaited us when we arrived, but Baker refused to elaborate on what I already knew. Whether this was due to his natural reticence or a genuine lack of information I wasn't sure. All he would say was that Professor Harries had been the victim of an unfortunate accident and that Sir George Wallace had requested our (or his) presence.

Our conversation was limited as we walked. Baker seemed to have closed in on himself, perhaps resenting the presence of a senior officer in what would otherwise have been a major opportunity to display the full majesty of the law. I might have been doing him an injustice, but either way I could have reassured him. I was feeling remarkably like excess baggage on the journey. If there was any investigating to be done, Baker's local knowledge would more than match my Scotland Yard training.

It was thus in a rather foreboding and gloomy state of mind that I recognised the tree that had so terrified me on my way to the village. Still in darkness but stripped of the mist, it was almost as disturbing: a twisted and gnarled trunk with limbs that seemed to threaten, even in their stationary state. At some time it had been struck by lightning so that the top was split and blackened, and the whole thing was quite dead.

I was startled as Baker's voice muttered from beside me, 'Best turn off into the Manor road now, sir.'

The first few hundred yards of the road leading to Banquo

Manor were indistinguishable from the one we had just left. The trees pressed in on either side and a slight curve ahead of us hid any discrepancies from my eye. The footprints I had noticed before stretched ahead, linking us to the Manor. We trudged silently, and although only a handful of minutes passed before we found a pair of huge iron gates on our left, it seemed like an hour.

'What's at the other end of the road?' I asked Baker, gesturing ahead.

'Little Applecombe, sir. But that's about twenty miles away. Nearer than that there's the other end of the drive. It's a half-circle, do you see, sir?'

We moved on down the drive, the crunch of snow under our feet an odd echo of the gravel that was probably underneath. The drive was indeed semicircular, and I estimated the radius at about four or five hundred yards. A fairly sizeable clump of trees in the area enclosed by the drive shielded us from direct sight of the house and it was only after we were a third of the way around that I raised my eyes to find Banquo Manor looming above us.

It is odd that I always use the word 'looming' in connection with the Manor. It implies bulk, but Banquo was in fact quite small as such houses go. It was an ugly thing – tall and uncompromisingly rectangular, as if built from a child's building blocks. It had been constructed about a century before from an orange-tinted stone found in the local quarries. Tall narrow windows looked out on to the drive, bordered by the same white stone that formed the mock-Tudor battlements crowning the house. The whole of the area that fronted the hall curved out smoothly from the body of the house, with four pillars flanking the main doors and supporting the domed roof of the portico. The simple dwelling of an upright man.

Yet, as always, I was struck by a note of incongruity about the Manor, almost as if the house I knew was just an intricate mask hiding something much older and much, much stranger behind it. Some of the house fronts near to the house where I lodged were nothing but flat screens, masks hiding the line of the underground train tunnels and the steam from the ventilation shafts. Other residents had protested when they were built, but I had found the concept amusing, and supported it. There the illusion was one of conformity and normality. Here, the frontage had the opposite effect.

For a few seconds as I trudged towards it, the face of the building appeared to be perfectly flat, and the portico curving out to greet us was nothing but clever shading on a two-dimensional backdrop. The impression lasted only a moment, and then Baker and I were walking up the steps of an undeniably real building. With a last glance to see whether I was going to usurp his authority, Baker took a step forward and grasped the bell pull. By my watch it was almost a quarter past nine.

Deep within the house there was a booming and within seconds I could hear footsteps approaching. The door swung open, held by a middle-aged man with an expression of contempt etched on to his face. His butler's uniform was immaculate, but his expression was beginning to fray around the edges and I wondered if our business there might be more serious than I had thought.

'Ah, Sergeant Baker,' he said with perfect diction and evident relief. His expression turned to me. 'And you are…?'

'This is Inspector Stratford, Simpson,' Baker anticipated.

'Of course,' said Simpson, as if he had been expecting me all along. 'I'll show you into the study, gentlemen.'

'What's happened?' I asked as we were neatly shepherded inside the hall and across to a large door on the left.

'I'm sure Sir George will explain, sir.' So saying, Simpson knocked and speedily opened the door.

'Sergeant Baker and Inspector Stratford have arrived, sir,' he announced, gesturing for us to enter. Crossing the room to meet us, followed by the worried gaze of the room's other occupants, came George Wallace. I had never met the man, but from my aunt's description, it could only be him. He was short and chubby; not a young man any more, but with a childish, insecure face that belied his age despite a flourishing moustache. He gave me a dubious look, my third in five minutes, and turned to Baker.

'Baker, good of you to come so promptly,' he began.

'That's my job, sir,' said Baker. 'May I introduce Inspector Stratford from London?' Mentally I blessed the man: he could have made things very awkward, but he seemed prepared to play it with a straight bat. Wallace extended a damp palm. I shook it and muttered a greeting.

'Richard's sister, Catherine, is asleep upstairs,' Wallace said in a low voice. 'I had to sedate her after the accident. Poor girl was in shock.'

I nodded and Wallace led us to the far side of the room, where the other occupants were arranged.

'This is Susan Seymour,' he said, introducing me to a tall slim woman in a lacy green dress that made me think of Aphrodite rising from the waves. I took her hand as Wallace continued: 'Susan is – was – Richard's fiancée…'

'Miss Seymour,' I said quietly, 'my condolences.'

'For what?' she asked simply.

I was nonplussed by her composure. 'For the… the tragic death of your fiancé,' I said finally. Perhaps it was the shock of events, but she seemed to me to be completely devoid of any emotional reaction. Or, I suddenly realised, perhaps she too had been sedated.

She nodded. Her hand was cool and confidant in mine, and I reluctantly released it before I crossed over the boundary of good manners.

Wallace dragged us away from Miss Seymour and introduced us to his wife. Elizabeth Wallace was tall and stately, and as fragile as a porcelain figure. She had obviously been a great beauty when Wallace married her, but time had undermined her good looks with a network of fine lines as if a skeletal autumn leaf had been laid against her skin

'And this', Wallace said, guiding a large, rather surly young man across the room to us, 'is one of our visitors: Herr Kreiner. He's a protégé of Dr Friedlander, who is –' He glanced around. 'Where is the Doctor?' he asked peevishly.

'Still in the laboratory,' Herr Kreiner said. One of his eyes had a white pressure mark around it, as if he had been wearing a monocle for the first time and trying too hard to force it into his eye. There was something about him that I distrusted on first sight. I had seen his type before in the Rookeries and Stews of London: stupid, easily led, believing that the world owed them a living and they would take it any way they could. Teuton or not, I resolved to watch him carefully.

'This is a terrible business,' he said, shaking his head sorrowfully. 'Poor Rupert…'

'Rupert?' I queried.

His face froze for a moment, but I could see a lurking phantom of panic in his eyes.

'He means Richard,' a voice interjected from the doorway. 'Richard Harries.'

I turned, to see that John Hopkinson had entered the room.

I had completely forgotten about Hopkinson. Thanks to the walk through the snow and the anticipation of trouble, the death of Gordon Seavers and the real purpose of my visit had slipped entirely from my mind. My surprise was so total that all I gained was a confused impression of a tall, thin man with straight brown hair. There seemed to be an old-fashioned air about him, but I couldn't immediately tell why. Neither could I fathom my immediate identification of the man. I had not met him before, yet recognition was total. He was carrying a decanter of whisky and two glasses, and as he entered the room his eye caught mine. There was a sudden flash of… puzzlement? Uncertainty? Then it was gone and I was left wondering if I had ever seen it. Had he realised that I was a police officer, and did he know why I was there? If so it was perfectly masked when Wallace introduced us, and I decided to wait for a more opportune moment before questioning him about the missing letter. Now was the time to deal with the death of Richard Harries.

'Where did the accident occur?' I said decisively, turning to Wallace.

He winced at the recollection.

'We moved the equipment in here, but the accident took place in the conservatory,' he said. 'Richard used it for his experiments. I didn't mind… Had no use for the blessed place myself.'

I noticed a flicker of expression on the face of Elizabeth Wallace, but whatever crossed her mind went unsaid. I glanced towards the almost unidentifiable debris on the desk.

'Well,' I said turning to the others, 'if you would all be so good as to wait elsewhere, the sergeant and I will see each of you in turn. In here. I intend running through the incident with each of you – for the sake of completeness.'

I watched Miss Seymour as I spoke, wondering what her reaction would be. In point of fact she failed to react at all, but out of the corner of my eye I saw George Wallace flinch. I turned to him.

'Sir George, if you could stay first and enlighten us?' He nodded weakly. His wife, taking the hint, gently shepherded Mr Hopkinson, Herr Kreiner and the elfin Susan Seymour from the room.

Before Wallace could move, I sat in the comfortably upholstered chair behind his desk. Second-guessing me as usual, Baker was already manoeuvring a chair into position beside Wallace. I took a large notebook and fountain pen from my pocket. Baker walked round to stand beside me, and as Wallace sat down I placed my elbows firmly upon his blotter, steepled my fingers and stared across the burnt-out equipment, waiting for him to start.

THE ACCOUNT OF JOHN HOPKINSON (5)

It took us several minutes to recover from the ordeal of the experiment, and then to varying degrees. Somehow, Simpson was there, helping Susan – pale and tense – to support Elizabeth and guide her towards the relative comfort of the drawing room. George and I carried the unconscious Catherine up to her room. Dr Friedlander went ahead of us opening doors. I left George and the Doctor to check her pulse.

When I arrived back at the conservatory, Simpson and Friedlander were talking in low voices by the shattered remains of the equipment. A single valve had survived, standing upright amongst the shattered remains of its fellows. The intricate wiring within the glass bulb contrasted with the devastated and tangled mass that surrounded it.

'I was just saying, sir,' Simpson explained as I entered, 'that we really ought to move Professor Harries.'

He glanced across at the dead man, face down over the further end of the table – the furthest that we had been able to move him so far.

'It doesn't seem respectful to leave him like that,' he added. I nodded.

'The trouble is', Kreiner said, 'that the table is rather in the way.'

'So I've just realised.'

I walked over and examined it closer, doing my best to ignore the stench of charred flesh from the other side.

'And because of the trestles, we can't lift it out of the way very easily,' I added.

'Too heavy, sir,' said Simpson, who tapped the corner nearest him. 'Oak top and trestles. Very unusual, but very heavy. Even heavier with all this on it.' He gestured at the debris littering the middle. 'Can we clear it all off?'

'We could,' I said slowly, 'but it would take some time.

Perhaps it would be best though. Then we can lift the top off and move this trestle.'

I gave it an experimental kick. It failed to move at all.

Wallace came in as we were preparing to sweep the first pile of blackened wires and broken glass on to the floor. There was no sign of the Doctor. Perhaps he was ministering to the ladies.

Kreiner again outlined the problem that faced us.

'Best to keep it all together, though,' George said, leaning over the mess, feeling around the edge amongst the soot and glass. 'Ah, yes, here we are.'

He scraped some of the mess of black away and I could see that underneath was a lip of wood. The equipment had been mounted on a separate board – scarred and pitted now, even burnt through in places, but still intact.

'My desk is pretty clear, and it should be big enough. We'll put it in the study.'

Kreiner helped him to prise up the wooden board and Simpson opened the door to allow them to carry it out into the corridor.

The lights dimmed as they left, and Simpson glanced up at the bulbs, his concern assuring me that it was not my eyes that were at fault.

'We'd better move the table then, sir,' he suggested and I edged around it so that I could pull the body away and slump it into a chair. This meant of course that it watched us with its single recognisable eye as we manhandled the table top into a gap between the piles of papers and boxes – a film of greasy black dust now trailed across them The wooden slab was every bit as heavy as we had feared, so we left the trestles in place, and steeled ourselves to the task of moving Harries. Simpson looked pale and was breathing heavily. When George and Kreiner reappeared a moment later, he muttered something to George, who nodded.

'Yes, yes, you had better. I did notice,' he said, and Simpson left us.

George and I carried the body, Kreiner – looking somewhat frail from the experience and getting paler by the minute – opened the doors for us and guided me backwards up the stairs, which now seemed steeper than before with a curve that went round for ever, rather than the mere ninety degrees it had been. Somehow we managed to get Harries to his room and on to his bed without any of us actually being sick or fainting. Harries's bare teeth were clenched tight together as if he was as nauseated as we were, and I tried not to look at the devastated remains as George pulled a sheet over them.

Susan Seymour and Elizabeth Wallace were sitting side by side on the couch in the drawing room. The Doctor was engaged in a low conversation with Susan Seymour, who seemed to have recovered much of her composure, though she was still pale. Elizabeth was shaking slightly but otherwise seemed almost back to her usual self. Her husband took her hand in both of his, and she looked up at him.

'We, er – we put him on his bed.' George answered her silent question. 'It seemed best.'

'And how is Catherine?'

'I've given her a sedative. She'll sleep for a while; should be over some of the shock when she wakes up again.' George sat down beside her, still holding her hand. 'I telephoned Baker while I was in the study. He's the police sergeant.'

'And what did he say?' Kreiner asked. 'Something about lead piping and billiard rooms, maybe?'

'Fitz,' the Doctor admonished quietly but firmly.

George frowned, as uncertain of the allusion as I was myself. 'He said he would come over. Shouldn't take him too long. Not far.'

As he spoke, the Doctor drew out his watch and examined it. Then he wound it slowly with his thumb and forefinger before returning it to his waistcoat. 'Time, I think,' he said quietly, 'is of the essence.'

'Oh, don't worry,' I told him, 'just routine – as they say.' My own voice was loud with nerves. 'He'll ask a lot of stupid questions, then call the undertakers for us. Just an unfortunate accident, that's all.'

'Just an unfortunate accident,' echoed George absently.

'Feel free to query the adjective,' I told him. Then I caught sight of Susan's face, the streaks from the tears catching the light as she looked over towards me. 'I'm sorry,' I murmured, 'I need a drink.'

I closed the door behind me as I felt the colour rise in my cheeks, and wished, not for the first time, that I could reconcile my sarcasm to some sort of tact on occasion.

After a few deep breaths, feeling a little more recovered after the events of the evening, I decided that the decanters had probably been taken to the kitchen, and I made my way in that direction. The corridor from the dining room was dim, the lamps low. As I neared the kitchen, I heard a footfall behind me and ducked instinctively into the shadows.

A door I had not noticed before had opened silently behind me and a tall, white apparition stepped as if from the wall into the corridor. It peered around, suspicious, and I saw that the white was the colour of the overalls the man wore. With piercing eyes, the figure's face turned directly towards me, glaring at my silhouette, apparently annoyed that I had seen him – then he turned abruptly away. Simpson wheeled round and set off down the corridor away from me, heading towards the butler's pantry. Puzzled, I continued to the kitchen.

Beryl was there, although at first I failed to notice her. She was curled up in a wooden armchair in the corner beside the stove. She stirred as I reached a decanter from the table and startled me somewhat as her face lifted out of what had appeared to be an empty bundle of clothing.

'Oh, hello, sir,' she said, and uncurled a little into a more decorous shape. 'I was asleep, sir. Mr Simpson said we'd all to wait until Mr Baker had been. But I'm so tired, and it's cold in here.'

'Baker won't keep us long, I'm certain,' I assured her and handed her a glass of whisky. She eyed it dubiously, then sniffed at it. 'Go on. It will warm you up.'

She hesitated, then sipped at it, choking slightly as it burned its way down. Her hand went, surprised, to her throat.

'Oh!' she exclaimed and I laughed.

'Finish it up,' I told her, 'then we'll go through to the drawing room. No point in you freezing out here when there's a good fire in there.'

'But Mr Simpson said –'

'Never mind what Mr Simpson said. This is what I say, all right?'

'All right, sir.' She smiled and shivered, drinking more of her whisky, beginning to enjoy it.

'Where is Simpson, by the way?' I tried to sound uninterested.

'He went down to the cellar – to see to the generator.'

'Ah.'

Beryl giggled. 'He doesn't like doing that. Says it's like hell's pit down there, rats and things.'

That explained one thing, anyway: Simpson had just been attending to the important work without explaining it all. I decided that he was probably not proud of this more menial of his duties.

'He told me about what happened.' Beryl's large eyes caught the light, glistening as she looked up at me. 'I didn't really like Professor Harries, but for that to happen...'

She shivered again and tightened her hands around her glass. I refilled it for her, letting my own stand empty on the table nearby.

'Was it very terrible?' she asked quietly.

I sat gently on the wooden arm of her chair and patted her shoulder lightly. 'It wasn't pleasant. But it's over now. You'll soon be home, tucked up warm.'

Beryl glanced towards the outer door. 'I don't know, sir,' she murmured.

'Why? What is it?'

'Well, sir – it's just… well, walking all that way. In the dark. After what happened.'

I took the empty glass from her and placed it on the floor beside me. Then, as she was still shivering, I put my arm around her shoulders. She was quite cold and I could feel her smooth skin trembling beneath the thin fabric of her dress. It seemed odd that she was wearing so little on such a chill evening. Perhaps it had got colder since she had struggled in, drenched, in her long cloak. For a moment Beryl was still, then she drew her feet up on to the seat of the chair, kicking off her shoes and massaging some warmth into her toes with one hand, her knees up under her chin.

'You'll be able to sleep here tonight if you want. I'm sure no one will mind. We'll find you a bed somewhere.'

She relaxed a little at that, pleased to be able to put out of her mind the prospect of a long walk in the dark. I felt her unwind as she nestled her head against my shoulder, her fair hair spilling over the black of my jacket, and smiled, her mouth stretching across her white teeth. I laughed back at her innocent, guileless face, but she didn't mind, just wriggled closer and warmer, her dress rising up over her legs above her knees as she moved, although she seemed not to notice.

I stayed with Beryl for a while, and when we heard the doorbell and I suggested that we go through to the drawing room to see the sergeant, she assured me that she was much warmer. I escorted her back down the corridor, the lights now brighter, presumably due to the efforts of Simpson and the generator in the cellar. As we emerged into the dining room, I remembered that I had originally left to get a drink, and it occurred to me that probably some of the others could do with one as well. Beryl offered to go back for me, but I was afraid she would catch cold again, and anyway, I was not too sure about the impression it would create after my absence if the maid returned with the refreshment – or for that matter if we returned together after so long.

'You go on in,' I told Beryl. 'I'll be with you all in a short while.' And back I went to the kitchen to collect glasses and decanter, hoping that we had not emptied the last one, and that a suitable time would elapse between Beryl's entry and my return.

THE REPORT OF INSPECTOR IAN STRATFORD (5)

The conservatory was in shadow when I entered. Wallace's description of Richard Harries's fatally flawed experiment had intrigued me, and I wanted to see the scene as soon as possible. Leaving Baker in charge of questioning Herr Kreiner, I had followed Wallace's directions through to the back of the house.

Pale-blue moonlight cascaded in through the glass roof, barely illuminating the untidiest room I had ever seen. I could just about make out two trestles standing in the centre of the room; a large table top stood beside them, scarred with an irregular pattern of scorch marks that identified the location of the ill-fated experiment. The area between the trestles was piled high with junk of every kind: books, glassware, paper, boxes and other items of scientific detritus. I guessed that they had been shifted from the surface above to make way for the equipment.

The sweet smell of charred meat hung in the air – not entirely unpleasant until one remembered the source.

'If the state of this conservatory reflects the state of mind of its former occupant then Richard Harries must have been a very disturbed person, wouldn't you say?' The voice hung on the air, vibrant and eager. In the jigsaw pattern of moonlight and shadow it was difficult to trace where it came from, but I thought the man was located over by the garden side of the conservatory, where Richard Harries (or, more likely, Simpson operating under Harries's instruction) had covered the glass with black cloth and wooden boards in a haphazard arrangement.

'I rarely draw sweeping conclusions from scant facts,' I said to the shadows.

'Very wise. Conclusions are like London buses: if you jump on one without looking you invariably end up heading the wrong way.' The voice seemed to be elsewhere in the room now. Had its owner moved, or was I misjudging his location?

I took a step forward. 'My job here is purely to establish what happened – Dr Friedlander.'

'What happened?' The voice was closer this time, over near the bookshelves that lined the wall adjoining the Manor proper. There was an oil lamp and a box of matches on a side table. I moved closer and set flame to wick. 'A search for absolute truth,' he continued. 'You're a philosopher, then? And please – call me "Doctor": Friedlander is such a mouthful, I find.'

'I'm not a philosopher: I'm a policeman. Inspector Ian Stratford, Scotland Yard.'

As the light from the oil lamp slowly spread across the conservatory I found myself staring at a man of medium height wearing a long coat of some material that reflected the light in a soft sheen. His waistcoat was cut from a cloth more suited for carpet bags than for formal attire, and his cravat was in imminent danger of coming undone. He struck me immediately as a student of the Bohemian persuasion, but there was something about his poise, his immense stillness and concentration, that spoke of experience, of life lived to the full but also of a boundless enthusiasm. He held a book in his hands, and for all the world it appeared as if he had been reading it in the near-darkness.

'Surely crime is a philosophy of its own,' he said, not raising his gaze from the page. 'One man obeys the law, another chooses to break it. Two different views of life and social responsibility.'

'Crimes are committed by criminals,' I said firmly. 'Criminals are either desperate men attempting to better their situation by breaking the laws by which society lives or unhinged men who refuse to accept that they are bound by society's rules. Either way, they must be apprehended and punished.'

'And so falls several hundred years of debate,' the Doctor said, smiling at me. His eyes were a startling blue. 'I have to say that Professor Harries's taste in books is remarkably catholic.' He gestured to the shelves from which he had removed the volume he was reading. 'Complete runs of several scientific journals, leather-bound of course – must have a fit postman – as well as books on everything from archaeology through orchids to signs of the Zodiac. Irving Braxiatel would have a field day in here.'

'And Irving Braxiatel is…?'

'My –' he hesitated. 'My colleague and occasional collaborator in adventures of the mind, the soul and the body.' With an emphatic thud he closed the book he was holding. 'The *Necronomicon* of Abdul Alhazared: possibly the most misunderstood, mistranslated and misused book the human race has ever produced.'

My eye was caught by a slip of paper protruding from between the pages. I moved closer to the Doctor and removed it. Written in a childlike script was what appeared to be a series of notes on the history of the book:

Al Azif circ. AD 730 in Damascus. Trans to Greek AD 950 by Theodorus Philetus, all copies burned AD 1050. Retrans. Greek from Olaus Wormius Latin ed. Both supp. by Pope G.IX. Spanish trans. around AD 1600? Prob. from orig. Arabic. Cf. quote:'To things immortal, time can do no wrong/And that which never is to die, for ever must be young.' Poss. Blake? Check roots against Alhazared.

'Harries's writing?' I asked, showing the paper to the Doctor. He nodded. 'I imagine so. Inspector, I have a most terrible suspicion that –'

A squeal from the far side of the room cut across his words. We both whirled round and scanned the room for the source of the noise. Even as my eye encountered the large wooden cage which almost filled one windowsill, the door to the cage swung open and two hellishly large rats leaped out. For a second they paused, their tails flicking restlessly behind them as their noses twitched, searching the air for danger. A glance passed between them as if they were discussing their next move; then they scurried in opposite directions along the sill. One I lost sight of as it darted behind a pile of books; the other paused beside a broken pane of glass. Daintily placing its forepaws on the razor-sharp shards, it looked out upon its new kingdom. Then it was gone.

'I don't like rats,' muttered the Doctor darkly. 'I once had a friend who was almost eaten by one.'

'If they were the ones Harries used in his experiments, shouldn't they have been locked up?'

'They were.' He crossed the room to where the cage stood vacant and examined the wire door. 'The cunning little brutes have removed the hinges.' He glanced up at me, and there was something brooding in his eyes. 'There's a word for what that man Harries has been doing to the laws of nature.'

It suddenly struck me that I was treating the Doctor as a fellow investigator rather than as a witness to a fatality. Attempting to pull control of the conversation back to where it belonged, I said, 'I doubt if there is anything significant here, but Sergeant Baker and I can give it a thorough search after Simpson has caught the rat. What I need to do now is view Professor Harries's body. Are you acquainted with its location?'

'Indeed, and if you don't mind I'll examine the body with you.'

'You're a medical practitioner? I had assumed you were a doctor of science.'

He gave me a quizzical glance. 'I am qualified in many things, Inspector Stratford, including several that have yet to be invented.'

I followed the Doctor through the house to the main staircase, matching what I remembered of the journey to the conservatory to what I could see now. I had already decided that a thorough knowledge of the immediate geography could be valuable. From the study I could hear Baker continuing the questioning of the maid. Odd girl... She had given me the most appealing glance when I had passed her in the corridor earlier. Perhaps she disliked and feared Richard Harries as much as everyone else in this unusual household. Baker could reassure her. She was local, with a large family in the village. I wondered if Baker would start on Simpson. I hoped not, I was looking forward to tackling him myself. And Hopkinson.

The Doctor showed little inclination to speak as we scaled the stairs. I had hoped that he would continue with whatever he had been about to say earlier, before Harries's rats interrupted us, but it seemed that my wishes were in vain. At the top of the stairs he turned right into a panelled corridor lined with doors. A right-angled turn at the end led us into a similar passage with a door set prominently at the end. Typical of Harries to take the master bedroom, I thought, then frowned. I had never met the man, yet my objectivity seemed to be shading with the tints of other people's opinions. The Doctor turned the handle and entered the room, crossing straight to the window and staring out across the gardens. Steeling myself against the smell that had begun to seep out, I walked across to the bed.

In my career as a police officer I have seen death in many ways: in mortuaries, on streets, dragged out of stinking rivers; knifed, beaten, mutilated or just quietly and inoffensively dead. In all my time nothing had prepared me for the sight as I pulled the stained and stinking sheet from the thing on the bed. Yet at the same time my feelings had been and have been echoed, both before and since the time I first set eyes upon the remains of Richard Harries. It is the disquieting feeling I get now when I walk down a street and see a half-demolished building in a derelict slum area. Harries's face was like that. One side of it was still intact, although the skin was red and blistered and the eye had run and spread. The other side was ruined, stripped of all humanity. It had been burnt down to the skull and beyond. The bone was blackened and cracked like rock and the eye was just a curdled white lump in the socket. The line of teeth, roughened and blistered by the fire, stretched up to the end of his jaw in an insane grin. The worst thing about Richard Harries was not his appearance, or the smell, or even the frozen laugh. It was the knowledge that everything I could see in his exposed face lay under my own as well.

I pulled the sheet entirely off and bent to the gruesome task of searching Harries. I found nothing but everyday items: a few coins, a bunch of keys, a handkerchief. I could not examine the body closely for other injuries without removing his clothes, a process that I did not relish, so I confined myself to an examination of the exposed areas. There were no injuries apart from the obvious ones and if any were covered by his garments then the body would have had to be redressed after death. I could not imagine any circumstances, however unusual, that would have required that. Perhaps it had been an accident.

As I worked I became gradually aware of a scratching noise, like fingernails tapping irregularly on wood. At first it did not bother me, but it became increasingly irritating as I worked. Eventually I glanced up, ready to deliver a mild reproof to the Doctor, but before I could say anything I noticed that his hands were behind his back as he gazed out of the window. Whatever the noise was, it had nothing to do with him.

Whether or not my reaction had alerted whatever was producing the noise to my interest I could not say, but it died away slowly, as if the thing that was causing it were scuttling away into the distance. Harries's remaining rat, the one that had stayed in the house? The thought made me uneasy – not only was the thing intelligent enough to dismantle a cage door hinge, but it also seemed to me that it might be spying on us.

Trying to distance the thought from my mind, I rolled up Harries's sleeves and trouser legs to check his limbs. As I pulled the trouser legs back I noticed something strange. There seemed to be an unusual amount of play in the knee joints: as I moved the leg around it seemed to move sideways as well as forwards and back. I was about to comment on this to the Doctor when he answered my unspoken question.

'The severe electric shock he received caused all his muscles to spasm,' he said in a low voice. 'The effect would have been most marked in the long extensor, long adductor and sartorius muscle tissue. His knees just couldn't take the strain: shattered straightaway.'

I finished rolling the trouser legs down, feeling queasy as Harries's legs moved around as if attached by nothing but string. I was just pulling down his right sleeve when I noticed something that I had missed before. It was an array of dots on the inside of the elbow. They fitted into a fold in the skin and it was only by straightening the arm that I had noticed them. Looking closer, I saw that they were holes, some old and dimpled, some dark and new. No particular pattern was formed, rather they were distributed randomly over a small area. I looked up at the Doctor. His eyes met mine, and he nodded.

'Cocaine,' he said simply.

'How can you tell?'

'There are signs – some physical, most behavioural. I knew as soon as I met him.'

My mind raced, sorting out connections, relationships, causes and effects. An addict, living in the same house as a physician... Was it too much to suspect that George Wallace had been supplying his friend with cocaine? And did that give me enough grounds for suspecting that Richard Harries's death was more than just an accident? The use of stimulant drugs, although not illegal, accreted crime around it as the mental state of the user became warped. I had never worked on a case involving drugs without also finding blackmail, theft... or murder.

'Was Harries murdered?' I asked.

'Yes,' the Doctor said, and nodded sadly. 'Yes, I think he was.'

'How was it done?'

He crossed the room to the bed.

'You remember the equipment in the study?' I had not examined it yet, but I remembered the burnt objects on the table. I nodded. 'It's always difficult to tell, when dealing with people who don't quite understand what they are doing, but looking at the equipment now I think two of the wires have been swapped over. To put it simply, instead of stepping the voltage down to a safe level I think it was boosted to a very *un*safe one.' He shook his head sadly. 'I was in the audience of the American Institute of Electrical Engineers when Tesla allowed half a million volts to pass through his body and walked away unscathed. I once did something similar with a charge of distronic radiation on a Zygon ship in Scotland. It's not the voltage that kills you, of course: it's the amperage. But what Richard Harries was doing was far, far more dangerous. When you mix electricity and the power of the mind you're in danger of unleashing uncontrollable amounts of Artron energy, and that, I suspect, is where Harries was unwittingly heading.'

'Artron energy?' I said, as sarcastically as I could. His words smacked of fakery, of 'mesmeric powers', 'ectoplasm' and 'the aether'.

He smiled at me boyishly, as if he knew what I was thinking. 'Artron energy is to normal energy what movements within the deeps of the sea are to the waves on the surface. Very slight in humans, but in some other –'

'This is all very interesting,' I interrupted heavily, 'but my primary concern at the moment is to determine who, if anyone, could have killed Richard Harries, and why they did it. The "how" can come later.'

'As far as I can see,' the Doctor said, 'anyone could have tampered with the equipment. They could have got in either through the conservatory doors or through the French windows. But it would have had to be someone who understood what they were doing.'

'Which would include…?' I prompted.

He smiled dazzlingly. 'Me, of course. Fitz possibly – let's give him the benefit of the doubt.'

'Fitz?'

'My associate – Herr Kreiner. Mr Hopkinson I will have to reserve judgement on, as I've only just met him. Sir George Wallace has been living in the same house as Richard Harries for some time, so we should assume that he's picked something up along the way, and the same applies to his sister Catherine.'

'And what about Miss Seymour?' I asked.

The Doctor was immediately watchful. 'Yes…' he said cautiously, '*she* would certainly have the knowledge. Perhaps more so than the rest of us put together.'

I made a mental note to follow up on that intriguing comment later, but for the moment there was something else about Miss Seymour that I wanted his opinion on. 'It strikes me,' I said, 'that her attitude towards the death of her fiancé has been suspicious to say the least.'

'How so?'

I frowned. 'The best way I can put it is that there is a marked lack of compassion in her manner.'

'That's been worrying me as well,' he said quietly. 'Compassion seems to be conspicuous by her absence.'

'So, what you appear to be telling me is that I can't rule out anyone except for the servants.'

'Didn't I mention the servants?' he asked. 'They too have been around Richard Harries's experiments for some time, and Simpson at least strikes me as being a lot more intelligent than he lets on. Oh, and don't forget the absent Mr Seavers –'

A wave of coldness ran through my body. 'Gordon Seavers? But he's –'

'Sir George mentioned his name when Fitz and I arrived. I gather he's expected at any moment.'

Gordon Seavers was dead. That was why I was here. But the

news had apparently not percolated through to Banquo Manor yet. Why hadn't John Hopkinson told anyone that Seavers had killed himself? Everything seemed to link back to him, and I remembered the sudden flash of recognition between us. Where had we met before? Suddenly I wanted very much to talk to John Hopkinson.

'Is something the matter, Inspector?' asked the Doctor.

I was torn between telling him about Seavers and letting the matter ride until I could confront Hopkinson. Professional feelings won over humanity. 'Just feeling tired,' I said. 'I've had rather a busy day.'

'I would suggest you ask Simpson to find you a room here – I'm sure Sir George won't mind. It will save you making the journey to the village and back again. Especially in this weather.'

'Thank you,' I said, but my words were lost on the Doctor's retreating back. Like a searchlight, his attention had been directed elsewhere.

He turned back to me as he reached the doorway to Harries's room. 'Footprints,' he said succinctly, his eyes wide with sudden enthusiasm.

'Footprints?'

'In the snow. They might show if someone had entered the conservatory from outside in order to tamper with the equipment. I'll go and check.'

'There's no need, Doctor,' I called as he sprinted away down the corridor, 'Baker and I can check later on.'

'There's no present like the time,' he called back. I thought I just caught him muttering the phrase 'Artron energy' as his footsteps faded away into the distance. Well, good luck to him.

I took a last look around the room before leaving. It was remarkably bare, and I gained the impression that it was less of a bedroom and more of a functional utility for Harries. If he could have fitted a bed into the conservatory, I think he would have done. My attention was attracted by a book holding down a sheaf of papers on a desk in the corner. Out of curiosity I crossed to pick it up. The papers seemed to consist of a journal entitled *Archives de Neurologie* for July of the year. It was opened to the first page of a paper with a long French title, of which the only words I could recognise were 'hysterical' and 'paralysis'. The author had the unarguably Germanic name of Freud, and a few sheets of manuscript paper beside the journal bore witness to Harries's attempts to translate the paper.

A man who understood technical French of a highly specialised nature well enough to translate? My respect for Harries increased slightly. The book that had been holding the papers down appeared to be a collection of poetry and I noticed a slip of paper emerging from between the pages. On the basis of the two books I had examined, Richard Harries had been an incessant memory-jogger. I opened the book to the page marked. The piece of paper was blank but there was only one poem on the page revealed. It was by Samuel Coleridge and a few lines in the middle had been underlined in a thick, wavering red penstroke:

> *Two lovely children run an endless race,*
> *A sister and a brother!*
> *This far outstripped the other*
> *Yet ever runs she with reverted face,*
> *And looks and listens for the boy behind,*
> *For he, alas! is blind!*
> *O'er rough and smooth with even step he passed,*
> *And knows not whether he be first or last.*

I shivered and decided to make my way down.

As I gained the bottom of the stairs I discovered Sergeant Baker standing foursquare and rocklike in the centre of the hall. 'Just sent the maid and the butler on their way, sir,' he said catching sight of me. 'No help there: they don't know a thing.'

'Ah – I wanted to talk to Simpson. I thought we might –'

'Anticipating your instructions, I persuaded Mr Simpson to prepare rooms for us here for the night, sir.'

'Oh. Well done, Baker.'

'And I took the liberty of questioning Mr Kreiner as well, sir.'

I sighed. 'That's all right, Sergeant. It saves me the trouble. Did he have anything interesting to say?'

'No, sir. Nothing except the accent in which he said some of it, which is as fake as a three-shilling note.'

I felt as if I was just running around distracting attention while Baker calmly and methodically plodded through the case. Nonetheless, I felt a certain pride as I told him of my discoveries. To his credit, Baker did not claim prior knowledge of Harries's drug habit or pretend that he had guessed about the murder. He merely nodded and said, 'Well, that is interesting.' And the sincerity with which he said it was better than any ironic praise.

'Indeed,' I acknowledged cryptically, and began to move across the hall towards the study door. Over my shoulder I said, 'Could you find Mr Hopkinson and ask him to step this way, Sergeant?'

Baker moved off, and I entered the study.

Less than a minute later I heard two sets of footsteps crossing the hall towards me. I let a few seconds elapse after I heard them stop, then I turned to face John Hopkinson.

'You wanted to see me, Inspector,' he said beating both Baker and me to the first words. He advanced across the room towards me, leaving the Sergeant to close the door. I used the time to fill in the details on the rough mental sketch I had of him.

He was as tall and as thin as I remembered, moving with restraint and precision. He now wore a pair of half-rimmed glasses through which he studied me with a curious and, I felt, faintly disappointed air. It was as if he had already decided how a Scotland Yard inspector should act, and I wasn't living up to his expectations. A faint glow of anger flared inside me: what right had he to expect me to play his games? Even as part of me realised how ridiculous I was being, I decided to dislike John Hopkinson.

'Yes, Mr Hopkinson,' I said, 'there are a few points I should like to clear up about the accident.'

'Accident, Inspector?' The light from the lamps reflected in his lenses, making walls of his eyes.

'You don't think so?'

He smiled briefly and sat down. 'I don't think you would be going to all this trouble if *you* did, Inspector.'

'Very astute of you,' I said. 'What do you think happened?' I moved back to sit on Wallace's desk, supporting myself with my hands.

'Harries wasn't a very well liked character, I'm afraid. When he died it was a bit too fortuitous for my liking.'

'If he was murdered, aren't you rather throwing suspicion on to yourself?'

Hopkinson smiled. 'All gifts have to be paid for, Inspector. If my suspicion is the price for Harries's death then I pay it willingly. After all, I have the best possible defence.'

Baker, silent beside the door, came suddenly to life. 'And what might that be, sir?'

'Innocence, Sergeant,' he replied. 'I didn't do it.'

'Can you tell us who *did* do it, Mr Hopkinson?' I said with as much calm as I could muster, cursing as I suddenly realised that Hopkinson had manoeuvred us into tacitly admitting that Harries had been murdered.

For the first time some animation appeared in his face. 'No, Inspector, I couldn't. I would like to, believe me, but I couldn't.'

Remembering Wallace's opinion of Richard Harries, I altered tack slightly. 'You say that Professor Harries was not a particularly pleasant person. Does anyone else in this house share your opinion of him?'

'I couldn't really tell you that either, I'm afraid,' he replied. 'I don't think George Wallace liked him – in fact, I don't know why he let the man stay in the house. Friedlander I don't know about – he only arrived just before dinner. Everyone else seemed indifferent – Including, oddly enough, his fiancée.'

'Yes,' I said, 'I had noticed that Miss Seymour seemed a little detached. I'd put it down to shock. Do you know of any other reasons?'

'Not entirely,' Hopkinson answered, trailing his sentence off into introspective silence. He seemed about to continue, then casually extended his long legs and folded his arms. I wondered at the sudden thaw that had occurred when dislike of Richard Harries (and, something muttered in the back of my mind, Susan Seymour) was mentioned.

'But I gather from Mrs Wallace that the engagement was all but off,' Hopkinson continued. 'Why, I don't know.' He looked at his feet. 'I wish I did. In many ways I know less than you, Inspector.'

'I doubt that, Mr Hopkinson,' I said, and our eyes met for an instant. I don't know what passed between us, but it was remarkably like understanding. 'You can, of course, account for your movements immediately before dinner?'

'Of course.' He smiled a self-satisfied smile.

'Then I won't ask you to,' I continued, '…yet.'

'Thank you,' he replied, either simply or sarcastically. I suspected the latter.

'Thank you, Mr Hopkinson. You have been of some slight help to me. You might ask Simpson to let us know which rooms are ours.'

'My pleasure, Inspector.' Hopkinson rose and turned towards the door.

I let him take two paces, then used my one, major piece of ammunition: 'Why did you not tell Sir George that Gordon Seavers had committed suicide?'

Hopkinson froze. Over his shoulder I could see Baker's face gaping in stunned amazement. Part of me realised that I had not actually told him about it yet, but my total concentration was focused upon John Hopkinson. He was perfectly still for one frozen instant in time, clenched hard but fragile like glass. Then he turned and was smiling mockingly at me, but I knew that he knew more than he would say. And he knew that I knew, but we were forced to play out the script as written.

'George has not been well,' he said. 'I had hoped to find an appropriate opportunity to break the news to him. No such opportunity has arisen. I'm sure you understand, Inspector Stratford.'

I understood. And for a moment I admired him: I had met few people who could carry through a bluff as coolly as he was doing. 'I am not sure that I do, Mr Hopkinson,' I said, calling the bluff. 'How long have you been here now? A whole day? And no time to break the news of the death – the suicide – of an old and trusted mutual friend? And even allowing for Sir George's health, not even telling his wife? I find that very odd, Mr Hopkinson.'

'It's been a very long and tiring day, Inspector. I should like to go to bed – if you have finished making vague implications. Was there anything else?'

'Just one thing. Where is the letter that Seavers received just before he died? The one that drove him to kill himself?'

He had known that the question was coming, just as he knew that by facing me down he had me beaten. 'I'm sure I don't know what you mean, Inspector,' he said, and turned to go.

I lost my temper.

'Oh yes you do. You know a great deal more than you are saying about a lot of things, Hopkinson. And if you won't tell me – as it seems you won't – then I shall still find out. I want to know what was in that letter, and who it was from. I'm pretty certain now, but I intend to find out for sure. Don't doubt it, Mr Hopkinson. Sleep well.'

He raised his hand in a sarcastic farewell and left. I heard him mutter something from the hall, but I didn't catch it.

There was an uncomfortable silence in the study for a few moments until Baker said, 'What do you think, sir?'

'I'm not sure,' I sighed. 'A murder – a technically minded one at that – and a man who doesn't bother to tell his hosts that one of the guests has done away with himself. It's a strange business, Baker. What do you think?'

'Must have been someone who knew what they were doing, sir. That's a fearsome pile of equipment. I wouldn't know which bit did what. So…' He paused. 'Friedlander, or Miss Harries, or Miss Seymour, or…'

'Susan Seymour?' I queried sharply.

'Why not, sir? She was the murdered man's fiancée, so she probably knew more about the experiment than most. She *has* been very distracted, almost cold, since we arrived. And her engagement had been broken off. If it was Harries who broke it off she might have been hurt enough to –'

'Point taken, Sergeant,' I muttered. 'What about Hopkinson?'

'Difficult to say, sir. We don't know how much he knows about the equipment. He is a solicitor, after all. Harries only wanted him for legal advice.'

'And Wallace?'

'If it were him, why call us in, sir?'

'In case Friedlander or Miss Harries realise about the sabotage. They're qualified to notice as well as to commit the act. And Wallace is astute enough to know that. It seems such a simple operation, just swapping two wires. I'm inclined to think that anyone could have done it – even the maid.'

'Beryl Green, sir?' Baker looked thoughtful for a moment. 'In fact, sir, you might be closer to the truth than you know. There's a bit of talk in the village about Beryl; not quite as white as she's painted, so they say. Not that I have any truck with gossip, of course. But I still reckon your Mr Hopkinson is well in the lead in the field of suspects…'

A knock at the door halted Baker in mid-sentence. It was unfortunate: his talkative periods were rare and always worth paying attention to. Resignedly, for I knew it would be quite some time before I could persuade him to talk again, I raised my voice and bade the person outside to enter.

It was Simpson.

'Sir George asked me to inform you about your rooms, gentlemen,' he began. 'If you care to stop for the night, I believe that the first two rooms at the top of the stairs are free.'

'Thank you, Simpson,' I said, and turned to Baker, hoping that he would finish his sentence. I opened my mouth, but I was still aware of Simpson's shadowy figure in the doorway. 'Is there anything else?' I asked, thinking that he was just loitering with intent to eavesdrop.

'Well, sir, it's just that… Well, when the sergeant was questioning me earlier, there was something I forgot to mention.' He looked between us anxiously.

'Come in and shut the door,' I said, and after he had done so I gestured for him to continue.

'I didn't mention this earlier,' said Simpson, not looking at either of us, but staring resolutely at the far wall, 'because I felt it was the business of the gentlemen concerned. However, on further reflection, I realise that it could have some bearing on the matter in hand. I shall now tell you about it.'

The flood of pomposity over, he paused for breath. I glanced at Baker and smiled. His moustache twitched in acknowledgement.

'You see, sir, I think I know who murdered Professor Harries.'

It was one of those rare occasions when I seemed to be thinking on at least three different levels. Simultaneously I was sifting through the evidence trying to identify his choice, wondering at the luck that had, apparently, come my way and guessing who had told him about the murder. Hopkinson probably. In a darker undercurrent, I was cursing him for falling over the answer before me.

'I beg your pardon?' stuttered Baker. I hoped that I didn't have the same expression on my face as he wore on his.

'Well, sir,' said Simpson, 'it must have been someone who didn't like Professor Harries, mustn't it?'

'Yes, it's conceivable,' I replied.

'The Doctor, sir – Dr Friedlander,' said Simpson, pulling his rabbit from the hat with aplomb. We said nothing, and he eventually continued: 'I was just preparing dinner, earlier on, and I needed some herbs from the garden. I was kneeling down, cutting some mint for garnish, when I saw the Doctor and his companion, Mr Kreiner, leaving the conservatory. They were obviously concerned that nobody saw them, and it was only the fact that I was kneeling down that prevented my detection. This was before they made their appearance in the house, sir, claiming they had just arrived.'

'What action did you take?' I asked.

'Action, sir?'

'Did you notify your master?'

Simpson was scandalised. 'That's not my place, sir. I am only telling you now because of... because of events, sir.'

There was a muffled thud from outside the door. Baker, standing beside it, opened it quickly. He could see nothing out of place from his viewpoint, closed it again and shrugged at me. I returned to Simpson.

'Is there anything else you think you ought to tell us, Simpson?'

'No, sir.'

'Very well, Simpson. You can go.'

'Thank you, sir. I'll just be retiring now.' His extracurricular duty discharged, the butler left the room.

'Interesting,' was the only thing I could think of to say.

'Indeed, sir,' Baker rejoined. 'Especially as mint dies back during cold spells, and it has been, as you'll have noticed sir, snowing outside.'

I frowned. 'But Simpson should know that. He's been butler here for how long?'

'Many years, sir. Longer than I can remember, actually. And yes, he should know that.'

I tried to say something to Baker, but all that came out was a huge yawn, followed by a sheepish grin.

'There's nothing else we can do tonight,' said Baker, eyes twinkling. 'I suggest we get some sleep, sir. And start afresh tomorrow with Miss Harries and Miss Seymour, if Miss Harries has recovered from sedation. I'd be interested to know what she thought of her brother.' I nodded, too tired even to say anything. Whilst we had been questioning Simpson, exhaustion had descended upon me like a cloud.

We left the study and walked towards the stairs. Someone had dropped a vase by the banisters; blue porcelain fragments lay on the deep pile of the carpet like angular pools of water. Next to one of the fragments something glittered in the light from the lamp in the hall. I bent down to pick it up, and found to my surprise that it was a perfect circle of plain glass attached to a ribbon.

'Mr Kreiner's monocle, I believe,' Baker said. 'I think we were overheard, sir.'

'We can confront Herr Kreiner and the Doctor tomorrow. If they're not here, we'll just take it as an admission of guilt and apprehend them before they can leave the country.' I sighed. 'And to think I only came here to collect a letter.'

'Saved me the price of a stamp, sir,' said Baker smiling at me before vanishing into the first of the two rooms that had been allocated to us.

I undressed quickly, washed, and climbed into a bed that seemed large enough for a regiment. It settled around me, leaving me lost and floundering in the centre. Finally I found the edge of the mattress and spent the rest of the night poised between empty air on one side and suffocating stuffing on the other. I slept badly, awakening regularly every few hours. Shortly after dawn the sky outside my window was milky and opalescent and the sun was just a brighter area with no boundaries. It seemed only a few minutes later that the horizon was lemon-sharp against a blue background so deep that it seemed to go on for ever. If I dreamed then the memories fled before morning.

As I had suspected, Baker had already arrived by the time I found the others in the study. What I was less prepared for was the presence of his associate. How, I could not fathom, but as soon as I set eyes upon the tall, lean man I knew why he was here. He had come for me. It seemed that he recognised me just as instantly, for he greeted me by name, and with such assurance that George thought we were already acquainted. As he introduced himself (and even his name seemed familiar, although I did not then know why) I had a chance to study Inspector Stratford.

He was, as I have said, a tall and thin man, his shape emphasised by the ample figure of the sergeant beside him. His face was slightly narrow, matching his nose, and he exuded an air of calm and confident efficiency and authority. He made me feel uneasy; he had the advantage and he knew it.

Although his eyes had not shifted from their study of me, I realised that Stratford had been talking to George, and presently we were sent to wait in the drawing room while Stratford and Baker continued their interview with George and also with Dr Friedlander. It seemed that Stratford was glad of all the help he could get, and finding a forensic scientist already waiting at the scene of the crime must have seemed too good a stroke of luck to waste.

The waiting seemed eternal. I remember little else about it except hazily, in unconnected snatches and random order. It seemed that the whole day, from my arrival until now, was simply a prelude to my session with Stratford. With the certainty of one of Harries's rats I had been steered through the maze of the last week in order to account for myself to the man from Scotland Yard who feigned interest in the timely death of Richard Harries. It could hardly have been better, in fact, which was in itself a bitter irony. I suppose that my nerves had balanced on the knife-point of Banquo Manor for longer than I care to speculate; I felt that everything was unfolding for my sake, whereas now I see that the events had a different inevitability – a whirlpool that sucked me in with Stratford and the rest rather than revolving about me. I have always been a little vain.

Beryl in particular seemed to share my mood as we waited. Silent. She shifted uneasily from one foot to the other as she stood opposite Simpson by the door. The effect it provoked in me was not one of sympathy: her reflection of my suppressed feelings irritated me still further. 'Oh, for heaven's sake, girl, sit down,' I told her, a little sharply. I softened my tone, sensing that Miss Seymour was watching me: 'And you too, Simpson. You make me nervous there.'

'Thank you, sir,' murmured Beryl as she and Simpson selected a chair each.

The silence broken, it seemed all the more oppressive when it began to reassert itself. 'You must be tired, Miss Seymour,' I ventured, since she was still looking at me. 'I know I am. And you, Elizabeth.'

'I shall be all right, thank you, John,' Mrs Wallace replied with the glimmer of a smile. 'I think you need some sleep though, Susan.'

Miss Seymour was not so sure, however. 'No thank you – really.'

'Are you sure?' Kreiner asked her. 'I mean you've been through a lot, what with –' He stopped, as if unsure of how to describe things. 'Everything,' he decided.

'I'm fine, Fitz,' she snapped. I don't know if I was more surprised at her sudden temper or her use of his Christian name. But Herr Kreiner seemed unperturbed. In fact he took it so much in his stride that I began to wonder if they had perhaps met before, though I could not see how that would be possible.

Even then I did not believe that telepathy was really possible. But as if in response to my thoughts, Susan's face clouded over and she stared at Kreiner in apparent confusion. 'I'm sorry, Herr Kreiner,' she said after a moment, 'but have we met before?'

Kreiner seemed startled by the question. Startled and troubled. He was about to reply when George Wallace entered.

'Ah, George. How is Catherine?' asked Elizabeth immediately.

'She is still sleeping.' Wallace lowered himself into an armchair. 'I think she'll sleep until the morning.

'Good. Sleep must be the best thing,' I said, hoping to persuade Susan Seymour to take the rest she undoubtedly needed.

Again, Kreiner agreed: 'He's right, Susan.'

'You must rest,' added Elizabeth, and this seemed to begin to convince Susan.

'Well, perhaps. In a minute.'

'I think they are right, Miss Seymour.' George smiled at her. 'And Elizabeth, you should get some sleep too, my dear.'

They went eventually. I forget if Baker came in before or after their departure to say that they might. Beryl too was dispatched, having been questioned, and given a bed in the servants' quarters. I doubted her parents would miss her.

We sat in silence. Simpson was so deep in uncharacteristic reverie that I forgot for a while that he was there – if indeed he was – and George and Kreiner both seemed unconcerned.

By the time Stratford wanted me, I had my nerves under better control. I decided that I had to make the most of my predicament and hope that I was mistaken in my diagnosis of the Inspector's intentions. But I knew in my heart that I was not. I put on my spectacles and took a deep breath before entering the study.

'You wanted to see me, I believe, Inspector,' I said, but the voice was not my own.

'I did indeed, Mr Hopkinson.'

He was leaning against Wallace's desk, the wreckage of Harries's career cluttered across the top. Baker stood beside me. 'Just one or two little points I'd like to clear up about this accident.'

'Accident?' I had felt rather than heard the slight hesitation as he chose the word.

'You don't think it was an accident then, Mr Hopkinson?'

My legs were about to give way, and I sank into the chair in front of the desk hoping it looked as if I had intended to. I talked to cover my weakness: 'I don't think you'd be bothering with all this if you did,' I told him. 'That's not quite the same.'

'And what do you think happened?'

I pretended to consider, in fact concentrating on keeping my hands steady as I pressed the moist fingertips tightly together in front of me. 'Harries was not a very likeable character, I'm afraid. When he died it was a little too neat in my opinion.'

Stratford raised an eyebrow and suggested that perhaps I was putting myself under suspicion by admitting my dislike for Harries. I had little doubt that I was under suspicion already, but pleaded confidence in his ability to detect my innocence.

'I didn't do it,' I told him; I felt it was a pathetic thing to say. But it sounded smug.

'Can you tell me who did?'

I told him that I neither knew nor cared. I was floundering now; if he failed to see the perspiration on my brow it could only be because he was distracted by the sound of my racing heart.

'Does anyone else here at the Manor share your opinion of Professor Harries?'

I almost laughed – he could not be so naïve. I watched as he toyed with the blackened base of a shattered valve, seemingly uninterested in my answer. He was trying to trap me.

'I couldn't really say,' I lied. 'I don't know that Sir George cared for Harries overmuch. I'm not sure about Dr Friedlander or Herr Kreiner, but they have only just arrived. I don't believe they'd met Harries before this evening Everyone else apart from his sister seems remarkably indifferent. Including his fiancée,' I added, not because I wanted him to know – perhaps he already did – but because I wanted to believe it myself.

'She does seem a little detached –' He did know. 'Have you any idea why?'

I had, of course: it was obvious given the conversation I had overheard and Gordon's predicament. But I was not going to play into Stratford's hands quite that easily. 'Not really,' I told him. 'But I gather from Mrs Wallace that the engagement was not going smoothly.' I hoped she had noticed. 'It seems that I know even less than you, Inspector.'

It sounded lame. He knew that I was lying, and his smile said so as clearly as his sarcasm.

'Quite probably, Mr Hopkinson. Quite probably,' he humoured me. 'You can of course account for your movements this evening.'

It was not a question, but I answered anyway. 'Of course.'

'In that case, I shan't ask you to – not yet.'

The menace was sharp in his voice, and I muttered my thanks. With that, he dismissed me. It was over. A wave of relief washed over me and I felt my skin cool beneath its sheen. I could hardly leave the study quickly enough.

I should have realised, of course, that he had not been at all interested in my answers so far. He had been waiting for me to give in to my relief. My hand was on the door handle when he spoke, as I think I had known he would. But I still reacted. My hand gripped the handle and my whole body froze, rigid.

'Why didn't you tell Sir George that Gordon Seavers is dead?'

As I struggled to control my clenched hand and search for a

plausible answer I heard a voice reply, a calm and quiet voice. Reasonable and secure. It was my own. 'George has been ill,' my voice said confidently. It felt ready to crack at any moment. 'I hoped to find an opportunity to break the distressing news to him gently, so as not to upset him. No such opportunity has yet arisen.'

I listened, detached, to the strange sound of my own voice. Too precise, I thought vaguely: he can tell you're a solicitor, pleading for someone else, someone guilty. Queen's English, M'Lord. 'You understand I'm sure, Inspector.' I rest my case.

Stratford was less willing to accept my defence. 'How long have you been here?' he asked, suggesting that I had ample time to tell George of Gordon's suicide.

'Goodnight, Inspector. Or was there something else?' It was senseless to argue.

'Just one thing.'

I knew what he was going to ask. And I had no answer. Of course I had taken the letter, and he knew it. Who else could have done? I had realised that the envelope was missing as soon as I had burned its contents, but it had been too late then.

Stratford was still talking, although I had denied all knowledge of the letter. He paused, and I spoke without waiting to hear if he had finished. 'I wish you more luck with your windmills than that Spaniard had with his.' An appropriate allusion since the whole room, and in particular Stratford's face, seemed to be revolving like a giant windmill, and I was impaled at its centre, Quixotic fool that I am.

Whether my hand was still on the doorknob or not I do not know, but I almost fell through as the door opened towards me. I breathed deeply for a few seconds, then returned to the drawing room, hoping I would not collapse before I could reach a chair. The hall began to straighten out and I could hear the sound of my feet on the floor again as the rushing of blood in my ears faded slowly into the distance.

Herr Kreiner accosted me as soon as I returned to the drawing room. 'Have you seen the Doctor?' he asked. He seemed flustered, urgent.

'No,' I confessed. 'I'm sorry. He's not with the inspector. But he can't be far away.'

'No,' Kreiner said. 'No, of course not. He's around somewhere. Just haven't seen him for a while, that's all.' He nodded to himself. 'I'm not worried,' he assured me. But I knew he was saying it to reassure himself.

'You've worked with Dr Friedlander for a while, I imagine, Herr Kreiner?' I asked him.

'What? Oh yes, quite a while.' He smiled thinly. 'Seems like centuries, actually,' and he gave a high-pitched nervous laugh. 'He'll be around somewhere,' he repeated. Then as an afterthought, 'Call me, Fitz won't you? Everyone does.'

'Do they?' I said. He didn't respond. But we were still standing together just inside the drawing room, and as much to make an excuse to move as anything, I asked, 'Are you a forensics expert too, then?' I had assumed he was, of course.

'What? Oh yes. Yes indeedy.' He nodded vigorously, the way people do when they are either telling an obvious truth or an unprepared lie. 'Smudge of paint here, fingerprints there. Dee-en-ay stuff. You know.'

I didn't. 'Dee-what?'

He coughed as if to cover embarrassment or a silly mistake. 'Sorry, new technique. Not really on the market yet, y'know.' His manner was strange, but not intentionally so, and not in an intimidating way. I put it down to his having spent so much time abroad, away from native English-speakers. Though I did wonder where the Doctor had learned to speak our language so well.

'Maybe he's turned in already.' I suggested as Herr Kreiner – Fitz – continued to pace up and down.

'Who?' he asked.

'The Doctor.'

'Oh, right. Doesn't sleep much, actually. I believe.' He paused and shuffled his feet uneasily.

Simpson was still standing just inside the door. He coughed politely. 'Dr Friedlander did ask if his room was made up earlier, sir,' he offered.

'Did he?' Fitz was at once elated, relieved. Then he huffed and sank into a chair. 'Typical. You'd think he'd tell us if he's going to push off and grab some kip, wouldn't you?'

'Not really, sir, no,' Simpson said. He leaned forwards slightly, towards Fitz Kreiner. 'Are you feeling tired yourself, sir? You seem a little worn, if you don't mind me saying.'

I was surprised that Simpson ventured such an opinion. But Kreiner merely shrugged it off. 'Oh, I'm fine,' he said easily. 'Don't worry about me. Wide awake. Full of life. Not ready to drop yet.'

'You dropped the accent though,' I pointed out. Was it my imagination, or did Simpson hastily conceal a hint of a smile at my observation?

'Oh, that. Yes.' Kreiner waved his arms about rather more than was strictly necessary as he blustered. 'Well, actually that's just for professional purposes you know. People expect German experts to be, well...' His voice tailed off.

'German, sir?' Simpson suggested.

Fitz did not reply. He was looking at Simpson, his head slightly to one side as if considering whether he trusted the man or not. He continued to stare as I poured myself a glass of whisky and sat down on the other side of the room. I needed some time, some peace and quiet during which to marshal my thoughts.

I stayed in the drawing room only long enough to drink a second glass of whisky. Simpson left to sort out rooms for Baker and Stratford, which saved me from having to decide whether the inspector had asked me to send the butler to him

113

again or whether I had imagined it. Suddenly I was immensely tired, as if today's events were finally over and I was now free to retire from the stage until morning. Once in bed I was asleep in a moment.

The next thing I knew, Harries was leaning over me, his face scarred and ripped, but mercifully obscured for the most part in the shadows. His teeth glinted in the dark as if he were insanely grinning, while his single eye gave him a permanent, mocking wink. A syringe containing some vile, bubbling fluid was clenched in his monkey-like hand. I tried desperately to move away, but the bed seemed to suck me down. A panicked thought fled my mind as Harries leaned closer – the whisky, there had been something in the whisky. But that hardly explained the corpse grimacing over me.

I thought at first that I was still asleep, but the noise convinced me that this was no nightmare despite its slowed and distorted action. As Harries pressed the syringe towards my eye the scratching grew louder, and I could see – for I could no more close my eyes than cry out or escape – that the sound was that of his teeth as they ground against each other in anticipation.

The needle met my pupil, and the world exploded.

The light was the sun, and out of it flew the bat, swung in a wide arc by Joe Wells. I had no time to move, and as the ball struck my ankle I screamed and fell, the bone once more shattered. But the nurse was there. The white dress clung to her body as if wet and her hand held up a scalpel. Her fingernail scratched along its handle as her tongue moistened her lips.

'It's all right. You were dreaming.' Miss Seymour put her arm around me and I relaxed as she wiped my soaking forehead. I looked up at her, grateful, and saw my mistake. It was not Susan Seymour, but Catherine Harries. But was there something odd about her? Her eyes? Her hair? Even as I watched, one of her eyes blistered and boiled away and the snakes that I had mistaken for her hair writhed still more and strained to reach me, their tongues darting back and forth with a strange scratching sound.

With a jolt the room was empty apart from me. And the eyes. I was awake now; I knew that, because the fear I felt was so real that I could taste it. The pain in my ankle had dissipated to the dull throb to be expected after the day's exertions.

But still there were the eyes – tiny black eyes, gleaming in the night as they caught the first hint of dawn through the curtains. The scratching quickened into a scuttle as the eyes disappeared and something long and thin, with ridges or scales, flicked my face as the creature turned and leaped from my bed. I jumped the other way, reaching for the nearest lamp. The room seemed empty. Had the rat too been part of my nightmare?

I left the light on and climbed carefully back into the bed, still damp with my sweat. Was it only my shivering as I slipped back into a fitful sleep, or was there a faint scuffling sound – as if something was trying to scratch its way out of the room? Or into it.

THE REPORT OF INSPECTOR IAN STRATFORD (6)

I woke the next morning to find a cup of tea by my side and Beryl over by the window. Looking at her, silhouetted by the bright morning light, I momentarily wished it the other way round. She turned and smiled as if she had read my mind.

'Did you sleep well, sir?' she asked, a knowing smile upon her face. I muttered something approximating to 'Good morning', and floundered to the edge of the bed. The fact that the pyjamas that Simpson had laid out for me the night before were far too large did nothing to make me feel any easier.

Beryl just stood there watching me, the light streaming around her body like water around a curved stone in a brook. Her half-smile made me distinctly uneasy, as if she were waiting for something she knew was bound to happen. I dismissed her curtly, and as she left with a disappointed flounce I began to review the events of the previous day.

It all added up to a large zero: one body, a multitude of suspects and no obvious clues to point me towards a solution. All I could do was proceed slowly, feeling my way around the case and pretending that I knew what I was doing. My actions for the morning were pretty well set anyway: I had yet to question Miss Harries, Mrs Wallace... and the strangely distant Susan Seymour. Somehow I wished I could ask Baker to see her. Police questioning can often be mistaken for petty prying and I had no wish to be cast as the villain in her eyes. Quite the opposite. But it was my duty, and the opportunity to see her alone was something I looked forward to even as I dreaded it.

I suddenly remembered Dr Friedlander. Simpson's revelations of his presence in the conservatory before his apparent arrival at the house could well form the start of a case against him. Fired with enthusiasm and the warmth of the tea, I washed and dressed.

On the way to the door, and I hoped a large breakfast, I paused by the window. The snow-covered fields and woods stretched out before me like a rumpled bedsheet, and I felt an urge to walk out of the front door and keep going. All my happiest memories were linked to that countryside – staying with my aunt, walking the hills and vales all day, and returning in the evening with aching feet and an easy mind. Walking had always helped me clear my thoughts. Whenever things got too much for me I returned to Three Sisters, and to peace.

With an effort I tore my gaze from the hidden paths and pushed it ahead of me to breakfast.

On my way through the hall I met Sergeant Baker heading in the opposite direction.

'Good morning, sir,' he said. 'On your way to breakfast?'

'Yes, have you eaten?'

'I'm afraid not, sir. My views on a good breakfast don't seem to coincide with Sir George's. I'm sure I can find something around, though.'

'I'm sure you can, Sergeant,' I said. 'I've been thinking about what Simpson told us about the Doctor and Herr Kreiner's presence in the conservatory. I'd like to speak to him again, confront him with what we know. Can you get hold of him and tell him I want a word?'

I entered the dining room to find Simpson in the process of serving a young woman seated at the large table. She looked up with a smile of greeting which quickly changed to surprise.

'This is Inspector Stratford, ma'am,' murmured Simpson. Relief filled Catherine Harries's face as I crossed the room and took her hand.

'Miss Harries,' I said, 'I am sorry to make your acquaintance under such tragic circumstances.' As I spoke I searched her face and wondered if her good looks had been reflected in her brother; and also found myself morbidly attempting to delineate the shape of her skull, muscles and tendons beneath her fair skin.

I sat down opposite her as she said, 'I'm so pleased to see you, Inspector. Richard's death has… has confused me so much. I feel much safer with you in the house.'

'I'll serve your breakfast now, sir,' said Simpson.

I could not help being flattered by Miss Harries's trust in me. 'I'll do my best to keep you safe,' I said, not sure how to respond to her words.

'Your kippers, sir,' intoned Simpson, depositing a plate in front of me.

Breakfast seemed to be composed of a mixture of cold leftovers from the night before and dishes prepared and preserved by the cook before she left. There was ham and devilled kidneys as well as the fish, and a plate of devils-on-horseback, which I tucked into with relish. During these dishes, and the following selection of toast and marmalade, I cajoled Miss Harries into giving her version of events. It tallied almost exactly with everything that Baker and I already knew. Without mentioning murder, because I didn't know how much Miss Harries had been told and I wanted to avoid any unnecessary shock, I managed to establish three more things. First: there was still a long period of time during which the equipment had been unattended and could have been sabotaged. Secondly: Catherine Harries did not have an alibi for a significant portion of this time. Thirdly: Richard Harries had not an enemy in the world.

One of my sergeants when I was just an innocent young constable told me that negative information could sometimes be more useful than positive. I was doubtful then, but I didn't dare ask him why. I am even less sure now.

'A cup of tea for you, sir,' said Simpson and, so saying, placed a cup of tea in front of me.

Catherine Harries leaned forward confidentially. I glanced sideways to find Simpson poised by the door with a tray in his hands. I caught his eye, and he left with that insufferably superior expression still dripping from his face. I wondered exactly how many conversations went on that Simpson couldn't help overhearing.

'Inspector Stratford, is it true that my brother was murdered?' Seeing the stunned look on my face she continued in a rush: 'I'm sorry to be so blunt, but it was something Sir George let slip last night after he sedated me. He thought I was asleep, but I wasn't – not quite. He was talking to the Doctor. Is it true? I must know.'

She bit her lip and gazed anxiously into my eyes. My mind rebelliously conjured up images of Susan Seymour and the beauty of her eyes.

'I'm afraid it does seem to be true, Miss Harries. We do think that your brother was murdered.'

She gasped and closed her eyes. 'You don't know who did it?'

'We're not entirely sure that it was murder, but that is the theory we are working on. We have not discovered who the murderer is yet, or even if it was someone inside the house. But we *are* working on it.'

'You think it might have been someone from outside?' Miss Harries seemed to be genuinely incredulous and I wondered at how easy it was for her to suspect her friends. Did she know something that I did not?

'It's a possibility that we cannot overlook,' I admitted.

She shivered and hugged herself. 'I feel so helpless. I feel as if whoever did it is still wandering about the house – and he might kill someone else.'

Her fingers began to knead the material of her dress as she sat, arms folded and hands clutching shoulders. She didn't look at me, but stared blindly at the cooling cup of tea before her.

'I had the oddest dream last night. At least, I think it was a dream. It was difficult to tell. I don't know what it was George gave me, but it left me feeling most peculiar. I kept waking up during the night feeling very restless and thirsty. But I was too tired to move. Then, once I woke up, it was still night because I

could see the full moon shining in through the window, and…
I could hear someone else in the room with me. I couldn't hear
any breathing, just the rustle of clothes as he moved around the
room. I couldn't move, I was too terrified. I didn't dare turn over,
in case… in case – oh, I don't know. Eventually I think I fainted.
I must have slept for quite a while because when I woke up
again the moon was gone. But he was still there.'

She looked at me, cold and piercing. A chill ran through the
room. 'I could still hear him in the room. And he was making
noises, groans. I was so scared I was trembling and crying, and
praying for my life in case he heard me.'

Her eyes were wide and dilated; not looking at me, but beyond
me into the recent past. 'Then the groaning stopped and I heard
him move. I thought he was going to kill me, or – or…' Breath
in short gasps now, fingers crushing the fabric of the dress and
bruising the flesh beneath. 'But then I heard him scrabbling at
the door, and he was gone. I couldn't sleep after that. I'm so
tired now.'

Her eyes abruptly focused back on mine. 'I'm so glad you're
here now. I feel much safer having met you. You seem so… so
competent.' One of her hands sought mine across the table and
she gazed long and searchingly into my eyes. I was confused, I
felt there was some message she was trying to get across to me
but which I could not read.

'I'll just clear the dishes away, sir,' said Simpson, entering the
room. How much had he heard?

The spell was broken. And soon after Catherine Harries
begged leave to see Sir George Wallace. I finished my cup of tea
alone.

THE ACCOUNT OF JOHN HOPKINSON (7)

After such an uneasy night I resolved not to bother with breakfast, and afforded myself a lie-in. That decided, I slept through most of the morning until I was awakened by Beryl bringing me a cup of tea. She perched on the side of my bed as I drank it, then went to help Simpson prepare lunch while I washed and dressed.

As I had suspected, lunch was fairly bland, but having missed breakfast I was hungry enough not to care. Even Inspector Stratford seemed subdued and I guessed that his morning's investigations had not thrown up anything of great interest.

'So, what do you intend now?' I asked him as he entered the drawing room. Everyone else seemed to have returned to their rooms after the meal. I was alone with Miss Seymour and Fitz Kreiner in the room when he joined us. He sat carefully in the armchair opposite the one I had chosen for myself. Miss Seymour seemed to notice neither of us, standing at the window staring out across the snow-covered lawn, though Fitz took a healthy and undisguised interest in our conversation.

'Oh, just one or two little routine matters,' Stratford replied easily. 'Finish questioning everyone; a few more words with you, Mr Hopkinson.'

'How nice,' I murmured. ('I'd like a few words, if I may...' I could hear Stratford saying it – see him as he did so. But when? And where? The inspector continued before I could further speculate.)

'And I shall of course need to examine the body properly.'

'The Doctor can help you with that,' Fitz said.

Stratford nodded. 'Except that I haven't seen him today. You wouldn't happen to know where he is, would you, Mr Kreiner?'

Fitz's eyes narrowed slightly. 'You're the policeman,' he said. 'You tell me.' He turned to me now. 'I told you I was worried about him. Yesterday – last night I told you.'

I nodded. 'Indeed you did.' I could not think of anything to add to that.

'His bed's not been slept in,' Fitz went on. 'I assume you know that. So why aren't you looking for him?'

'I'm sure we shall,' the inspector said. I caught the double edge in his voice, though I think Fitz missed it.

Miss Seymour turned from her contemplation to face us, as if she had only now realised that we were there at all. 'He never sleeps,' she said quietly, addressing Fitz. 'You know that.'

Stratford frowned, and looked at me. I shrugged.

'I suppose you will wish to question me, Inspector,' Susan continued. The light was behind her, but even in crisp silhouette I could tell that she was pale, and her voice was tired. Perhaps she too had slept badly. Probably we all had. Except Stratford.

'Yes indeed, Miss Seymour,' he told her, and I could see that he too had noticed her fatigue: 'When you feel up to it.'

'Why not now? I feel as up to it as I ever shall.'

'You shouldn't overdo things,' Fitz told her, shaking his head. 'Get some rest. Try to get some of your strength back while we look for...' He paused, looked at us. 'While we find out who's behind all this,' he said.

'I would rather speak with you when you are quite composed, Miss Seymour,' Stratford told her. Whether Stratford disagreed or whether his excuse was genuine I do not know. 'I should like to see the body again first. Then I shall question you and Mrs Wallace. And Miss Harries, of course.'

I wondered vaguely if Stratford had yet spoken to Catherine other than formally at lunch, but George came in before I could ask.

'How is Catherine?' asked Miss Seymour when we had done with the courtesy greetings, and I gathered that George had sent her back to bed for the afternoon.

'Just a few bad dreams, I think. She said she'd been sleepwalking.'

'Had she?' I wondered how she could know.

'Oh I doubt it. Anyway, I gave her another shot a while ago, so she'll sleep for a bit more. Should be as right as ninepence when she wakes up.'

'What about Elizabeth?' I asked him.

'She's gone off to get some sleep too.'

'I expect they both need the rest,' Susan Seymour said.

'Don't you, Miss Seymour?' asked Stratford.

'Obviously,' she said at once, again with more than a hint of sarcasm in her voice. Yet almost at once she seemed surprised at her words, and frowned. She looked from me to the inspector, then to Fitz Kreiner, her eyes wide and confused.

'Please com—' Kreiner again broke off, as if realising he was speaking out of turn. 'That is, please come over here and sit down,' he said after a brief pause.

She crossed to where Fitz was standing and sat down on the chaise longue nearby. 'I am wide awake now and I see no reason to sleep merely for the sake of it. Especially since you say that you will wish to question me, Inspector.'

He had no more answer to that than I would have had, so Stratford responded by asking Wallace if he could look again at Harries's body. George grimaced at the thought and Susan Seymour looked away.

'Yes, of course, Inspector,' said George after a moment. 'I'll show you.'

'Thank you, Sir George.'

They were gathering themselves for the ordeal when Sergeant Baker entered. 'Still no sign of the Doctor, sir,' he reported.

'I told you,' Fitz said again. 'What did I tell you? Missing.

Gone. We should find him. I mean, where could he have gone? In this weather.'

'The railway station,' Baker suggested.

'Caught a train?' Kreiner's disbelief was obvious. 'Where to, for God's sake? I mean... I mean we should be looking for him,' he finished somewhat sulkily.

'Indeed we should,' Stratford said. 'And we shall. But first things first.'

'The body?' Fitz asked. When the inspector nodded, he started towards the door. 'Then I'll come with you. Since the Doctor's not around, you'll need a forensic opinion from someone else.'

'Will I?' Stratford seemed almost amused at the thought. 'But I have already been given the Doctor's professional opinion.'

'Then it's time I gave you mine.'

'Oh?'

'The Doctor may have missed something that my training will pick up on. Or...' He let the word hang.

Stratford took the bait. 'Or?'

'Well, it's pretty obvious you think the Doctor's done a runner. If he's a prime suspect, then maybe he didn't tell you the whole story. Covered something up.' He nodded to emphasise his point. 'You need my help.'

Stratford nodded. 'Very well, Mr Kreiner. Let's hear what you have to say, shall we? Sir George, if you'd be so kind?'

Wallace, a little grudgingly, led Stratford, Baker and Fitz out and I watched them cross the hall to the stairs.

'What do you think he wants to see the Doctor about?' Susan Seymour was standing beside me, also watching the others climb the staircase and turning the corner out of sight.

'Oh, I don't know. Something Simpson told him perhaps. I think he saw the inspector after the Doctor left last night. Or maybe he's picked up on the coincidence of names that

Richard noticed.' I bit my tongue as soon as I'd said it – thinking out loud, not always a good idea.

'What coincidence?' she asked.

I pretended not to hear. 'Actually,' I said quickly, 'he's been acting a bit oddly recently as well.'

'What, Simpson?'

I nodded. It was a little disconcerting having Miss Seymour standing so close to me. She suddenly turned towards me: 'Oh, I wish I could just dematerialise and leave all this.' She leaned forward so that her head almost met my chest. As a result she did not see my surprise at her choice of phrase. I put my hand on her shoulder, to steady and reassure her.

'Yes,' I said quietly, 'we all do... We all do.' She looked up, apparently recovered, but her face reddened slightly. I spoke first to save her the further embarrassment of apologising. 'I think I'll go and hear whatever revelation Stratford is about to unleash.' I felt awkward standing so near to her. So close.

She smiled slightly, but her eyes were still moist. 'I'll come with you,' she said.

'Are you sure? It won't be pleasant, you know. I mean he's gone to look at the body.'

'I know, but I've seen it once.' She shivered despite her determination. 'I shall never forget that.' She swallowed and looked away, back towards the window. 'And I'd rather not be left here alone,' she added quietly.

'As you wish.' Perhaps I sounded too indifferent, so as we crossed the hall I endeavoured to change the subject slightly: 'Yes,' I said, agreeing again with her earlier sentiments, 'I think we'd all like to change places with the Doctor at the moment...' It seemed a worthy thought to both of us. At the time.

Despite my full night's sleep I felt tired and restless by the early afternoon. Partly it was due to an unproductive morning spent in Richard Harries's laboratory sifting through his papers. Mostly it was due to Susan Seymour. I had repeatedly tried to catch her eye during lunch but she had either failed to notice me or (my insecurities whispered) she was deliberately avoiding me. Either way, she was devoting too much time to looking at John Hopkinson, then dropping her gaze when he looked at her. Even after lunch I discovered them together with Herr Kreiner in the drawing room. Miss Seymour had the grace to blush. Hopkinson insolently returned my stare.

Where had I seen him before?

To my relief, Sir George Wallace and the sergeant entered the drawing room soon after me. I had been thinking about Harries and had already decided to make a more complete examination of his body than my previous one. I wasted no time in asking Sir George to accompany me upstairs. Fitz (Fitz *what*? I wondered) Kreiner elected to join us on the thin pretence that he could contribute on the basis of his professional knowledge. Baker and I exchanged amused glances at his presumption – it was obvious to both of us that the man was completely out of his depth – but I agreed on the basis that I would rather have him with me, where he might make some slip and give away his true identity, than out of my sight.

We left Hopkinson and Susan Seymour together – Baker, with misplaced tact, electing to join us. The true identities of Dr Friedlander and Fitz Kreiner worried me as we mounted the stairs. Kreiner I had tentatively pegged as a confidence trickster, an intruder pretending false knowledge as a means to somehow obtaining money. Too stupid to plan or execute such a scheme by himself, he obviously depended on some confederate for leadership, and Dr Friedlander was the obvious choice, but there was something about the Doctor that bothered me. He did not have the reactions of a confidence trickster: rather, he reacted like the only honest man in a world of confidence tricksters. He would bear further watching.

Sir George seemed tired and restless, running a finger around his collar as we mounted the stairs. He didn't seem to have slept too well and I noticed a faint red mark on his neck. Shaving cut? It did not look like one and unbidden images rose in my mind... But no, the very idea was grotesque. Elizabeth Wallace was, after all, a lady. Then, as a sudden revelation, I realised that Beryl Green the maid was not, and I wondered if she treated everyone with the same friendliness she had shown me that morning. And I wondered what George Wallace's reaction would be to a young, attractive, available maid. And then, like a game of patience where one difficult card leads to a run of moves so obvious they don't even require conscious thought, a lot of unconnected facts fell into place: Richard Harries and the evident dislike of everyone for him; the behaviour of Dr Friedlander; the suicide of Gordon Seavers; the murder of Richard Harries.

But as suddenly as it had occurred, my exhilaration faded. I may have stumbled across the reason for Richard Harries's death, but I still had no inkling who had killed him. If I was right then everyone had a strong enough motive.

I sighed and turned to George Wallace as we gained the upstairs landing. 'May I borrow your telephone for a while?' I asked. 'I had better report to my superiors on recent developments.'

'Of course, Inspector, of course. Telephone's downstairs in the hall. Feel free to use it whenever.'

'Thank you.'

We were at the corner of the corridor leading to Richard Harries's last resting place when I heard a familiar voice behind us. I turned to find John Hopkinson and Susan Seymour walking towards us.

'Do you mind if we join you?' asked Hopkinson.

'Professor Harries's… remains… are no sight for a lady,' I snapped. 'I would have expected you to show more consideration, Mr Hopkinson.'

'Actually,' Hopkinson said, 'it was her idea.'

'Every opportunity to gather data should be taken,' Susan Seymour said calmly. 'I have much theoretical knowledge of the inner workings of the human body, but little practical experience.'

It took me a second to register the casual import of her words, but when I did I could feel a chill run up my spine.

'And besides,' she said, a fearful look haunting her eyes, 'he *was* my fiancé, and it may be the last chance I get to see him. To remember him.'

'It may still be a shock m'dear,' said Wallace. 'I don't like to be indelicate in front of a lady, but sometimes in cases of electrical shock the burns take some time to develop.'

I looked questioningly at him. 'It's a new field,' he explained, 'but I've been reading up on it since we installed the generator. You see, sometimes the electrical charge, as it is called, actually travels along the nerves in the body. Thus the burns start from the inside and work their way out.'

Miss Seymour winced and Wallace began to apologise to her. 'It's up to you if you want to come in,' I interrupted. 'We'll all quite understand if you wish to stay outside.'

'Simpson and Beryl are around somewhere,' said Wallace helpfully. 'Or you could go and see if Elizabeth or Catherine is awake.'

'No,' said Miss Seymour resolutely, and I could tell from her eyes that the moment of vulnerability had passed. 'The concept of nerve conduction fascinates me. It parallels the Artronic resonators with which TAR–'

'Another time, Comp– er, Susan,' Herr Kreiner said quickly. 'I'm sure the inspector has more important things to do.'

'Indeed,' I said. There was something going on here that I just didn't understand. One moment Susan Seymour was vulnerable and frightened, the next she was cold and heartless. Could it be shock, and if so why wasn't Sir George doing something about it? I could tell from his expression that he was as bemused as I.

We entered the room. Someone had wisely opened the windows and the sickening charred smell had dissipated. The body lay sheeted on the bed, and without further ado I walked over and grasped the top of the sheet. 'Brace yourselves,' I said and pulled the sheet back.

What I revealed, pushed into a shape approximating a prone body, were a rolled blanket and three heavy bolsters. The body of Richard Harries had vanished.

I pulled the sheet completely off the bed. Behind me I could hear Baker cursing and Hopkinson pulling the cupboard doors open looking for the body. I could only stare numbly at the bed. Inspector Ian Stratford: the man who let a corpse be stolen from under his nose.

'You'd think that with a house full of policemen the crime rate might decline somewhat.'

My hand was shaking so much as I poured out the first glass of brandy that I did not dare to attempt the second. Susan was sitting on the edge of the chaise longue and sipped at the drink just as nervously when I handed it to her. It seemed to bring her back to life at once – her nerves seemed to have drained her energy while mine kept me on my feet, pacing to and fro in front of her.

I felt I was trapped in a play by Arthur Pinero. But I was unable to decide whether it was the frenetic action and confusion that made me think of farce (*The Magistrate*, perhaps? I wondered ruefully) or the depth of passion and emotion released that reminded me of Mrs Patrick Campbell as the tragic and fated figure of *The Second Mrs Tanqueray* that I had seen at St James's the previous summer. I did not try, but let my fear continue to fuse into anger and sarcasm.

'But no. A robbery now; and it's only the corpse that's been stolen. I mean, what does that –'

'John!' Susan stopped me with the authority of a schoolteacher. 'Calm down.'

'What? Oh, I'm sorry.'

Glumly I sat down beside her, realising that she had addressed me by my Christian name, and that I was now thinking of her in the same fashion. Fear brings people closer together.

'Why are you suddenly so tense?' she enquired.

'Oh, I don't know,' I lied. We were not yet that close. 'I'm worried, I suppose. I thought I knew just about what was going on here. Now this happens.' I reasoned that half the truth was better than none at all.

'I'm sorry,' she said quietly.

'What for? You didn't take it.'

'How do you know?' She smiled. 'Anyway, that is not what I meant at all.'

I began to stand up again but Susan put her hand on my shoulder. Her grip was surprisingly strong, and I found myself pushed down into the chaise longue. I fought down my nervous energy, turning it into speech: 'But there's just no reason for it. I mean, who would want a corpse? There's not a lot of demand for them these days, is there? Except apparently around here.'

'There must be some reason for it.' Susan was giving the problem considerably more thought than I. More than was necessary in my opinion.

'Yes, someone's gone mad. That's the reason.'

'Really?' The voice came from the door and I looked across to see Herr Kreiner. He was leaning against the door frame, watching us intently. I wondered how long he had been there. I wondered when Susan had noticed him for she seemed not to be surprised. 'Do you think so?' he continued, pushing himself upright from his casual posture and crossing to help himself to a brandy.

I did not. But my brain refused to accept the events so far as connected or logical. 'Well, it's got to be, hasn't it? There's no motive – at least you can credit the murderer with that.'

'I don't know that "credit" is the word I'd choose,' Kreiner said as he slumped down in a chair and swirled the liquid round inside his glass. He stared into it for a moment before dipping in his index finger, shaking off the excess liquid and then licking the remainder from it. There was something so absent-minded, so natural, about the gesture that it did not seem at all uncouth. Only somehow naïve.

I assumed of course that both he and Susan had realised that the murderer and whoever moved the body were different people. 'There is no reason why the murderer should move it,' I told them.

'A murderer has to be mad as well,' Kreiner said with an exaggerated heaviness.

'Rubbish,' I retorted, too strongly, taking out my glasses and polishing them vigorously on my handkerchief by way of distraction. It was an act I often used with clients. 'Give him a decent reason for it and any man will kill. That's all war is – legalised murder. The reasons may justify it sometimes.'

'Or the principles?' Susan wondered.

My polishing act did not appear to have distracted her from my somewhat flimsy argument so I put the spectacles on and peered over the top of the frames at her. 'Yes. Or to save oneself or one's friends.' That had not worked either. I had merely succeeded in losing my own concentration and slipping up again. I tried looking through the lenses instead.

'So you think that whoever killed Richard Harries was sane and had a motive?' Kreiner asked. The notion evidently amused him.

I was still staring through my spectacles at Susan. From the way she met my gaze, she seemed to think that I was studying her even more intently than before. Another act. Then I remembered that Harries had loved this woman – had been loved by her. For a time.

She continued to regard me steadily, and I could not tell her that the glass in my spectacles was clear; that my eyesight was perfect; that it was all an attempt to seem erudite, wise. I looked away. 'I think killing Richard could have been quite easy for a sane man,' I said. Odd that I should feign a disability, albeit minor, while I did my best to disguise the slight limp of which probably only I was aware in any case.

'Perhaps you're right,' said Susan. She was looking at Kreiner now, as if to gain approval for her concession. I felt ridiculous suddenly and removed my glasses. Susan took this for surprise at her words; perhaps it was. 'I don't mean that I condone it,' she continued quickly, standing up and turning back towards the windows – her musing ground. 'But... but I can sympathise with the murderer... in a way.'

Her hands twisted around the brandy glass and I was afraid she would spill the remains of her drink. Instinctively I stood up and took a few steps towards her.

'But not with whoever stole the body.' I tried to swing the conversation back to the area that worried me most.

'Therefore,' Kreiner said as he joined us at the window, 'whoever stole the body was mad, and therefore cannot have been the murderer, who was sane. Is that your argument?'

Susan turned to face me again, to see my answer.

'In a nutshell,' I confirmed.

She smiled. 'Now you are talking rubbish.'

'It seems sane enough to me,' I joked.

'Then you must be mad.' Kreiner responded at once. It was a joke, but even so I felt the blood freeze in my face... But he went on: 'The body was stolen by the murderer. For a reason.'

'What reason?'

'Well, I don't know.' There was more than a hint of exasperation in his voice, as if this whole debate were merely some side issue unconnected with the events of real importance. 'Suppose the body had a clue on it. A clue to the murderer's identity.'

'A good point,' I conceded.

'Thank you.'

'But why not just remove the clue?' I asked him. 'Why not leave the body?'

'Well... perhaps he didn't know what the clue was. Or perhaps...' He floundered, then a thought came to him: 'Perhaps the body itself is the clue.'

'Or perhaps it isn't, and he's simply trying to confuse us,' Susan suggested.

'Well, if that's the case, then he has certainly succeeded,' I said.

But Susan was sure Kreiner had hit upon the answer.

'What difference does it make anyway?' I asked her.

'I know you didn't move the body,' she said quietly. Kreiner had turned away and was staring out of the window, across the grounds. I don't know if he heard, if he was listening, even if he was at all interested.

'Do you?' I asked.

She frowned. 'I think so, yes. Yes, I'm sure you didn't.'

'So?'

'So I know that you're not the murderer either,' she concluded with flawed logic.

'And that makes a difference, does it?' Kreiner spoke without turning.

I stared at Susan, anxious to see her reaction to this. Again she avoided my gaze, this time looking down at her brandy, warming the bowl of the glass in her delicate hand. 'Yes,' she said softly.

'Well, it must be reassuring to know that you're safe in here with him,' Kreiner said. He did turn now, and there was a boyish grin on his face.

She looked up at him, her eyes colder than before. 'Oh shut up, Fitz,' she said, her tone suddenly and markedly harsher than normal. Then, more gently, she added, 'You're still worried about the Doctor, aren't you?'

'Aren't you?' he asked, his own tone serious for once.

'Me?' She seemed surprised. 'Obviously.' Then immediately, as if she had not answered, she said, 'No, why should I be?' Before I could express surprise, though, she was speaking again, quickly with realisation. 'You think he took the body, don't you?'

'No,' Kreiner replied. But he spoke so quickly that I knew he was lying. He gave a short, humourless laugh. 'I mean, why would he?' He looked at Susan intently, and when he spoke again there was a severity, an undercurrent to his words as if he were trying to tell her something more than his mere words articulated. 'Even if there was something about the body as we said. Some clue. Some artefact that he wanted.' He continued to stare at her, as if to see what effect, if any, his words had.

She smiled and her eyes thawed a little. 'I'm going to see the inspector,' she said with resolve, and stood up. It was as if Kreiner had not spoken.

'What on earth for?' he asked abruptly. 'You've seen him before, haven't you?'

I too was surprised and neglected to rise.

'I think he wants to question me,' she said simply.

'Lucky you,' Kreiner responded.

He probably wanted to see me as well, I thought, less than happily.

'I wish you weren't so sarcastic.' I wondered if she was talking to us both, or just to Kreiner. 'I'll tell him about the body being a clue,' she added.

'Oh good,' I said, only half sarcastic myself. 'And tell him how it exonerates me too, will you? That should just about make his day.'

'All right, I will. Here.' She handed Kreiner what was left of her brandy, a little less than half a glass, and took his empty glass in return. 'I think you need this...'

'Thank you,' he muttered, but she was gone.

I watched the door close, as Kreiner swallowed the brandy. I was suddenly aware that I had not had a drink myself and went to pour one.

'So what has happened to your friend the Doctor, do you think?' I asked Kreiner. We were sitting opposite each other, each nursing a brandy glass. In other circumstances the situation would have seemed amicable if not cosy. As it was there was an air of suppressed tension between us. As if we were both awaiting a crash of thunder having already witnessed the distant lightning.

He shrugged. 'I really have no idea.'

'But you're worried.'

'Of course I'm bloody worried.'

I stared, probably I gaped. There was no call for that sort of language, and from his own embarrassed expression I saw that he knew that.

'Have you been with the Doctor long?' I asked in an effort to change the subject and also to glean information for my own edification.

He smiled. 'He's annoying and a pain sometimes. But you soon miss him when he's not there.'

'And Miss Seymour?' I asked innocently. 'I get the impression you knew her already. Both of you.' I made it a statement rather than a question. This approach is, in my experience, more likely to solicit an honest reply.

'You mean –' He broke off. I wondered what he had almost said. But he went on before I could enquire. 'No,' he said quickly. 'I never saw Susan Seymour before we arrived here.' He nodded emphatically. 'That's the truth,' he added, in the manner of one who is telling only the half of it.

I could tell that I should let the matter drop, at least for the meanwhile. Our conversation turned instead to politics and the situation in Germany after unification. It did not really surprise me that, while his ideas were to say the least progressive, Herr Kreiner seemed to know very little about either, though he blustered a fair deal. I was intrigued, I confess. But my own preoccupations and the current circumstances contrived to blunt my interest and our talk meandered over easy subjects for a while.

George Wallace had joined us and we were all three sitting talking when Elizabeth came in about half an hour later. 'Ah, there you are, John.' She seemed relieved to have found me, and I soon knew why.

Stratford had sent her. I braced myself mentally, and made my way towards the study.

THE REPORT OF INSPECTOR IAN STRATFORD (8)

I spent the afternoon in a state of some confusion. No matter what I was doing, my thoughts kept flashing back to the scene in the bedroom, pulling down the sheet to find Harries's body missing. My mind revolved around that point, going in ever-decreasing circles. I spent some time using Sir George Wallace's telephone, trying to get through to Chief Inspector Driscoll and failing miserably. I was shoved up, down, sideways and backwards between a succession of secretaries, sergeants and pen-pushers – without any result. The man was in a meeting, but no one knew where, with whom, or for how long. I left a message and gave up.

After that, I finally managed to question Miss Seymour about her movements of the previous night. I tried to be as tactful as possible, bearing in mind the death of her fiancé, but my mind lagged far behind my tongue and I am sure I offended her more than once, judging by the lapses into silence that she displayed and the regal, almost arrogant gaze with which she occasionally deflected my clumsy questions. In my thoughts I was still staring blindly at a pile of bolsters and blankets piled into human shape. What loomed largest in my mind was embarrassment. I cringed to think that my first action had been to pull the sheet completely off, as if I expected Richard Harries to be hiding at the foot of the bed. It had been John Hopkinson who took the most practical action: checking the cupboards to see if the body had been hidden in there.

Miss Seymour could add little to my meagre store of knowledge, apart from the interesting supposition that Richard Harries's body either was, or contained, a clue to the murderer. That, she suggested, was the only possible motive for the theft.

As soon as she left, Baker turned to me: 'Do you think she's right, sir?'

'About the body, yes. Although it might just be a red herring.

About Hopkinson being innocent? No, I don't think so. At least, he may well be innocent, but it doesn't naturally follow from anything she said.'

'She may have taken it herself, sir.'

Good old Baker, investigate every possibility. 'Not without help, I don't think.'

'Then maybe she had help, sir.'

But there was a difference between theory and wild speculation. 'Yes, possibly,' I said, unconvinced. Then I remembered something. 'Baker, any sign of the Doctor yet?'

'Ah, no, sir,' said Baker.

'I am getting sick and tired of talking to people who claim not to know anything,' I snapped. 'Let's do something practical for a change – let's search the house.'

Baker's eyes brightened. 'Yes, *sir*!'

We started at the top of the house. The quarters occupied by the scullery maid and the kitchen maids were sparsely furnished and freezing cold, with threadbare bedding. Improving biblical tracts were fixed to the walls. A single change of uniform hung in each closet, along with a few personal items: Sunday bonnets, worn gloves, a once beautiful pair of dancing shoes. The Doctor was not there.

We then moved down to the next floor, where the various household maids, the cook and the undercooks resided. The rooms were better furnished and more comfortable, but they still had the feeling of places barely occupied apart from during sleep. Still no sign of the Doctor. By the time we got to Simpson's room I was more circumspect – the man was actually still in the house, after all – but while Baker stood at the door, ready to intercept the butler should he appear, I searched everywhere the Doctor could hide (and, frankly, anywhere Richard Harries's body might have been hidden). I tried to get some impression of Simpson's character from his possessions, but all I could tell was that he was almost fanatically meticulous at what he did: his clothes were neatly hung, his loose change was stacked in piles of different denominations (and in date order of minting, I noticed). Beside the coins was a pile of six white squares made of some hard, cold material. Cards for notes, perhaps?

The next floor down contained the various guest bedrooms, and we quickly went through them, taking particular care with Miss Seymour's and Miss Harries's rooms that we did not trespass upon their proprieties. We also missed out Sir George and Elizabeth Wallace's room, as Elizabeth Wallace was resting within and, we assumed, would have alerted us had she discovered either the Doctor or Richard Harries. Apart from that one room we covered the floor from one end to the other, and found nothing. Not hide nor hair of the Doctor. That left the ground floor and the cellars. The first we could afford to treat lightly, as we had spent so much time in its various rooms during the course of the day, and so Baker and I concentrated our efforts on those areas usually hidden from guests: the kitchen, the scullery and Simpson's peculiar pantry – peculiar because, due perhaps to Banquo Manor's odd architecture, it seemed more spacious than its cramped position beneath the stairs would indicate. The cellar was dark and enshrouded with spiders' webs. A furnace roared away to itself in a corner, a half-filled coal bunker beside it. But no bodies resided between the racks of fine wine or under the shovel. In short, neither the Doctor nor the body of Richard Harries was anywhere within the walls of Banquo Manor.

Leaving Baker to explore the exterior of the house, and having taken a cup of tea and washed the grime of my search from my face and hands, I took the opportunity to seek out our hostess, Elizabeth Wallace. She had woken from her sleep as we explored the cellarage, and I found her in the kitchen directing the urbane Simpson and the harassed Beryl in the dinner arrangements. She readily agreed to answer a few questions.

'I'll just carry on now, ma'am,' came Simpson's voice, floating after us from the kitchen.

I spent some time questioning Mrs Wallace about Richard Harries and his relationship with the other members of the household. She could not add anything that I didn't already know, although she herself didn't like Harries and she didn't know anyone who did. I tried to draw out why her husband had allowed Harries to live with them, but she avoided the bait with the dignity and grace befitting the Lady of the Manor. My theories remained unconfirmed, and I changed the subject to the time of the murder.

'And so, after the aperitifs, where did you go, Mrs Wallace?'

'I went out to the kitchen to see how Simpson and Beryl were coping with the food. It was all cold of course: Richard had insisted that we send all the servants away, save Simpson and Beryl.' She smiled bitterly. 'Quite inconvenient for most of us. Less so for George.'

I filed that away as another prop for my theory. Unfortunately I had quite a few props up on one side, and almost none on the other. I continued: 'This was because of Professor Harries's experiment?'

'Yes.'

'I see. So you were all three in the kitchen the whole time? No one could have slipped out to the study?'

Mrs Wallace cast a regal glance at me. 'Not at all, Inspector. We all carried things through to the dining room at one time or another. Any one of us could have slipped away for a moment.'

She had seen what I was getting at with no difficulty, and my respect for Mrs Wallace increased. I had seen many people in her position bluster, 'Surely you can't suspect me, Inspector?' but Elizabeth Wallace automatically included herself in the list of suspects. I liked her.

'I know for a fact that Simpson was outside for a time,' I said, trying to provoke some reaction from behind her well-bred mask.

'Quite probably, Inspector. As I said, I wouldn't have noticed.' Nothing.

'And equally well, neither Simpson nor Beryl would have noticed if you had left them.'

'Of course not.' But as an afterthought, 'Though I didn't.'

'But if you had?'

'No, they wouldn't have noticed.'

The door behind Mrs Wallace opened, and Baker's considerable bulk squeezed through the gap. He looked as though he had news to impart.

'Thank you, Mrs Wallace,' I said smoothly. 'I don't think I need detain you any longer.'

'Thank you for being so courteous at such a difficult time,' she replied, rising gracefully from her chair.

'Could you ask Mr Hopkinson to step this way?'

'Of course.'

She left, shutting the door behind her.

'I've been checking the routes away from the house, sir,' Baker said with suppressed excitement, 'and I think I've found a fresh set of footsteps belonging to Dr Friedlander. They lead away from the conservatory and veer off towards the station.'

I was cautious. 'How do you know they belong to the Doctor?'

'Distinctive footwear, sir. Those boots of his were never made in England, I'll be bound.'

I could feel Baker's excitement transmitting itself across the space between us. Warmth spread through my stomach and the embarrassment of the morning fell from me as I sprang to my feet.

'So it could have been Friedlander who killed Harries and then moved his body?'

'Seems likely, sir,' said Baker. 'And the sooner we set out then…'

'…the quicker we can catch up with him,' I finished. I got up and we crossed to the door. Just as we were about to open it there was a knock and I remembered Hopkinson. I had no time for him now and thought quickly. Perhaps he could tell us more about Friedlander's supposed plans before we set out after the elusive Doctor.

THE ACCOUNT OF JOHN HOPKINSON (9)

Despite my apprehensions, Stratford did not appear to want to see me on a matter of any great importance. Indeed, he seemed more interested in appropriating the services of Herr Kreiner on an expedition into the grounds in search of the good Dr Friedlander.

Kreiner for his part seemed nonplussed. But there was no mistaking the excitement that seemed to link those twin custodians of the law, Stratford and Baker, in its embrace. I shrugged dismissively as the front door closed behind them and left them to their business.

'I shouldn't worry too much, my dear. I've just about given up all hope of finding out what's going on since the inspector got his claws in.' Wallace's voice greeted me in the hall, escaping from the open door of the drawing room. I smiled in agreement and went in.

Susan and Elizabeth were also there, and I drew up a vacant chair beside them.

'Even so, it worries me,' said Susan, and Elizabeth agreed.

'Yes, me too, George. I'd like to be able –' She broke off as the door opened to admit Simpson.

'Have you finished with the coffee, ma'am?' he asked Elizabeth, ignoring my hand poised over a clean cup.

'Yes, thank you,' she replied absently. I relinquished my hope of coffee and allowed the butler to remove the tray. It seemed that he had still not forgiven me for catching him doing something useful. Simpson smiled at me benignly and turned back to Elizabeth Wallace.

'What shall I do about dinner, ma'am?' he asked her seriously.

'Dinner?' demanded George. 'What do you mean, what shall you do?'

'Well, sir,' began Simpson, seemingly prepared to outline in minuscule detail the problems and possibilities of the culinary strategy.

Elizabeth checked him in time: 'We'll have whatever you and Beryl can manage between you, thank you, Simpson.'

The butler raised an eyebrow. 'Very good; and for how many will it be?'

While Elizabeth described at length the problems involved in obtaining any information from either Baker or Stratford, I watched George. He seemed preoccupied with something on the carpet. He eventually traced it to Simpson's feet and I too noticed that his shoes were wet through, dripping on to the floor and soaking into the pile of the carpet.

'You been doing the gardening as well, Simpson?' asked George, his tone only just hinting at admiration for the butler's depths of versatility.

'Sorry, sir?' Simpson followed George's gaze. 'Oh, no, sir; I was outside for a little while earlier on.'

'Whatever for?' asked Susan, not unreasonably.

'Yes, it's not exactly warm.' I remembered Baker covering his well-insulated form with an overcoat.

'We're short of herbs.' This apparently explained everything. 'I went into the kitchen garden to find some thyme.'

'You're not attempting to serve a hot dinner, are you?' Elizabeth was horrified.

'No, but –'

'Yes, well never mind the blasted herbs,' George interrupted irritated at the fuss, 'just get on with the dinner.'

'Very well, sir.'

Simpson made good his escape. The farce was continuing it seemed, but it was about to tip into the tragedy it echoed.

THE REPORT OF INSPECTOR IAN STRATFORD (9)

Leaving Banquo Manor was as I imagine walking into the Arctic wastes would be. The snow covered everything around us, hiding differences, making unevenness even. It seemed to glow of its own accord and I had to narrow my eyes into slits if I wanted to see anything comfortably. The trees lining the drive reached up skeletal hands in supplication to the blank sky. Each bare branch held its own layer and for a moment it appeared that the white snow was the tree and the darker branches underneath merely shadows cast by the sun overhead. Then my perception shifted back, and the trees were trees again.

I felt good standing outside the front door of the Manor with Baker by my side. Even the sullen presence of Herr Kreiner, desperate to locate the Doctor and reluctant to accept the fact that his friend was almost certainly a murderer, was not enough to dent my enthusiasm. The frustrations and troubles from inside the house faded away, to be replaced by the happiness I always felt out of doors. I took a deep breath, and the frozen afternoon air stung like needles in my lungs.

The ground in front of the Manor was a mishmash of tracks. From this three sets emerged. Two I could immediately identify: those belonging to Baker and myself from the night before. The third set could only belong to the Doctor, but they deviated almost immediately from ours, heading out at right angles to the driveway towards a distant line of trees. I looked over at Baker, engulfed in an elephantine overcoat and flapping his arms to keep warm.

'It looks as if the Doctor wasn't trying to get to the railway station after all,' I muttered.

'I *told* you,' Kreiner said. 'The Doctor never runs away. He's always there, in the thick of it, confronting –' his eloquence seemed to peter out – 'whatever needs to be confronted.'

'Oh, I don't know, sir,' said Baker. 'That's a short cut to the village.' He indicated the path taken by the Doctor with a nod of his head.

'So why didn't we come that way last night?'

'It can be treacherous, sir. I didn't want to risk it at night. Especially with a superior officer. The Doctor obviously had more confidence than me.' A frown passed over Baker's face. 'Perhaps the gentleman met with an accident, sir.'

'I hope not,' I said. 'He's our main suspect at the moment, and I don't want to lose him now.'

Kreiner snorted as we took one last look at the façade of the Manor behind us, then set off after the Doctor.

Soon we were in the trees. Their lines were abbreviated by winter so that they were just black slashes on the white parchment of the snow. High above our heads the branches fanned out so that we were walking in a maze of elongated cathedral windows – stained glass bleached to black and white. The trees were set far enough apart for us to walk abreast with the Doctor's footprints forming a line between us; but the size of the forest was such that a clear line of sight petered out within fifty yards. A slight wind blew, but the trees were so old and firm that they scarcely showed the breeze. The cold began to bite home and I huddled deeper into my coat. I felt as if the joints of my fingers were on fire.

I think we had been travelling uphill for some time, although the white blanket covering the ground made such judgements hazardous. It certainly caused me to misjudge the height we had reached. When we emerged from the treeline we were almost at the crest of the hill, and I saw with considerable surprise that it was one of the highest points in the area around Three Sisters, and certainly the highest within the grounds of Banquo Manor.

'Nice view,' Kreiner said with what I took to be a measure of sarcasm.

I turned slowly. Behind me, over the tops of the trees that were reaching blindly for the sky, I could see the chimneys of the Manor House. On my left as I faced the Manor was the snaking black line of the railway, straddled by the block of the station. I completed the circuit; ahead of me was the crest of the hill, and just before the top was a small wooden hut barely large enough to hold two men. I looked questioningly at Baker.

'Belongs to Sir George Wallace,' said the sergeant. 'It's to do with this grotto of his.'

'Grotto?' I asked, wondering if I had heard Baker correctly.

'Yes, sir. Sir George has some plan to make a cave in the hill. Says he wants to be able to come up here in the summer and sit in a cool cave overlooking his grounds with a bottle of crusted port. Started last summer blasting a cave out of the hillside, then called a halt when the weather drew in come autumn.' Baker sniffed. 'Can't see why he wants it, myself. I suppose the view is quite good, but it's a fairly sheltered spot.'

'Perhaps he has a taste for the artificially picturesque,' I said, slightly stunned at Wallace's Napoleonic ambition. 'But what's this about blasting? You mean he has access to explosives?'

'Yes, sir. Keeps them in the shack, he does. Blasting powder, Express Dynamite, Saxonite, detonators; he's got it all.' He chuckled. 'Some of the poachers around here would pay a pretty penny to get their hands on that, I can tell you.'

'I don't understand,' Kreiner said.

'Fishing, sir. Drop a lighted stick of dynamite into the water, then scoop up all the fish that drift to the surface after it's gone off. Stunned or dead, it makes no difference, sir. They all go into the pot.'

I shuddered. Ever since the Yard had been bombed in 1884, the Metropolitan Police went in fear of explosives. I had been in the force for several years then, and had recently been transferred to London for personal reasons. If I hadn't taken a day's leave on private business, the infernal device might have claimed my life. A number of my colleagues were maimed in the explosion.

'I hope the stuff's kept under lock and key,' I muttered. 'Poachers or whatever, it could be very dangerous in the wrong hands.'

'Don't worry, sir,' said Baker as he walked over to the shed. 'It's sturdier than it looks, and it's always kept locked. I check it whenever I'm in the area.'

He grasped the padlock on the door and gave it a tug

'Hmm. Where does Sir George get it from?'

'I believe it comes via a colleague of the late Professor Harries. A foreign gentleman sends it over. Swedish, I believe.'

We walked on, past the shack. There was a small, grimy window in one side, and on a sudden suspicion I walked over and peered in.

'Anything interesting, sir?'

'Nothing that looks remotely like Dr Friedlander or Richard Harries,' I replied. We walked on.

As it turned out, we did not have to look much further for the Doctor. As we topped the crest of the hill the ground fell away steeply, almost like a cliff face, where the dynamite had been used to artificially gouge half the hillside away. Baker extended an arm, partly to prevent me from slipping and falling into the grotto but mostly, I realised later, to preserve the evidence. The signs of a fight, where the snow was churned into slush. The broken branches. The splash of blood, bright crimson against the virgin snow.

Thirty feet below us, down in the artificial hollow where George Wallace was intending, next summer, to sit with his bottle of crusted port, the Doctor's body lay crumpled, face down. His arms had been broken and twisted grotesquely by the impact with the ground, his legs seemed to be buckled beneath him, and his head was hidden by his hunched shoulders.

'No!' Kreiner cried, and threw himself towards the edge. Baker and I grabbed hold of his arms.

'It's too dangerous!' Baker shouted as Kreiner scrabbled closer to the almost sheer drop. 'The sides are covered with ice and snow. You'll never get down in one piece.'

'It's true,' I said, knowing that Baker was, in part, talking to me as well as to Kreiner. I grabbed him by the shoulders and stared deeply into his eyes until his gaze locked on me and not on the wild phantoms of his own grief. 'It's true. Mr Kreiner – Fitz – you have to keep control. We need you.'

'But –' His struggles began to subside. 'But the Doctor… the Doctor…'

'He's dead,' I said.

'You can't know that. We need to get down there. We need to –'

'Kreiner, trust me. He couldn't survive more than five minutes in this weather without protection. The fall must have broken most of the bones in his body. He's dead.'

A great sob racked Kreiner's body, and as I let go his shoulders he slumped to his knees, heedless of the white blanket covering the ground. Turning to Baker, I said quietly, 'Can we get down there?'

'There are other routes round to the bottom, sir, but they're all pretty treacherous. I wouldn't want to risk it, sir – not without proper equipment. Simpson might be able to help, but we'll probably have to wait for a thaw. I suggest we get back, sir – we've found what we came for.'

Slowly, the first flakes of a new snowfall began to drift from the silent clouds above us. As they settled, tears began to run down Kreiner's face and mingle with the snow.

THE ACCOUNT OF JOHN HOPKINSON (10)

I met them in the hall, quite by chance. Stratford was leading the way, Baker close behind him. Fitz Kreiner brought up the rear, his head bowed and his expression sullen. At first I mistook his demeanour for thoughtfulness, but as he looked up I caught his eye. And I could see the depth of sadness that lurked behind his eyes. In that moment, without asking, I knew what they had found.

As we stood, sullen and subdued on the hallway, Stratford offered a brief explanation. Baker asked Stratford who was to break the unpleasant news to the others. I offered, but the inspector insisted that he should. I did not argue. I was too shocked. I felt empty, as if someone I had known for many years – not just one day – was gone. The Doctor had surprised me initially by his enthusiasm and energy. Now I could understand at least some small part of what Kreiner must be going through. He had known the man for years, had worked closely with him. They were, in short, friends. Even after our brief acquaintance, I could recall how his eyes had danced with light. And now those eyes, were closed for ever. The dancing was finished.

Kreiner and I waited in the hall while Stratford and Baker went to tell the others what had occurred, and I was glad not to have to be there. We just stood, sharing the silence. For how long we stood there, I don't know. But eventually, Kreiner looked up at me. I took my cue, and placed my hand on his shoulder. His mouth curled into an approximation of a smile, though his eyes still had a dead, moist quality. Still without a word, we rejoined the others.

I felt numbed when we got back to the drawing room. The pale voids of the others' faces, I imagined, echoed my own. Only Stratford seemed to be coping; death was a part of his job.

As we entered, Simpson left to finish laying for dinner. I hoped he would have the presence of mind to lay the right number of places: one too many would be unfortunate to say the very least. Stratford followed close after him, taking Wallace with him presumably for some discussion of events.

'John, what's happening here?' I realised I had sat next to Susan on the chaise longue.

'I don't know. I wish I did.' I turned to the policemen. 'Any ideas, Sergeant Baker?'

Mention of his name seemed to jolt Baker out of his reverie – for the shock appeared to be having a delayed effect on him. He mumbled a few words about finding the inspector as he shuffled out towards the study and his mentor.

'It's almost dinner time.' Elizabeth was holding back the tears. 'Best to carry on as normally as possible, I suppose.' They got the better of her. 'Only it isn't normal, of course,' she sobbed and Susan guided her to a chair.

'Come along, Mrs Wallace. You'll be all right in a minute, once you're over the first shock.'

Kreiner watched them. He was tense, angry. His hands were bunched into fists at his sides as he walked slowly across to where Susan was standing beside Elizabeth.

'Don't you feel anything?' he hissed at her as he approached. Whether he had forgotten I was there or was so bound up in his emotions that he just did not care, I don't know.

'Steady there,' I said quietly. But I may as well not have spoken.

'He's dead,' Kreiner went on. His voice was as tense and knotted as his fists. 'Stone-cold dead. I saw him. In the snow. You know he couldn't...' He broke off, as if unsure what he was saying. 'The inhibition, it affected him too. You know it did,' he said. Something like that. 'He was just lying there. And you can't even...' He shook his head.

Susan looked up at him, and even from where I was I could see the tear stains down her cheeks. Despite Kreiner's anger and rebuke Susan had felt the loss as keenly as I had. More so. Had I been less caught up in the moment, had I been able to distance myself from the events and their shadows, I might have wondered why she was so affected. And why Kreiner thought she should be.

'You don't feel a thing, do you?' he demanded. 'Nothing at all?' He was close enough to reach out and touch her now. And he did. He caught her by the shoulders, gripped her tight. I saw the startled look in her eyes, and I took a step backwards myself.

'Compassion!' he shouted at her, shaking her like a doll.

She blinked again. Her mouth opened in surprise and she pulled herself free as I closed on them. I put my own hand on Kreiner's shoulder and gently pulled him away. He was almost in tears. Perhaps he merely had to vent his frustration, his anger, his brutal sadness on someone. But that someone could be me rather than Susan, I decided.

He stared at me for a moment, as if suddenly aware that I was there. 'No compassion,' he said quietly. 'None at all.' Then he seemed to sag under my grasp. He murmured something else as he turned and walked slowly, stiffly from the room. I wasn't sure, but it sounded like he said, 'So there's only me left now.'

Behind me, Susan was once again seeing to Elizabeth Wallace who, had watched these events with a mixture of apprehension and incredulity. 'Come through to dinner,' Susan said gently, helping Elizabeth to her feet. And I wondered what had brought Kreiner to the conclusion that there was no feeling for others in this gentle, thoughtful woman.

I needed to be alone, so I remained in the drawing room as they went in to dinner. I stared into the fire, but it held no solace. Above it the brass plaque taunted me with my own polished reflection, distorted by the grooves of the engraved letters – as if it knew the answer, and that answer was an image of myself. I still felt completely numb as I stood by the fire, and murmured the engraved words:

> If you can look into the seeds of time,
> And say which grain will grow and which will not,
> Speak then to me who neither beg nor fear
> Your favours nor your hate.

Something clicked inside my mind as I smashed my fist down on the stone mantel, and as the pain slowly permeated the empty numbness, Stratford's face floated up into my memory, distorted by time – a younger reflection – and I knew where we had met before.

I got away from the group in the drawing room as soon as I could without being obvious about it. The conversation was going around in circles and my head was spinning at the same rate. The death of Dr Friedlander – the fight – left me stranded. It did not fit in with my tentative theories at all, but if I scrapped them where did that leave me?

Back at square one.

I walked across the hall and entered the study. I switched the lights on, crossed the room and slid into the huge leather chair behind the desk. I liked that chair. It gave me a sense of power, a sense of importance. It made me feel that, with just a little thought, the whole puzzle would become clear to me.

There was a knock on the door, and I inwardly cursed. It looked like my peace was going to be short-lived. 'Come in,' I yelled. The door opened and Baker appeared.

'Not disturbing you, am I, sir?'

'Of course not,' I lied.

'It's just that I was feeling a bit out of sorts in the drawing room. Not exactly my cup of tea, sir, trying to talk to the gentry.'

He sat down in one of the chairs opposite the wall and laced his fingers behind his head. I stared at a bare piece of wall to one side of the door. There was silence for some time.

'At least we can rule the Doctor out now,' said Baker eventually.

'Yes, but if not him, then who?' I said despondently.

'Back to Mr Hopkinson, I suppose, sir.'

'I'm afraid we are. But Miss Seymour was right.'

Baker frowned. 'About what?'

'About his seeming as surprised as the rest of us when Harries's body vanished. And he was visibly shocked when we told him about the Doctor.'

'Could have been a put-on, sir.'

A silence again. This time it was broken by me. 'Do you ever get the feeling that things are slowly but surely getting out of hand, Sergeant?'

'Yes, sir. But never as much as I do now.'

'Thank you for the vote of confidence.'

He looked over at me and smiled. 'You're doing all right, sir,' he replied in a slow and measured voice, and I felt something lighten inside me. 'So what do we do now?' he continued.

'Only one thing we can do at the moment,' I said, rising from the chair. 'Go and join the others for dinner.'

Dinner was thin on the table, but we were not hungry. Only Sergeant Baker, now over the worst of his shock apparently, was able to more than pick at his food. Perhaps for him a reasonably sized meal was a mere bagatelle in culinary terms. I watched Ian Stratford carefully but surreptitiously as Simpson crossed from the door and whispered to him; and suddenly he, like me, was years younger – standing in front of my desk as I waved him to a seat. An image of the questioning of the evening before, almost. But in reverse, another out-of-joint reflection.

He was nervous, still in his coat, his fingers playing along the rim of his hat. Forgive me for not standing – fractured ankle... Now, what can I do for you, sir? (Can't remember his name. Oh well, just preliminary after all.)

'A matter of some delicacy... I wonder if... possibly... You see, she's been...'

Ah, yes – I quite understand. Not the first case of this type we've dealt with. Most unfortunate... My sympathy, sir. (How can I palm this off on Gerald? God – I don't want it! More Gerry's line; 'delicate', what a word... He'll love it. Just his biscuit.) Now, perhaps you could tell me...?

'Of course. That is – my wife...'

Stratford's face froze, mouth open; his private agony stilled. Until it found voice and screamed at me across my desk...

I was suddenly back in the dining room at Banquo Manor: older but no wiser, fork held stationary in front of my mouth. Stratford mirrored my action across the table – his mouth open to receive the meat; Simpson was still beside him.

The scream stopped – cut off. Choked off. Abrupt. Susan's knife slipped from her hand and fell in slowed motion. It crashed at last into her near-empty plate, spun, lifted – blade uppermost – above the china, then dipped back on to it, echoing itself and clattering us back to reality before settling.

Stratford was already on his feet, typically the first to recover. Across the table from him, Fitz Kreiner was a hair's breadth of elapsed time behind. Perhaps he was as used to this sort of happening as Stratford. Forensics must have its own drama. And nightmares.

'Catherine,' murmured Elizabeth, her face stone – immobile, cold, pale. It had certainly been a woman's scream. Or a girl's. I followed Stratford and Kreiner, Baker on my heel catching his arm on his chair in the hurry. Thoughts and movements were becoming muddled. Simpson somehow held the door open – had he been in front of us?

So many stairs...

The fact that Harries's body was back on the bed, the sheet that had covered it pulled to his feet, failed to surprise me. I realised somehow at the back of my mind that I had heard Simpson's hushed words to Stratford, that this is what he had been telling the inspector. Stratford was already kneeling by the supine figure of Beryl Green, his finger on her bruised neck feeling for the pulse.

'What was she doing in here?' His professional, almost dispassionate tone told us immediately that she was dead. Almost dispassionate.

'She found the body was back when she came in to change the sheets.' Simpson's voice seemed unaffected. His face was not: grief, horror, sadness all met in his eyes. 'I left her sitting over there.' He gestured towards the overturned chair by the dressing table; she had stood up hurriedly. 'I came to get you while she got over the shock.'

'You left her in here – with that?' Kreiner asked.

I could only agree with his incredulity. If the sight and smell of Harries's body made *me* feel ill, God alone knew how it would have affected a sixteen-year-old girl, however sophisticated. Beryl. Oh, Beryl.

'Well, I covered it up first, of course, sir.'

'Of course.'

'She must have uncovered it again,' Stratford mused, pulling the sheet back over the wreck of humanity on the bed.

'Could she have died of fright when she saw it again, close up?' Baker's suggestion was a weak one and he knew it.

'Why go to the other side of the room to do it?' Kreiner asked him.

'She could have staggered back, knocked over the chair –'

'No,' said Stratford, 'she couldn't.' Stratford could not have failed to see the marks as Baker had. 'She's been strangled.' He thought for a moment. 'Baker, ask Miss Seymour if I could see her for a minute in the study, would you please?' The inspector was back in control. Baker departed on his appointed task.

'It's time I got this sorted out,' Stratford decided, and for the first time I felt that he was addressing us as equals.

'You know who did it?' Kreiner asked. I was surprised he seemed slower to realise than I had been.

'Oh yes, I think so.' Stratford's eyes were on me as he answered.

Simpson raised an eyebrow, but said nothing.

Stratford knelt by the body again. 'There's only one person we can't account for,' he went on, lifting Beryl's hand from its rest beside her head. He brushed the fine blonde strands away from it and pulled something from her clenched hand. 'And this rather confirms it all.' He smoothed out the scrap of paper and held it up for us to see. It was part of a page from a small pocketbook, but before I could read the words written on it or make sense of the tiny scrawled dates and numbers, he had spirited it away.

As Stratford strode from the bedroom it was with the relieved confidence of a man whose work is done. Kreiner and I exchanged glances and followed. I could see some of the line of argument the inspector must be pursuing; but why did he wish to see Susan? As Simpson carefully closed the bedroom door behind us, the final part clicked into place. Or so I thought.

I leaned back in the leather chair and steepled my fingers on the desk blotter in front of me. Baker stood by the study door and Miss Seymour sat demurely in a chair drawn up in front of the desk. There was a puzzled, faintly questioning look on Baker's face, and the ghost of a similar expression in Susan Seymour's eyes. Neither of them quite realised what was going on, but they could both sense something of the triumph that filled me. The look that they shared was one of reassessment. For once in this case things were going my way, and I felt as if I could not make a wrong move. I felt in command.

In my right hand was the piece of paper I had found in Beryl's dead fist, grasped tight like a talisman.

'I realise, Miss Seymour –' and my voice was deep and confident – 'that this is a rather sensitive matter for you, but would you like to tell me why you were breaking off your engagement to Richard Harries? I believe I already know, but I need confirmation.'

Susan Seymour's delicate head dropped, and a rose-tinted blush stole across her delicate cheeks. I suppressed the feeling that I could sense moving within me and continued like a professional. 'I can assure you that it is vital that I know.'

'I found that –' she paused, hesitant, like a deer startled by a noise – 'that the more I got to know him, the less I got to like him. It is as simple as that, Inspector.'

'What in particular, Miss Seymour? Perhaps it had something to do with this.' I opened my hand to display the scrap of paper. A calculated risk, but one that immediately paid off. The colour heightened in her cheeks and she drew herself up.

'Yes, Inspector, that was the reason.' Over her shoulder I could see surprise almost comically etched into the lines of Baker's face.

'I realised earlier on today,' I said, softer. More conciliatory.

'Finding the evidence was another thing entirely.' I indicated the torn paper in my hand. 'Fortunately, your fiancé kept meticulous records. The scientist in him, I expect. Beryl must have found the records in his desk, and was killed for her discovery. The murderer failed to notice the one page left in her hand when he tore them from her grasp. How many people was Richard Harries blackmailing, Miss Seymour?'

The expression on Baker's face was as if I had begun to tap-dance on the table. Yet another rabbit pulled from the Metropolitan Police hat. I was lucky. They were both so far off balance after my revelation that it did not occur to either of them to ask me about the identity of the killer. Although I had a fair idea, I needed more time to consolidate my position on that.

'I'm not sure,' sighed Miss Seymour. 'Sir George Wallace, certainly… That's why George allowed Richard to stay here. As part of the payment.'

'And was Gordon Seavers, back in London, being blackmailed?'

She nodded. 'I think that's why he stayed away this weekend – he didn't want to face Richard.'

I winced, remembering my reason for arriving at Banquo Manor. The letter… the suicide of Gordon Seavers…

'Miss Seymour, has no one in this house remarked upon the fact that I happened to be in the area when your fiancé was murdered?'

She looked up, startled. 'Why no… I think we all assumed – at least, I assumed – that it was just a coincidence.'

I looked down at the blotter, then up at her uncomprehending eyes. 'I arrived here following the suicide last week of Gordon Seavers, at his London residence.'

Susan Seymour went white. Her hands convulsed on the arms of her chair and she opened and closed her mouth as if the words she was trying to form did not even exist. Then a sudden rush of tears filled her eyes. 'Poor Mary,' she sobbed. 'Poor, poor Mary…'

I think that was when I realised that I had actually fallen in love with Susan Seymour. The characteristic compassion for the feelings of others that she possessed immediately made her think of Seavers's widow. She was so beautiful and my heart began to ache in a way I hadn't felt for many long years.

Then she realised. 'But surely, John…'

'Mr Hopkinson was staying with Gordon Seavers when the suicide took place,' I said levelly, and the flash of terrible anger in her eyes gave me the strength to add, 'And we have reason to believe that he removed a vital piece of evidence from Mr Seavers's body…' I am not sure if she was even listening.

'Why didn't he tell us?' she said. 'Why didn't he tell us?'

'That is a question which the sergeant and I would also like to ask him,' I said rising from my chair. 'Perhaps we should have a word with Mr Hopkinson.'

Baker opened the door for us and we exited to the hall. The drawing-room door was open and I could see John Hopkinson moving back and forth inside the room. All the strands were coming together now and I was looking forward to the long deferred pleasure of confronting him. I turned to the sergeant.

'Baker, find Sir George and his wife – and Catherine Harries. Ask them to meet us in the study.' As Baker turned to leave, a sudden thought struck me. 'You had better ask Simpson to join us as well.'

Baker moved off towards the stairs, and just as I was about to face John Hopkinson I felt a delicate hand on my arm. I turned to meet Susan Seymour's eyes, disconcertingly close to my own. Close enough so that I could just lean forward and kiss her, had I wanted to.

'I never stopped loving him you know,' she said. 'Even though he did some terrible things, I never stopped loving him. He wasn't evil, Inspector. Just different.' She looked up at me appealingly. 'I wanted you to know.' I looked down into her meltingly soft eyes and felt old wounds opening inside me.

'Miss Seymour, I was married once,' I said softly to her. 'After everything my wife did, I still love her. I understand you, Miss Seymour. Believe me, I understand you.'

'Inspector I… I didn't realise.'

'My name is Ian,' I said, and smiled.

She smiled back. 'And I am… Susan,' she replied. Then, more positively, 'Yes, I *am* Susan.' I smiled, grateful for the familiarity with which she was treating me.

Together we walked in to face John Hopkinson.

He was talking in a desultory manner to Fitz Kreiner when we entered the drawing room. His glasses were in his hand. 'What can I do for you, Inspector?' he asked, replacing his glasses upon his nose.

…And suddenly we were in another place, another time, but following the same actions. He replacing his glasses, asking what I wanted, but somehow the situations were reversed and he was questioning me. Then, like snow melting in my hand, the moment – the recognition – was gone, and we were back in the Manor…

'I should like to see everybody in the study in ten minutes,' I said. 'Don't go anywhere in the meantime, Mr Hopkinson.'

'Got it all solved?' he asked, half sarcastically.

'Yes, I believe I have,' I said, and had the pleasure of watching his face change, retreating behind his lenses to hide all expression. I turned towards the door. 'Perhaps Susan and yourself could wait here while I go and help the sergeant to round everybody up.'

Without waiting for an answer I turned my back on the disconcerted John Hopkinson and left the drawing room.

Stratford had left the door open. But before I could move to close it Susan clutched my arm.

'He thinks that Catherine...?' She broke off, unable to complete the question. She hardly had to, for I could see as clearly as Stratford the way in which events had moved along. I sat down slowly on the chaise longue, and Susan (still holding my arm) had no choice but to sit beside me. Kreiner was pacing up and down in front of the fireplace.

'Oh I think he's pretty certain,' I told her, hoping that she would not be too shocked.

'How can he be?' she asked quietly, staring across at the window.

I took her right hand between both of mine, grateful for its warmth.

But before I could speak, Kreiner answered her question: 'We were all at dinner when Beryl was killed. Even Simpson was in the room.'

'Everyone except Catherine, that is,' I said.

Susan turned from Kreiner back towards me. 'But she can't have – I mean, she isn't... She can't be...'

'Have you any other suggestions?' She had not.

'What did Stratford want to see you for anyway?' Kreiner asked abruptly. Was he trying to deflect the topic of conversation, or was he merely trying to satisfy his own curiosity?

'About Richard.'

'Ah.' We both let her continue in her own time, if she felt she wanted to.

'Did you know he was blackmailing George and Gordon?'

'Yes,' I admitted.

'No,' Kreiner said at the same moment. He shrugged and waved a hand for me to continue.

'At least,' I said, 'I was fairly sure he was. I knew he was blackmailing Gordon Seavers.'

'But why?'

'Some of Gordon's early work – his first few papers – was not entirely his own, shall we say? It would have damaged his career had it become known. He got them from a colleague at Oxford and published them after the chap died.'

I imagined that George had been easily trapped. His misdemeanours (if that is the right word) were already apparent to me, unless George had been less captivated by his maid than he had seemed. I was considering whether to mention any or all of this to Susan and Herr Kreiner when I noticed the figure standing in the doorway. I had no way of knowing how much Stratford had overheard, but from his words as he stepped fully into the room it seemed that he had heard enough. This time he took care to close the door.

'Perhaps now you will allow me to see the letter that you removed from Mr Seavers's house, Mr Hopkinson.'

There was no point in continuing to lie. I remembered Gordon's body, crumpled on its side on the floor of his study, the blood trickling along the handle of the paper knife and dripping stickily through his fingers.

I remembered his face smiling down at me as I lay similarly on the grass waiting for a physician. Why hadn't he gone with the others, back to the pavilion? It was only a sprain, it would soon heal. God, it hurt. But he had known my ankle was shattered...

'What, and have to listen to Joe telling us how he took four wickets with four balls again?' he had said. 'No thanks. Pity he's not so accurate with his batting, isn't it, John? I think I'll stay in your somewhat dubious company, if you don't mind...' His face changed, the smile dropped, concerned: 'Does it hurt very much?'

A tear escaped from my eye, though not from the physical

pain. I brushed it away, hoping Stratford had not noticed; certainly he was tactful enough to show no sign of it.

'I would, Inspector, but I've burnt it I'm afraid.' I tried to be slightly more flippant, more than he would expect me to be. I hoped. 'Sorry about that.'

'Never mind. It's you I want to see now.'

'I see. Where's Catherine?'

He did not seem at all surprised by my sudden question. 'She's in the study, with the sergeant.'

'She'll deny everything, of course,' Kreiner said from the other side of the room.

'Oh yes. Vehemently.'

Susan was looking bewildered still. 'So,' I said – mainly for her benefit rather than to show Stratford that I knew the situation as well as he – 'she'll say she didn't try to kill everyone her brother was blackmailing, or who knew about it – as Beryl must have done if she found the notebook in Richard's bedroom – so as to preserve his "good" name. What will you do then?'

'It shouldn't be too difficult to convince a jury that she's the only person who could have killed Miss Green, and so she must have killed the Doctor as well.'

'Are you sure?' Kreiner asked.

'You have a better hypothesis?' Stratford enquired.

Kreiner shrugged. 'I thought we agreed that whoever killed the Doctor surprised him at the edge of the cliff. There was a struggle, and the murderer succeeded in pushing him over.'

I could see where he was going. 'You're saying you don't think Catherine was strong enough? Even with the element of surprise?'

'There was a struggle,' he pointed out. 'We could see that. And the Doctor was stronger than he appeared, believe me.'

'Nevertheless,' Stratford intervened, 'people can call on

surprising amounts of strength when they are emotionally roused. Psychotic.'

'Aren't you overlooking something else, Inspector?' asked Susan, and I saw that she too had realised that the explanations thus far had one large flaw in their framework.

'Am I, Miss Seymour?' Surely he could not have missed it. Could Ian Stratford have even less imagination than I had at first suspected?

'She is hardly likely to have murdered her brother only to try to protect his honour, is she?'

'She will have to have done, I'm afraid. Unless of course it really was an accident, which might be the other plausible explanation. Whatever, it certainly unbalanced her. You see,' he went on, fixing me with a level gaze, 'I cannot in any way prove that Richard Harries was killed by Mr Hopkinson.'

Kreiner gasped out loud. And I was aware of Susan's gaze on me. Amazed? Horrified? I could not look to see. I stared at my feet, not sure what to do or say.

'Besides,' said Stratford, his voice seeming to be filtered through water, 'knowing what sort of a man Harries was, I'm not positive that in his position I would not have been provoked into doing exactly what John did.'

I don't know which surprised me most – his sentiments, his insight or the use of my Christian name. 'You're very clever, Inspector,' I said quietly. 'And also very generous. Thank you.' I looked up at him, and thought I caught the faintest trace of a smile.

'Now, I had better go and see Miss Harries.' He turned and left the room.

'This I have to see,' Kreiner said as he followed. Whether through tact or by chance he closed the door behind him.

I realised that Susan was holding my hand between hers. Had it been worth it all? I thought back to the shooting star, and how it had finally decided me – an omen; how I had managed to unbolt the conservatory door into the garden while Harries obliviously explained his mad ideas – the part of the wall exposed: the door. Fortunate. Getting everything arranged in the few minutes I was absent from the drawing room and returning unobserved had been more than merely fortunate.

Susan squeezed my hand slightly and I was back in the present, a weight lifted at last from my mind.

Baker had already located Catherine Harries and asked her to join us. I left him to find Simpson and the Wallaces and returned to the drawing room. Hopkinson, Susan and Kreiner were talking in low voices as I approached, but I heard enough of what Hopkinson was saying to convince me that I was right. He had known about Harries's blackmail sideline, and also about Gordon Seavers's involvement.

'Perhaps now you will allow me to see the letter you removed from Mr Seavers's house, Mr Hopkinson,' I said as I entered. He glanced up with a flippant, supercilious expression on his face, but perhaps I was getting better at reading his demeanour because I could see something else behind the mask. Just as he used his glasses as a shield, the sarcastic exterior covered the true feeling he would – he could – never show. I could see why the glasses were necessary. His eyes gave too much away. For once the light hindered him, passing through the lenses and highlighting his eyes rather than glancing off and hiding them. His eyes were bruised with hurt, and they shone with the moisture of unshed tears for the life of a friend.

'I would, Inspector, but I've burnt it, I'm afraid. Sorry about that.'

'Never mind. It's you I want to see now.'

'I see. Where's Catherine?'

'She's in the study with the sergeant.'

Kreiner startled us both by saying, 'She'll deny everything of course.'

'Oh yes,' Hopkinson said. 'Vehemently.'

So he had guessed about Catherine Harries as well. I wasn't surprised: she was the only person without an alibi when Beryl was killed. Clumsy, but then if Beryl had discovered Richard Harries's notebook she had to be killed quickly. Catherine Harries may not have been involved with her brother's nefarious trade but she obviously loved him enough to protect his memory, just as she had to kill him to protect his honour. Hopkinson and I tried to explain this to Susan Seymour.

'She will have to have done it, I'm afraid,' I said eventually. 'Unless of course your fiancé's death really was an accident, which might be another plausible explanation. Whatever happened, it certainly unbalanced her.'

Now it was time. Everything else had come out, and I had to stop Susan from getting any closer to John Hopkinson. 'You see,' I continued, 'I cannot in any way prove that Professor Richard Harries was killed by Mr Hopkinson.'

Silence.

John Hopkinson: staring at his feet.

Susan Seymour: eyes fixed unblinkingly on me.

Fitz Kreiner: still about five sentences behind everyone else and struggling to keep up.

And myself? Complete, satisfied – job well done, Inspector, thank you and goodnight. Hopkinson's reaction told me everything I wanted to know. The suspicions I had begun to feel when he was the only person to say he actively hated Richard Harries, added to my knowledge of the blackmail and the suicide of Gordon Seavers, seemed to indicate only one answer. He had crept out before dinner, sabotaged the equipment and thus killed Richard Harries in revenge for the death of his friend.

Catherine Harries was just a complication, albeit a deadly one. That was why I had been going round in circles. There were two cases, not just the one I thought I was investigating.

('So who stole the body of Richard Harries?' a still, small voice inside me asked. 'And why was it stolen? Who killed Dr Friedlander?' 'Details, details,' answered the bulk of my mind. 'Catherine Harries was unbalanced. Who can say what her motives were?')

'Besides,' I said out loud, breaking the heavy silence, 'knowing what sort of a man Harries was, I'm not positive that in Mr Hopkinson's position I wouldn't have done the same.' It was a peace offering of a sort; an apology for taking Susan Seymour away from him. She wouldn't stay with a murderer, even an unproven one.

'You're very clever, Inspector,' he said quietly, 'and you're also very generous. Thank you.'

'Now I'd better go and confront Miss Harries,' I said, and left the room. I could get the full story from Hopkinson later.

Out in the hallway I became aware that Herr Kreiner was following me, like a lost puppy. 'And what about me?' he asked.

'Are you confessing to something?'

'The Doctor – Dr Friedlander, that is – is dead. And Comp–' He swallowed. 'I'm alone here. I've got nowhere to go.'

'I'll need to take a full statement from you,' I said, not unkindly, 'and then I suggest you go home. Will it take long?'

'About a hundred years,' I thought I heard him say as I moved off. I had no time for him now; I half-considered telephoning Chief Inspector Driscoll and reporting, but decided against it. Better to extract a full confession from Catherine Harries first.

Just as I was about to enter the study, George Wallace opened the door.

'Ah, Inspector,' he said, and I could hear the strain in his voice. 'Baker's here with Miss Harries, and Simpson is just coming. I'm off to find my wife. She's having a rest upstairs, you know.'

'Very well,' I said. 'In that case I'll fetch Mr Hopkinson, Mr Kreiner and Su– Miss Seymour. I need everyone together for what I have to say.'

Wallace began to walk up the stairway as I turned back again towards the drawing room, gesturing to Mr Kreiner to follow me. It was finally all pulling together.

If only I had known.

THE ACCOUNT OF JOHN HOPKINSON (13)

We were still talking: I trying to justify myself, Susan biting her lower lip and trying to look noncommittal. I talked, she perhaps listened.

'Mr Hopkinson, can you spare a minute?' Stratford's voice startled me for a moment, partly because it was even louder than my own, which had already been strengthened by my nerves and my dispelled fears.

'Inspector,' Susan beat me to the reply, 'are you sure about Catherine?'

'Yes, I am. Although I haven't told her yet.'

'Why not?' I asked, but as I spoke my words were drowned...

THE REPORT OF INSPECTOR IAN STRATFORD (13)

I missed Hopkinson's words as a woman's scream cut sharply through the conversation. It reached a peak of pain and disgust, then ended – abruptly. Not Susan: she was here with us, thank God. Not Catherine Harries. She was with Baker. It had to be Elizabeth Wallace. But surely she was with her husband…

'Come on,' Kreiner shouted, pulling himself together. We all ran for the hall. Baker was emerging from the study and behind him I could see a white-faced Catherine Harries.

'Is Miss Harries all right?' I asked.

'Yes, sir. What was –'

'Stay with her, Baker.'

Hopkinson, Kreiner and I pounded side by side up the staircase. Somehow the silence we ran towards was more terrifying than the screaming…

The door was standing open, gaping. And we could see through to the bedroom beyond. But despite that we still went in: I first I think, despite the fact that both Stratford and Kreiner had reached the doorway before me. We were drawn in by the scene before us. Tempted closer by its very horror, by our own fear.

They were frozen in tableau, like the close of a Greek tragedy. Two bodies lying twisted, motionless, silent.

Silent.

Silent as we were until we could breathe again, until we had taken it in and begun to realise at least something of what we were seeing.

'Oh, my God!' I murmured. Beside me I heard Kreiner's sharp intake of shocked breath.

'We were wrong,' said Stratford, but he was not disappointed. He was horrified.

George Wallace lay half off the bed, his face turned away so that the fear was partly obscured; the bruises on his neck were not. Elizabeth was further back against the wall, as if she was still cowering away from whatever had killed her husband.

Even as I watched, Elizabeth Wallace's head peeled stickily away from the wall and fell forward on to her chest. Someone had slammed it into the wall so hard that the skull had shattered. The plaster around the resulting dent was cracked and powdered, some of it settling like snow on to what had once been the back of her head. Strings of clotting blood joined her to the wall. A small drop of red fell forlornly from her mouth to her dress.

Beside me Hopkinson turned away and retched, while Kreiner just stood, mute and shocked. I was numb, cold, as dead as Wallace and his wife. Four deaths and nothing to show for it. What was I doing there? Was that all my training had equipped me for? Standing still while, all around me, strangers died.

In the mirror on the dressing table I could see the reflection of Wallace's face. I could not decipher his expression. What had he thought of as he died? Whose death was he mourning, his wife's or Beryl's?

Why did I think he was grateful for his own?

There was a rough irregular hole beneath his right ear. Whoever had strangled him had pressed hard enough to rupture the skin.

'Everyone is accounted for...' said Hopkinson behind me. 'Apart from Simpson.'

'And he was with us when Beryl was killed,' I said flatly.

'So either he and Miss Harries did it together,' I said quietly.

'Which, at best, is unlikely,' Kreiner pointed out, not unreasonably.

'Or it was an outsider.'

'No!' Hopkinson exploded. 'A passing tramp nipped in to steal the silver and kill a few of the gentry? Or a lunatic conveniently escaped from a nearby asylum? Come on, Stratford, it just won't work.'

'In that case we'd better get everyone into the drawing room...'

'And hope they're not all in it together,' Hopkinson finished. I turned to look at him. He raised a questioning eyebrow, and I couldn't help but smile back.

We walked out, leaving the Wallaces together, parted in death.

THE ACCOUNT OF JOHN HOPKINSON (15)

It was odd walking down the thick-pile stairway towards the others gathered in the drawing room below. It was odd, looking back, that we missed the obvious connection that Mr Kreiner's forensically trained mind was able to make. It is odd, given what had gone before, that Stratford and I were able to treat each other civilly, let alone on equal terms. It was odd at the time because, while two of my friends lay lifeless above us, I saw their departure from this world as little less than the inevitable consequence of the events in Banquo Manor to date.

In short, I was becoming anaesthetised to death – even the death of my closest friends. Stratford too was finding this – I could tell from his cautious smile as we left the bedroom. The deathroom. To speak to those downstairs who had yet to learn... Odd, I had never envisaged myself as the messenger of death. Had anyone warned me I should play the role I would have expected to deliver my lines badly. I was now being given more than enough rehearsal time – but the lines still sounded as tactless, as unprepared, as gauche, as I had feared they might.

I could feel their eyes on us as we descended the stairs. Baker trusting, depending on his superior officer. Susan Seymour – hurt, worried, pained. Catherine Harries – watchful, careful. What could we tell them? That two people, two friends of theirs, had died in unimaginable agony a few feet from where they stood?

We descended the stairs in silence and they watched us from the hallway. As we reached the bottom, Hopkinson stepped off the stairs and crossed to Susan Seymour's side. I was left on the last tread, alone apart from the unexpectedly supportive presence of Herr Kreiner by my elbow.

'They're dead,' I said. 'They've been killed... murdered...' My words trailed off inadequately, lost in the force of their accusing stare. I was alone and pierced by their grief, their disbelief, their pain. What else could I have said? But that was where I lost – not their confidence, I still had that. But I lost Susan Seymour at that time and in that place: she turned to John Hopkinson at her side and collapsed on his shoulder, crying.

Baker stared levelly at me.

Catherine Harries winced and looked away.

Simpson entered from the kitchen corridor. 'I couldn't help overhearing...' he began. I had no time for that.

'Simpson, is there a firearm in the house?'

'Yes, sir – the master keeps a shotgun in the study.'

'Then go and get it, man.'

THE ACCOUNT OF JOHN HOPKINSON (16)

Looking back I can see that Stratford never lost his presence of mind. He may have been short on imagination, but since he sent Simpson for the shotgun so quickly I can only assume that he realised almost immediately and instinctively what it took Kreiner's cautious words to tell.

'The noise,' he hesitated, 'that must have been...'

I nodded, unable to speak. Stratford seemed content to remain silent, waiting for Simpson to return.

'But we went up at once,' Kreiner went on. 'I take it that no one has come down since and...' He broke off, but I could see what he was trying to say.

'And there's no other way down,' I finished for him.

He swallowed emptily. 'Yes, so...'

'So whoever killed them,' continued Stratford, apparently taking an interest at last, roused from his thoughts, 'is still upstairs.'

His eyes flicked upwards almost subconsciously, and I felt rather than noticed Susan's follow their direction. I watched her for a moment, felt her weight on my shoulder, felt secure in her eyes as they looked up the stairway, wide and afraid. For a moment I was lost, was safe, in her eyes as they followed the direction of my anxiety. Then she turned slightly and looked back at me. Our eyes met and for a moment we were both transfixed, then I looked away embarrassed. Upwards, towards reality.

Towards death.

THE REPORT OF INSPECTOR IAN STRATFORD (16)

Suddenly, without any conscious effort on my part, my years of training surfaced, pushed forward and took over. There was a suspect – faceless admittedly, but a suspect nonetheless. And there was a location: he or she was confined to the upper floor unless he or she wanted to risk serious injury by shinning down a drainpipe.

'Baker,' I snapped professionally, 'stay here with the ladies. Hopkinson, Herr Kreiner, you will accompany me upstairs.'

John Hopkinson looked directly into Susan Seymour's eyes. Her hand reached up to caress his cheek. 'Be careful, John,' she whispered.

Hopkinson disentangled himself from Miss Seymour and walked towards the stairs. I made sure I was one tread ahead of him all the way up.

THE ACCOUNT OF JOHN HOPKINSON (17)

We took the steps quickly although we were in no hurry – where could the murderer go? In a way it was a relief that none of our closed circle could be held to blame; in another it was terrifying to consider the ease with which Banquo Manor had been penetrated.

We paused at the top of the stairway. I had assumed that Stratford had some sort of plan worked out that would enable us to conclude our unpleasant business with little difficulty. Kreiner also deferred to him, assuming the same. But I could see at once in his eyes (so unlike Susan's – so little depth, yet so much more experience) that I was wrong. He was as much in the dark as I was – just as frightened, just as worried, just as alone.

A pause. He could hardly allow us to see his anxiety – his mind.

'Right,' said Stratford. A decision. 'You take the right side of the corridor, and I'll take the left. Kreiner, you follow us and stay in the corridor. Make sure that nobody tries to sneak past.' He moved quickly over to his side and opened a door, the door to the room he had slept in the night before. He hesitated for a moment, then saw me watching and went in.

I opened the corresponding door on my side of the passage and matched Stratford's actions. We were all scared, and we all knew it. But at least Ian Stratford knew what he was doing, what to do and how to approach whoever was up there with us. At least my hope that this was the case was all that persuaded me, almost provoked me, to enter the black pit that was Catherine Harries's bedroom.

THE REPORT OF INSPECTOR IAN STRATFORD (17)

I pushed the door to my bedroom open and rapidly stepped back. My bedroom – the room I had spent one night in, mainly asleep. I wished that Simpson had been faster with the shotgun. I took two cautious steps into the room and looked around. Bed, wardrobe, chest of drawers. Door to bathroom. Possible hiding places: bathroom, wardrobe, under bed. From where I stood, just inside the doorway… You fool – what about behind the door?

Letting out a little yelp of panic, I whirled, slamming the door and taking two rapid paces backwards to avoid any attack. Nothing. There was no one behind the door. Panicky now, I jerked around to survey the rest of the room. The bed lurked in the centre, menacing me with its presence. I slowly bent and looked underneath.

Nothing.

'Stratford!' Herr Kreiner yelled from the corridor. 'Everything all right in there?'

'So far,' I shouted back, the volume disguising the tremble in my voice.

Two steps and I was at the wardrobe. The door caught on my first pull. I pulled again and it swung open. Slowly. I took a step back.

Nothing.

The bathroom. Five steps. Marble tiles and a huge bath.

Nothing.

Behind the curtains.

Nothing. The windows weren't even open.

How many rooms were there on this floor? Seven? Ten? I couldn't go through this for every single one. Just checking mine, a room I was familiar with, had almost reduced me to hysterics. I crossed the now safe room to the door. I couldn't let Hopkinson see me like this. Deep breath, two, three and pull open the door. The corridor outside was dark but I could just make out the figure of John Hopkinson at the end. He must have moved pretty fast to get there. Had that man got no nerves at all?

THE ACCOUNT OF JOHN HOPKINSON (18)

I knew that Stratford was a professional, but while I might suspect that the Metropolitan Police force held lectures on how to search a large bedroom in twelve seconds flat, it seemed impossible that he could have progressed to the end of the passageway in the time it had taken me to walk once round Catherine Harries's bedroom, cautiously pulling open all the cupboards and checking behind the curtains.

I hesitated a moment, gaping in awe at the figure silhouetted at the end of the corridor. I glanced back and saw that Kreiner, back by the stairs, was also watching the figure. And as I turned back, I realised that another large figure stood beside me, equally fascinated by the person at the end of the corridor.

The person beside me was Ian Stratford and we became aware of each other at the same moment – the moment that the figure at the far end of the passage became aware of us and moved towards us, and came out into the light of the one dim lamp still burning in the corridor.

THE REPORT OF INSPECTOR IAN STRATFORD (18)

The door to my right, the door through which I had seen John Hopkinson disappear a few moments before, opened.

John Hopkinson walked out. He looked to his right along the corridor and I could see his mouth moving, forming the word 'Inspector'. Time seemed to be moving slowly, like treacle flowing past both of us. It was possible to believe that I could see every muscle around his mouth moving in sequence as Hopkinson mimed the three silent syllables of the word. I don't know if he actually made any noise at all. The buzzing in my ears was far too loud for that. I became fascinated by the almost imperceptibly small movements of his lips as they glistened in the light of the nearby lamp. I had once read *Confessions of an English Opium-Eater* by Thomas De Quincey in which he described the effect of drug-induced hallucinations; although, God knows, I had heard enough ravings from itinerant sailors dragged out of the drug dens of Limehouse to know the details. That was what I felt as I stood there. The slowing of time, the feeling that I was simultaneously too large and too small for the corridor, the feeling that my mind was disconnected from my body... But I was not drugged. I just did not want to look at the figure at the end of the passageway. I was frightened; no, I was terrified. My fear was something real and huge and outside myself, crowding in on me like the wings of death. Some part of me, some long-buried survival instinct that modern man has little use for, was warning me that to turn and look would be to risk my sanity. It knew before I did who it was down by the turn that led to Richard Harries's room. My subconscious mind was delaying me, in the same way that I am even now delaying the moment when I must face my memories again and describe what I saw.

John Hopkinson turned and caught sight of me. Our eyes met. I placed a firm hand on whatever instinct had raised its head from my subconscious and shoved down hard. Then I turned.

It was the Doctor. His fine hair was disarrayed and he seemed to be wearing a different jacket from the one I had previously seen him in – a darker, more sombre colour – but he was undeniably the same Doctor whom I had seen, dead, lying at the bottom of the hill. His skin was pale, suiting his Bohemian raffishness, but not as pale as death, and his limbs were straight, unbroken.

'Doctor!' Kreiner cried. 'You're *alive*!'

'I was never anything else,' the Doctor said grimly, 'although someone in this house had other ideas. There is something terribly, terribly –'

He stopped as a hand emerged from the darkness behind him and rested on his shoulder. It looked companionable, reassuring even, until I noted the discoloration of the skin and the way the talon-like fingernails were digging into the Doctor's velvet coat. The Doctor raised his head slightly, and sniffed.

'The mistake I made', he said quietly, 'was in assuming that there was only *one* mystery in Banquo Manor.'

At that point the owner of the hand decided to follow it out of the shadows.

And I screamed.

Richard Harries's one intact eye glistened in the light of the lamp as it stared with amusement from the wrecked and pitted lunar surface of his face. His body, smaller and more apelike than it had appeared on his bed, lurched towards us from out of the shadows. His clothes were stained with the fluids of death and the exposed portions of his skull, burned to the bone by the explosion and surrounded by petals of flesh, resembled a peach half eaten through to the stone and left for a week.

You see, even as he lumbered towards us, even as my brain gibbered like a monkey within the cage of my head, police training took control. If I had remembered which pocket my notebook was in, I think I might automatically have started filling in details.

Harries was breathing, a ragged parody of human breath that tore into my guts. Hopkinson and I started to back away together, not taking our eyes from Harries. He came closer, step by dragging step, and the light fell more fully upon his face.

It was like wakening suddenly from a nightmare into daylight. The mask was convincing, perfect in every detail. As a delaying tactic it was beautiful. Someone more impressionable, less hard-headed and cynical than myself, it might even have driven over the edge into full-scale panic. Hopkinson was a romantic: I could tell from his grip on my right arm that he had not penetrated the disguise. It was very clever. Very clever indeed. I began to feel a grudging respect for whoever the murderer was, hiding behind the mask.

Then the smell hit me. The stench of charred and rotting flesh. And the hands raised up towards us. And the mouth twitched into a ghastly smile. And the eye moved its gaze from Hopkinson and fixed on to me.

And I woke up to the reality that this really was Richard Harries returned to us to extract vengeance for his murder. But from whom?

THE ACCOUNT OF JOHN HOPKINSON (19)

Stratford beat me to the stairs – just. The Doctor and Kreiner were breathing, metaphorically, down my neck as I ran. We had backed away from the grotesque, flesh-torn apparition in the corridor for only a few steps before our nerves snapped simultaneously and we all turned to run. Stratford beat me to the stairs because he did not look back; I did. And saw the fractured body of Richard Harries lumbering towards us, the shadows breaking into shards of light and dark on his pitted face, and one eye gleaming disproportionately after us. I passed Stratford several steps down.

We could sense Harries's presence behind us, at the top of the stairs, as we flung ourselves forward – not worried about falling so long as we got to the bottom. The hairs on the back of my neck bristled and I hoped it was my imagination that Harries was starting down the staircase after us.

But from the looks of horror and disgust on the faces below, I knew it was not.

'What is it?' whispered Susan, her eyes wide under her creased brow. But she knew the answer.

'Don't ask,' advised the Doctor.

'Nasty,' Kreiner gasped as he ran.

'Great Ras– Good God,' muttered Simpson and I noticed the shotgun he was holding as he snapped the breach shut and turned it towards us. Stratford and I hurriedly moved aside as we reached the foot of the stairs.

For a moment the Doctor stood in the centre of the staircase. His mouth hung slightly open, and an uncharacteristic frown furrowed his brow. Kreiner was ahead of him already diving down the last few steps. But the Doctor was still, and almost immediately I saw why. Simpson had the gun levelled directly at him.

'What are you doing, man?' Stratford demanded. Surely

Simpson could not have missed what was following behind?

For another lingering moment Simpson and the Doctor remained frozen, their eyes locked in some silent but deep communication. I have no idea what passed between them. But after that hesitation the Doctor continued down the stairs, as if challenging the other man to shoot him. Simpson tracked him for two steps with the gun before he swung it upwards again, back towards the real target.

Harries – what was left of him – paused, three steps down, as Simpson levelled the gun, then continued his slow, laborious descent. Simpson climbed up towards him, the shotgun held steady, his knuckles white against the gunmetal. He passed the Doctor still on the way down without comment and halted halfway to the landing, just as Harries reached it. Then he fired the first barrel.

The sound of the shot echoed round the hallway and for a moment we could see nothing through the smoke. Then it thinned and we could make out the figure of Richard Harries's body staggering back under the blast, his chest ripped open by the shot, and thick black clots of blood sprayed across the stairway. Simpson grimaced at the weapon as if chiding it for its inefficiency.

Susan turned away and buried her face in my chest. I held her close for a second.

She felt me freeze and turned back. She screamed. The sound drowned out Stratford's gasp and Kreiner's expletive. Baker was white as a bedsheet. The Doctor was tapping his chin, thoughtful rather than surprised.

Harries still staggered, but he did not fall. He steadied and pulled himself upright. And started down the stairs again. Close by me, Catherine watched, pale, fixed, her concentration focused on the horror approaching us. On her brother.

Simpson too was transfixed, unable to move, as Harries's

dead body lunged down at him. How could he have killed what was already dead? He recovered just as Harries reached him, and he fired the second barrel at point-blank range into the corpse's stomach. Harries reeled under the force and doubled up as if winded. Simpson backed away, lost his footing and grasped at the banisters for support. He was already off balance as Harries came upright again and reached out for him. Simpson swung the shotgun at Harries's shattered head – a long low arc. But too long, too slow, and Harries swatted the barrels back towards Simpson and followed through the action, catching him on the shoulder.

Simpson remained paradoxically still for a moment as he lost his balance completely and then, gathering sudden speed, his body smashed through the banisters and crashed to the floor below. He let out a cry of pain as his leg buckled under him with the force of the impact. Kreiner and I ran to help him, but the others still seemed too stunned to think or even move as Harries's blood-splattered form continued down the stairs. Towards us.

It took us only a few seconds to help Simpson up on to his undamaged leg, and supporting him between us we turned back towards the drawing room. But we had taken too long.

Harries had reached the bottom of the stairs, and now he blocked our path. We were trapped in the corner between the stairs and the dining-room wall where it protruded into the hall.

Or almost trapped. While Baker stood foursquare in front of Catherine and Susan, and while Harries turned to face us and lurched slowly forward, the Doctor and Stratford edged around Harries to the stairs as he turned to face us and lurched slowly forward. Stratford reached down from the broken hole in the banisters and Kreiner and I hoisted Simpson up until the Doctor and Stratford could pull him up on to the stairs. Kreiner followed. I lifted him easily (he was relatively light and I was terrified into depths of strength I had never known I was possessed with) and he stumbled through the gap in the woodwork above almost before the Doctor and Stratford had finished helping Simpson up. The Doctor supported the butler as they continued up the stairs. Stratford reached down again to help me, and Susan watched in horror from the hallway as I reached up to grasp Stratford's outstretched hands and pulled myself towards them.

Stratford had almost pulled me up when I stopped. Stratford pulled harder, to no effect, and the strain on my ankle tightened as Harries gripped me tighter.

Catherine had been standing behind Baker and Susan on the threshold of the drawing room. Now, as her dead brother started to drag me downwards, she came to herself again and ran across the hall and up the stairs to the others.

The sound of her running and the blur of her sudden movement distracted Harries for a moment and his grip slackened. Slightly. I just caught sight of Susan and Sergeant Baker running after her. Moments later, Baker's strong grip was added to Stratford's. Between them I could see Kreiner's anxious face, and the Doctor starting back down the stairs to offer his assistance.

It turned out to be unnecessary. My downward movement slowed as my rescuers reasserted themselves in the grotesque tug of war, and I managed to pull myself round slightly, freeing my other leg from where it had been trapped against the side of the staircase. I lashed out with my freed foot as soon as I was able, and caught Harries across the face, feeling the rotten flesh give as my shoe tore through it, and his hold on my ankle broke.

I was up on the stairway in a moment, thanking God that I was free and that Harries had chosen my left leg to grasp – my right ankle could never have stood the punishment.

I staggered up after the others while below Harries watched us for a moment, then returned to the base of the stairs, and started up after us. We were trapped, and all of us knew it. The staircase was the only way down from the first floor, and none of us could hold out much hope of getting past Harries, either on the stairs or in the narrow corridor above. Had we had time, we would have realised that we were now every bit as dead as he was.

It was the movement to help Simpson that was our undoing. After Harries, or what was left of him, had pushed Simpson from the stairs the butler had ended up in a crumpled heap at the bottom. Unfortunately, due to the idiosyncratic construction of Banquo Manor, the stairway was in the shape of an 'L' going up parallel to the dining room wall and turning right to join the upper floor. The bottom ten steps protruded out past the dining-room wall, forming a cul-de-sac approximately twelve feet square.

Simpson fell into this cul-de-sac.

Hopkinson immediately ran to help Simpson. Kreiner followed him after a few seconds. After that the events unfolded with the predictable and unstoppable momentum of a falling card house, leaving the Doctor and me watching in mute horror.

Hopkinson quickly checked Simpson over.

'He's alive,' he shouted, 'but I think his leg is broken.'

Kreiner helped Hopkinson to get Simpson up on to his undamaged leg and they turned to carry him over to us.

Richard Harries stood facing them. Kreiner shouted something, letting go of the arm that Simpson had draped around his shoulders. He slumped sideways against Hopkinson, and I could see him wince as his damaged leg touched the floor. Hopkinson stood still, assessing their predicament, but from where the Doctor and I stood it was clear there was no way they could get past Harries.

'Come on!' the Doctor shouted, and sprinted for the stairs. I thought he was getting out while he could, but then I realised what he was up to. The hole in the banisters that Simpson had fallen through was just above their shoulder level. There was a chance that we could get up there and pull them through. It was worth a try, and the Doctor had spotted it more quickly than I. I joined him on the stairway and together we hoisted first Simpson and then Kreiner up with us.

Down in the hallway, Baker was still protecting Susan Seymour and Catherine Harries. The women's faces were white and shocked. Baker's was grim, but I could see the strain beneath.

Harries had remained motionless, confused by the action around him. The sight of John Hopkinson vanishing from his trap (how much intelligence did he still possess?) galvanised him into action. The rotting body, swathed in the stench of decay, lumbered over and grabbed Hopkinson's foot.

There we stayed in a frozen tableau. Hopkinson was looking up at me despairingly as we grasped each other's forearm. Susan Seymour was crying in the hallway below. How easy to accidentally let slip and leave John Hopkinson to the cold embrace of Richard Harries. It was ironic that the three of us should be there: Harries, who had possessed Susan Seymour and then lost her; I, who had never possessed Susan Seymour and had still lost her; Hopkinson, who had taken her away from me. From us. In that way Harries and I were allies. How easy to let slip…

Catherine Harries broke the spell that held me by suddenly pushing past Baker's bulky frame and running for the stairs. I shook my head to clear the miasma of confusion and found my muscles acting of their own volition. With a massive effort I managed to pull Hopkinson from the grasp of the body beneath. Small pieces of wet flesh fell from Harries's hands as Hopkinson landed gasping at my side. Harries staggered backwards, and Baker took the opportunity to push Susan Seymour past him towards where Catherine Harries had paused on the lowest stairs in order to gaze at her dead brother with an oddly calm expression.

'For a moment,' Hopkinson muttered, 'I thought…'

'For a moment, you were right,' I said.

Together we manhandled Simpson up to the first floor. I turned to see Harries just starting up the stairs behind us.

'Are you sure those stairs are the only way down?' I asked Hopkinson.

'Unless you fancy jumping,' he retorted.

Baker seemed to take him seriously. 'How far down is it?' he asked.

Susan glanced over at him. 'Too far.'

The Doctor and Hopkinson led the way along the corridor. Together, like a grotesque three-legged race, Kreiner and I half carried Simpson, followed by Susan, Catherine and Sergeant Baker.

'He'll catch us up in a moment,' said Kreiner over Simpson's shoulder. He gestured to the nearest door on the right. 'Let's barricade ourselves in here.'

'No,' I said quietly. 'It's the Wallaces' room.'

Kreiner looked momentarily blank, then nodded in understanding. The bodies were still in there.

(And I had a sudden horrifying vision of the door to the room flying open and their bodies tottering blindly out at us... George Wallace and his wife walking towards us with their heads flopping loosely on their shoulders... Beryl staring coquettishly at me with blank, white eyes while her hands slid seductively round my neck... My stomach lurched and sweat broke out on my forehead and down the ridge of my spine. Why Harries? Why no one else – at least, not yet? Then with a sudden sense of jolting, as if I had fallen a few inches and jarred as I hit the ground, I realised that it was something to do with Harries's experiment. The electricity... the sudden power surge... something that hadn't been repeated in the other deaths. I could breathe again.)

'Mr Hopkinson's room?' the Doctor said firmly 'It's on the corner. If something goes wrong, we have two ways to run.'

'Yes,' I said and we hobbled down the corridor. Susan rushed in front of us to open the door and slammed it shut after us. As Simpson collapsed on to the bed I heard Susan lock the door.

Kreiner grabbed my arm and gestured towards the massive chest of drawers by the window. Together we slid it across the floor and blocked the doorway with it. It was a good deal heavier than Simpson, but at the moment it was a great deal more use.

The Doctor crossed to the bed and sat beside Simpson on the rumpled covers. With Susan Seymour's aid he examined the butler's leg. While Hopkinson piled more furniture against the door I crossed to the window where Catherine stood.

'How do you feel?' I asked as gently as possible. She glanced up quickly, like a startled rabbit.

'I don't... I'm not sure...' she said hesitantly. 'I think I'm dreaming all this. I feel so confused.'

'Don't worry,' I reassured her. 'It'll all be over soon.' I felt superfluous; what could I say that would not sound patronising?

Hopkinson glanced over to me from where he stood by the barricade. I crossed the room to where he stood.

'At least we know who the killer is now,' he said, and smiled. The smile faded from his face as he considered the implications of what he had just said. 'I suppose that makes me responsible for all this,' he said quietly. 'If I hadn't –'

I interrupted him brusquely. 'There's no time for recriminations now. We don't know what's going on here. Let's wait until we get out before assigning blame.' In a way Hopkinson was right, if he hadn't sabotaged Harries's equipment, none of this would have happened. But Catherine Harries did not yet know of Hopkinson's part in the death of her brother.

Death? However it was phrased, I did not think it was the best time for her to find out. There was enough tension already without my adding to it. I could not tell whether Hopkinson understood my reasons for cutting him off. He had his glasses on and I could not see his eyes very well.

Susan Seymour glanced over at Catherine. 'What do we do

now?' she asked, neatly summing up my feelings. Then I realised she was talking about Harries.

'We hope he goes past, then double back to the stairs,' the Doctor replied. 'How's that feel, Simpson?'

'It hurts a lot, sir. I don't think I can move it.'

There was concern in the Doctor's eyes as he gazed at Simpson. 'I think you can drop the "sir",' he said quietly. 'After all, you've dropped other parts of this façade. Under normal circumstances,' he went on, 'I would expect it to heal… quickly. Very quickly. But as things are…'

I did not understand what the Doctor was getting at, but Simpson obviously did. 'It's a… draining… time for all of us,' he replied. 'I'll just have to let nature take its course – human nature, that is.'

'Perhaps there's something I can do.' The Doctor seemed quite insistent. 'If only I could just flick a switch and make things better.'

'It's not as simple as that.' Simpson subsided, a spasm of pain crossing his face. 'There's a certain amount of unexpected improvisation going on, Doctor, but I'm still going by the script.'

'It's a clean break,' said Susan helpfully. 'So long as he doesn't walk on it, it's not serious.'

'Serious enough as far as we are concerned,' Baker muttered. 'Perhaps…'

The handle of the door turned. So much for Harries walking past. We could hear something scrabbling at the door, seeking to gain admittance. The scratching continued for a few seconds like a rat in the wainscoting, then it stopped.

A pause.

The door shuddered and bulged inwards slightly as something heavy slammed into it. Everyone took a rapid step backwards in reaction. The backs of my knees hit the bed and I fell awkwardly across Simpson, fortunately missing his injured leg. The hammering on the door continued over the resulting confusion as we disentangled ourselves. As I stood up I distinctly heard a small metallic *ping* from the lock as something gave.

'What the hell do we do now, sir?' asked Baker. A fine mist of sweat covered his forehead and he mopped at it with a handkerchief.

'We've got to find out what is going on,' I snapped, wishing I knew how to go about it.

'What good will that do?' The strain was beginning to tell on Kreiner: his voice had raised in tone and volume and I could see a tremor beginning in his hands. 'We can't get past him, we can't kill him...'

'It's OK, Fitz,' the Doctor said. 'Admittedly we can't kill him, because he's already dead. But if we can work out what's happened to him to make him this way, it might help us to find some way of resisting.'

The hammering on the door had almost faded into the background. Suddenly it was brought into sharp focus as the wood split down the length of one of the panels. A large splinter flew across the room, narrowly missing Sergeant Baker.

Hopkinson looked at me helplessly. I returned his stare.

'Any ideas?' I asked before he could.

'I think I can cast some light on events,' the Doctor said, rising from the bed and crossing to the window.'

'What do you mean?' Kreiner asked.

'Professor Harries's experiment,' the Doctor replied. 'It's obvious that it was much more of a success than anyone – including him - expected.'

'Yes,' I said. 'That's what I thought.' Straightaway I regretted saying it. The words sounded feeble, as if I were trying to steal his credit. 'But I couldn't work out what it was,' I finished, trying to repair the damage to my credibility.

'Consider the sequence of events,' the Doctor continued. 'Richard Harries was attempting a form of mental contact with his sister, correct? He was trying to establish a communion, a communication between their minds.'

'Yes,' said Catherine from behind him. 'Because we were twins he thought –'

'Exactly,' the Doctor interrupted. 'I think that he succeeded.'

In the silence that followed I thought I detected an irregularity in the thudding at the door. Then the impacts began to get heavier.

'Succeeded?' shouted Susan. 'It killed him.'

'Or so we thought,' I muttered, looking at the door. The split was gaping further open with every blow now, and as I watched the lock gave way and the barricade began to shudder under the repeated impacts.

'Indeed it did kill him. But the important thing is, the electric current was so great, and –' the Doctor glanced here at Simpson – 'was being boosted by a nearby Artron field flux that Harries knew nothing about, that before he died the telepathic contact that Richard Harries had been seeking was momentarily established. Maybe the residual energy from the murder a century ago helped things along. Nothing like the emotions generated between the victim and perpetrator of a particularly unpleasant murder to stir up the fields.'

'That does not', I said, 'explain how he comes to be trying to kill us. Or indeed why he's not still lying on his bed. What is it, some form of supernatural revenge?'

But the Doctor was not listening. 'Of course,' he murmured, turning to face Simpson, 'the murder. All those years ago. The energy from that would provide a natural source of local Artron energy. No extraneous emission, no anachronistic discharge. Just the sort of energy you'd need to power the dissipater.'

Simpson met the Doctor's level stare. 'Elegant,' he said quietly.

'Inhuman,' the Doctor replied. And it seemed to me that Simpson smiled at that.

The impacts on the barrier were much louder now and the door was visibly split in a number of places. The previous rhythm had been totally lost and the crashes were becoming more and more irregular. What was happening? I did not know how much of what we were saying could be heard by Richard Harries. I did not even know if he could still hear, although his sight was still functioning. Was he worried about how close we were getting to the truth? Perhaps there was something he wanted to stop us finding out about, something that we could use to stop him.

'I think that must be it,' Hopkinson said, following on with the Doctor's line of reasoning. Looking around, I saw a blank expression on everyone's face. Baker was mopping at his brow again, and Susan Seymour's eyes flickered nervously from person to person.

Catherine was twitching restlessly, keeping time with the relentless pounding on the door. 'This is ridiculous,' she said.

'By no means,' retorted Hopkinson, nettled that his reasoning was being dismissed.

'Surely I would know if contact had been made. There wasn't anything like that. Nothing.'

'As I remember, Catherine, you fainted before your brother… before he died. Isn't it possible that contact was established while you were unconscious? While your subconscious was in control?'

Catherine raised a hand to her forehead. 'I don't know… I… I don't…'

The Doctor leaned forward urgently, trying to convince us of his truth. 'Don't you realise? Don't any of you realise? It's not Richard Harries out there at all. It's Catherine Harries's subconscious mind that's controlling the corpse!'

'No!' screamed Catherine. 'It's not true!' She flung herself away from Hopkinson and collapsed hysterically into Sergeant Baker's arms. 'I would know. I tell you, I would know if I was doing it.'

'Not if it's all on a subconscious level,' the Doctor continued insistently. 'You don't even realise that you are controlling him. It's your instincts. You see, you don't want to see your brother disgraced as a blackmailer, and you want his murderer –' he broke off and glanced at Hopkinson – 'whoever that is, to be punished for his death. Your subconscious mind has two excellent reasons for wanting us all out of the way. In the simplest of terms, that is why your instincts want us dead.'

'No,' whispered Catherine, horrified.

'It is ridiculous,' said Susan. But there was doubt in her voice.

'No,' Hopkinson agreed, 'it's the only explanation. Some deeply buried part of your mind is using the bond between you and Richard, what there is left of him, to punish us – since you know we could reveal your brother as a criminal.'

The entire upper panel of the door burst open, spraying the room with splinters. Through the gaping hole we could all see the animated cadaver of Richard Harries now concentrating its attention on the bottom part of the wreckage. The light gleamed greasily from the exposed portions of his skull, and the line of his teeth was a malicious smile matched in his one remaining eye. He – it – would take great pleasure in killing us, and now that Catherine knew that subconsciously it was she who was responsible I could see that the overriding feelings of guilt would cause Harries to kill her as well – in a bizarre twin suicide. For with his unwitting controller dead, Harries too would return to death.

'What do we do?' screamed Susan.

Hopkinson was at a loss. 'I'm not sure. We must find some way of breaking the link.'

'But how?' I asked.

'If I might interject, sir.' Simpson had drawn himself up on the bed and was gazing at the Doctor. 'Not that I understand what is happening of course –'

'Of course,' the Doctor agreed.

'But if Miss Harries were to be rendered unconscious…?'

The Doctor nodded. 'It might give us a chance to render her brother into pieces. Well done, Simpson. You have hidden depths.'

The two of them appeared to be needling each other, and I could not work out why.

'I do have another suggestion,' Simpson added.

'I rather suspected you might.'

'Your… transportation… Doctor. If you could tell us where it is… perhaps we might use it to leave this place.'

'Nice try,' the Doctor said calmly, although I could tell that under his calm exterior he was furious. 'But you are, as always, missing the point. It's not *my* transportation. It doesn't belong to me. It doesn't belong to anyone.'

'There are… forces… out there that could help us, Doctor,' Simpson insisted. 'All I need do is call them. I have the means.'

'Baker and I are the only police around for miles,' I interjected, puzzled. 'Or did you mean the army?'

Neither man looked at me.

'All of our fates are in your hands,' Simpson told the Doctor. 'And the price is –'

'– too high,' the Doctor finished. 'We're getting out of this situation ourselves.'

Catherine looked beseechingly at us all. 'Is Simpson right?' she asked. 'If I can make Richard kill people, surely I can make him stop, if I think very hard?'

'Yes, make him stop, Catherine,' said Susan. 'Concentrate on stopping him. Please hurry, there's not much time left.'

Indeed, the barrier was beginning to shift under the repeated kicks. Harries had got an arm through the gap between the door and the frame and was patiently squeezing his body through.

Catherine closed her eyes and concentrated.

Nothing happened.

Susan reached over from the bed and grabbed hold of one of Catherine's hands. Baker put a fatherly arm around her.

Hopkinson, the Doctor, Kreiner and I stood shoulder to shoulder, waiting for the final breech.

'Before it's too late, Inspector, thank you for being so tactful,' Hopkinson said.

'There's no point in arresting you yet, Mr Hopkinson. Besides, I could hardly accuse you of killing the gentleman who is trying to break the door down. It's an interesting little legal problem, isn't it? We are about to be murdered by the man that you yourself murdered.'

The light shone from his lenses. 'That's not what I meant, Inspector.'

I looked over at Susan, clutching on to Catherine's hand for dear life. She was so beautiful and so far away. 'The problem with being cynical,' I said softly, 'is that you give up on lost causes before they are lost.'

Hopkinson looked serious. 'All cynics are romantics underneath, Inspector. That's why they become cynics.'

'I hope you're both very happy together, Mr Hopkinson.'

Hopkinson looked towards the door, or what remained of it. 'Yes, so do I,' he muttered.

I turned to see Catherine Harries screwing her eyes up in deep concentration. If this didn't work we were finished. I turned back. 'Can I ask you something, Mr Hopkinson?'

He nodded. 'Of course, anything.'

'Have we met before?'

Hopkinson smiled. And this was a real smile, not the mask he usually slipped on. His head moved enough so that I could see through his glasses to the compassion in his eyes. 'I was wondering if you remembered,' he said. 'It was some years ago. I handled the preliminary arrangements for your divorce.'

The door burst open. The barricade was down. Nightmare entered the room.

Richard Harries staggered towards Hopkinson and me with

outstretched arms. Most of the flesh had been ripped off by the attack on the door and I could see the muscles and tendons that were his hands clench as he approached.

And relax as he slowed.

And fall to his sides as he came to a stop, three feet in front of us.

'Point proven, I think,' said the Doctor

I smiled. 'Purely circumstantial,' I replied, and my voice shook with the released tension.

Behind me I heard Susan say, 'Well done, Catherine.'

Simpson was muttering quietly on the bed. Praying perhaps.

'What do we do now, sir?' asked Baker. Hopkinson glanced over at me.

'Tie him up and bury him in a sealed coffin,' I said, taking command again. 'That should be safe enough, and Miss Harries won't have to spend the rest of her life telling him what to do.'

I turned to her.

'Can you keep him stationary, Miss Harries?'

Her face was strained but her voice was perfectly calm as she replied, 'Yes, I believe so.'

'Right. Baker, Mr Hopkinson, Dr Friedlander – perhaps you could come with me. We'll need some chains to tie him up with. Miss Harries, Miss Seymour, perhaps you could stay here and keep the… keep Professor Harries still. As for you, Simpson…'

But Simpson was asleep on the bed.

'Protective healing trance,' the Doctor muttered to Kreiner.

'You mean –'

'I mean we were expected. Or half expected anyway. They couldn't be sure.'

'You sound surprised,' I said. 'I understood that the experiment couldn't go ahead without you.'

The Doctor glanced over at me, his gaze guileless and clear. 'Our contribution is vital,' he said. But I don't think he was talking about Professor Harries's experiment.

'Come on,' I said, and we edged around the cadaver and moved towards the door.

'We'll be back as soon as possible,' said Hopkinson reassuringly as we forced our way past the wreckage of the door.

Baker turned to me as we walked towards the head of the stairs. 'I'm not sure if I can credit all this about Dr Harries, sir,' he said. I could sympathise. Baker's previous experiences had hardly prepared him for what we had all gone through.

'What other explanation is there?' I asked.

'Well, sir, I read in one of the newspapers about this foreign doctor. He had this theory about people being buried alive, sir. Says the only way you can tell if someone is really dead is when they actually start to… well, to decay, sir.'

'I think you ought to read a different newspaper, Sergeant,' I replied as we descended the stairs.

'No,' said the Doctor beside me. 'I have met the gentleman. Hartmann, his name is; Franz Hartmann. He's an Austrian physician. I provided him with a couple of case studies for a book he's preparing on premature burial. They will make fascinating reading.'

'Look, it's perfectly simple to find out whether a man is dead or not,' I snapped. 'He doesn't breathe.'

'Perhaps,' the Doctor said. 'But there's an American colonel who wants anyone buried without an autopsy being performed to have a bottle of chloroform interred with them so that if they revive suddenly they can commit suicide painlessly and quickly. He doesn't think it's so simple.'

'It would never happen in England. But it doesn't really matter why Harries is up and about. The important thing is that Catherine Harries has some kind of subconscious control over her brother. That's what we've got to stop.'

'He was a foolish man,' muttered Baker. 'There's some things it's best not to meddle with, sir.'

The Doctor stopped on the last but one tread. He glanced up at Baker, his usually open, friendly face showing signs of irritation. 'You think so, Sergeant? It doesn't matter whether Richard Harries was likable or not; it doesn't matter whether he really understood what he was doing or not; what he *did* do took courage and commitment. Science is about taking risks, Sergeant. It's about carrying out experiments and taking any consequences on yourself. Harries wasn't afraid of those consequences.' He sighed. 'Times are changing, Sergeant. With the finish of the century so close, people are rethinking their attitudes, changing their approaches. Check the newspapers – discoveries aren't made by people any more: they are made by teams. The praise is spread out, but the responsibility? It could rest with anyone. No, the age of the gentleman scientist is over. No more Galileos; no more Newtons; nevermore a Faraday.'

The Doctor was genuinely angry as he stood there, two steps lower than Baker but somehow towering over him. Suddenly I understood him. He was a romantic, an idealist. He wanted to pin things down to people, not movements. There was no room in his mind for crowds.

There was an embarrassed pause. 'And that is why Romana has to be stopped,' the Doctor murmured cryptically to himself. 'Because she still doesn't understand that the morality of an organisation – a race – is no better than the morality of its most immoral member.'

THE ACCOUNT OF JOHN HOPKINSON (20)

'Where do we start?' asked Baker, ever practical, as we reached the hall.

The Doctor was already at the telephone, rattling its cradle. He glared at the handset for a second before slamming it back down. A moment later he was tracing the wire along the wall. He reached a frayed end and held it up for us to see. The other end of the wire was nowhere to be seen. 'Pity,' he murmured, 'I could have put it back together.' He sighed, then straightened up. 'You know the house best,' the Doctor said to me, as if I could produce a room full of chains and ropes (not to mention the odd thumbscrew) with absolutely no difficulty. I was explaining to him as patiently as I could that this was not the case when a thought came to me.

'Wait a moment, though,' I interrupted myself. 'That large portrait of Dodds – the one in the drawing room – that must be held up with something. It could be a chain fastening it to the wall.'

'Well, let's look.' Stratford led us into the drawing room.

It was the work of just a minute to climb up on a chair and to lift down the portrait to Stratford and Baker. It was heavy – more because of the plaster frame than because of the savage brushwork.

The Doctor peered closely at it as the two policemen lifted it from me. 'Well, it's no masterpiece,' he said in a tone that suggested he was more concerned with the painting than with the manner in which it had been hung. 'Look at that,' he went on, ducking under Baker's arm as he indicated an area of interest. 'The face in particular doesn't bear close examination, does it?' He shook his head. 'Pitted paintwork, disproportionate features – like the eyes.' He clicked his tongue in annoyance. 'Should be ashamed of himself, whoever painted this.'

The dim light caught the layers of paint (like make-up) as I stepped down from the chair, throwing shadows like tears or scars across Dodds's cheek. The lights were low, and the glow from the dying embers of the fire was all but extinguished.

Stratford turned the painting over as I brushed the dust off the embroidered seat of the Chippendale. The fastening was indeed a chain, but it was relatively thin and had been doubled in order to take the weight of the portrait.

'Rope might be better,' I suggested, hoping that the Doctor would not expect me to find him a few yards of that as well.

'Yes,' he agreed. 'The trouble is, we don't really know how strong the thing is.' He pulled experimentally at the chain.

'Do you mean the "thing", sir,' Baker asked, confused, 'or the chain?'

'Well, either, if it comes to that,' the Doctor answered, looking across from the chain to Baker. He seemed about to continue, but his voice caught in his throat. I followed his gaze over Baker's shoulder to the doorway.

Where Catherine Harries stood.

We were all surprised.

'What are you doing down here, Catherine?' Stratford asked. 'You're supposed to be with the others.'

'I thought I should tell you,' she said simply, not moving from the doorway. Her face was a blank, a contrast to the mask of concentration she had worn earlier. A white, Italianate mask of emptiness; unreadable.

'Tell us? Tell us what, Miss Harries?' the Doctor asked. His face seemed suddenly to have lost its boyish enthusiasm, as if he already guessed what was to follow.

'That you were wrong, Doctor.' Even the inflection was gone. My skin started to creep with a slow, scrabbling certainty. Beside me I felt Stratford tense.

'What about?' But I had begun to guess.

'About my subconscious control of Richard.'

'You mean that you don't have any control of him?' Stratford asked.

'Oh no. I can control him. I *do* control him.'

'Then what do you mean, miss?' Only Baker had not yet realised, as Stratford's short step backwards betrayed.

'The control is not subconscious. We know exactly what we are doing. We have always known.'

Baker's mouth dropped open, and with the immaculate timing of melodrama and the precision of the *commedia dell'arte*, Richard Harries's bloodied form stepped into the doorway beside his sister...

I had done it again. With my renowned clumsiness in total control I had once again misread the situation disastrously. Little things now began to add up in my mind: odd words, looks, gestures on the part of Catherine Harries. All of them pointers towards the inevitable truth. Inevitable only in hindsight, but that did not stop me from feeling like a complete fool.

Seeing Catherine Harries and her brother side by side for the first time I could appreciate the similarity in build. They were both short, but the base metal of Richard's stockiness and apelike stance were transformed in Catherine to the gold of a shapely figure, her femininity emphasised by the tightness of her dress. A chill ran through me as I looked between them – twins, but with a hideous difference. The stark skull and ripped flesh of Richard Harries was the blueprint for the beauty of his sister. Her beauty was a mask covering his truth.

'What have you done to the others?' asked Hopkinson from my side. I cast a sidelong glance at Baker. His face was pale and waxen, and the skin seemed to hang heavy on his bones.

(And under the skin I could trace the outlines of his skull, the rims of his eye sockets and the hard corners of his cheekbones…)

'Nothing yet,' smiled Catherine. 'The poor girl and Kreiner were so busy tending to the butler's leg that they didn't even notice us leave. They can't get away. Neither can you, not now.' She moved her right hand from behind her back. In it she held a massive revolver, pointed directly at my forehead.

'Wallace's,' muttered Hopkinson. 'She must have got it from his desk.'

'Why?' I whispered, 'Why now?' But she heard me.

'Because you know. You know about us!'

'You were in it together?'

'Of course. They were all so petty, so frightened of their

secrets coming out. They couldn't find the strength to take the responsibility for their actions. If Richard and I hadn't taken advantage of them, somebody else would. At least we used the money for good. For Richard's experiments.'

'His hellish experiments, you mean?'

Catherine's eyes blazed. 'But they worked!' she screamed.

'Look at him,' the Doctor said, stepping forward. 'Do you really think he can go on much longer? He's virtually falling apart as we watch. Do you think this is what he wanted?'

Catherine cast a possessive eye over her twin. 'Only his body, Doctor. Whatever remains of the real Richard Harries we share, now, as we've always shared everything. Richard and I were always close.' She smiled lasciviously. 'Very close.'

'You mean that Richard's mind…?' I asked.

'Oh, he's in here now,' she said, and it seemed for a moment as if something else were looking through her eyes. 'I can feel him moving around, swimming within me. I contain multitudes.' She smiled, like a shaft of sunlight, and I felt my skin prickle around my neck and shoulders.

'Doesn't that worry you?' Hopkinson asked. I think he had latched on to my tactics: try to keep Catherine talking until something, anything, happened. 'Doesn't it bother you that something else is experiencing your thoughts and emotions?'

Catherine turned to look at him. Simultaneously, the body of her brother turned to rake Hopkinson with a bloody stare.

'No,' she said. 'We could never be too close to one another. I loved me… him… I loved him.' She looked confused, not knowing where the mix-up had originated. 'And he loved me too,' she asserted. Her expression smoothed over and was replaced by a malign ingenuity. 'And I can see through his eyes too. I can move his body, use his strength to do things I could never do. Like kill you all.' And there it was again: another face, another person looking out through her.

She raised a hand and ran it though her hair. Hopkinson and I exchanged glances. She was tired. The strain was beginning to take its toll.

'I am my brother's eyes,' she said finally. 'He is my power. And you all know too much.'

Behind Catherine and Richard Harries, through the open door of the drawing room, I could see Susan Seymour walking calmly down the stairs. She opened her mouth as if to speak. If any such thing as telepathy existed without recourse to any scientific equipment then the shouts from the minds of Hopkinson and me should have stopped her from uttering a sound. But it didn't happen that way.

'Catherine?' she said. 'What –'

The words were lost in her scream as Catherine Harries and her dead brother turned to face the stairs.

'Run, Susan!' Hopkinson yelled. 'Get help from the village!'

Too late. Richard Harries was at the bottom of the stairs before Hopkinson had finished. Rooted to the spot with fear, all Susan could do was whimper.

And that is when Sergeant Baker did the bravest, most foolish, most suicidal thing I have ever seen. Before I could stop him, before I even registered what he was trying to do, he was running towards Catherine Harries. He was slow and noisy, puffing like the ancient steam engine that had brought me to Three Sisters, but his bulk was considerable and his inertia well-nigh unstoppable.

Catherine Harries began to turn as soon as she heard his wheezing. Her brother swung, puppet-like, away from Susan and towards us. The muzzle of her gun looked like a small cannon as she aimed it at Baker. Then he was upon her, and she went flying into the corridor.

'Compassion, get back upstairs!' the Doctor shouted to Susan. 'Get Simpson and Fitz and barricade yourself into another bedroom!'

Susan looked wild-eyed at Hopkinson.

'But John –'

'Do it!' the Doctor shouted. She turned and ran up the stairs. Harries took a long, lingering look after her, then staggered over to help his sister. I saw no more as Baker slammed the door shut and locked it.

'Well done, Baker,' I said.

'Only doing my best, sir,' he gasped, red-faced and panting.

Hopkinson crossed to the door and put his ear against it. With a free hand he gestured us to be quiet. 'Can't hear anything. No, wait… Catherine's saying something about… Thank God for that. She's told Harries to leave Susan alone, doesn't think she can get out from upstairs. She's probably right. She'd break a bone if she tried it… That's interesting: I think she's stopping Harries from breaking the door down. Something about an easier way. I wonder what she means… It's odd, it's as if she's holding a conversation with him, but I can only hear her side of it…' He paused for a moment. 'I can't be sure, but I think they've left.' Hopkinson straightened up, brushing the creases from his trousers.

'Shouldn't we barricade the door, sir?' asked Baker.

I considered for a moment. 'No, not yet. We may get a chance to slip out.'

'If they start to smash it down like they did upstairs we can't hope to keep them out for long,' said Hopkinson. 'At least, not without barricading ourselves in.'

'I realise that. But until they start, I think we'd do best to keep all our options open.'

The Doctor crossed to the French windows. It was pitch black outside and I could see his reflection staring back in at me, almost as if someone, some twin of his, was standing outside watching us. I shivered: I still had no idea how a man I had seen dead with his leg apparently twisted and broken beneath him could be standing before me, very much alive.

'When we were upstairs,' he said slowly, 'why did Catherine stop her brother from killing us when he got into the bedroom?'

'I don't know,' I said. 'I'd been wondering about that as well.' Not quite true. The thought had crossed my mind, but I had not worried myself about it. I'd had other things to contend with. 'She must have been mad for years. I don't think we can ascribe normal motives to her. She lives by her own rules of logic. Maybe she was frightened that a group effort could overcome him. And remember, Simpson had just suggested knocking her out to stop Harries. I don't think she wanted to risk that.'

'You don't think it was the sudden shock of contact and her brother's death that unhinged her?' Hopkinson asked.

'No, I think she's been mad all along. That's another thing that she and her brother shared – insanity.'

'Yes,' said the Doctor. 'I think you're right. This just pushed her into open homicidal lunacy. Which is rather a shame. A logical, reasoning mind would be rather easier to predict, don't you think?' He turned away from the French windows. 'I wish we knew what was going on out there.'

Baker walked over to the door. He had recovered from his exertions now and was mopping the last remnants of sweat from his brow. 'Can't hear anything, sir'

'One of us will have to go for help,' said Hopkinson sombrely. 'Since she's wrecked the telephone. Someone's got to make it to the village.'

We all stood staring at one another. Sizing each other up. Mentally drawing straws.

'I'll go,' we all chorused simultaneously. Hopkinson came off the rebound more quickly than any of us.

'You two are policemen,' he said. 'You're paid to take risks. I'm not. Given a chance I'd be on my way to Three Sisters instantly. I'm not being noble, I'm saving my own skin. And it's practical: I know the area.'

'So does Baker,' I pointed out. 'And come to that, my aunt lives in Three Sisters. I'm not exactly unfamiliar with the countryside myself.'

'And the grounds of the Manor? Under snow? At night?' queried Hopkinson. 'I think not.'

'He's right, sir. It's the best thing to do,' said Baker heavily.

'All right, Mr Hopkinson. Reluctantly I agree. Do you think your ankle can stand up to it?'

'How do you –'

'Never mind that. Can it?'

'I think so. So long as I don't fall on it.' He still looked puzzled and I confess I rather enjoyed his confusion.

'The hall could still be dangerous,' I said confidently. 'You can leave through the French windows. We'll barricade them after you. I'll light you a lamp before you go.'

Hopkinson moved towards the windows. The Doctor moved with him. I looked at him quizzically.

'I'm going with him,' he said in a tone that brooked no argument. 'After all, I'm dead already. What else can happen to me?'

I looked around the drawing room. There were two ornamental oil lamps on the mantelpiece. I hoped they were more than just ornaments and crossed to the fireplace.

Behind me the French windows exploded open.

Flailing his arms wildly, Richard Harries staggered into the room. Snow had built up on his shoulders, his head and the folds of his jacket, and the skin had started to peel from his face in long strips. With an inarticulate noise he lunged for the first person in his field of view. The Doctor.

'Quick, sir,' yelled Baker as the Doctor fell back with Harries's hands clamped around his throat. 'Do something.'

His words snapped me out of my frozen horror and I reached for the nearest heavy object and threw it at Harries. The impact of the heavy oil lamp knocked him back a few paces in a flurry of snow. Before he moved towards the Doctor again, Harries quite calmly crumpled the oil lamp into a useless mass before throwing it with venomous force at my head. I ducked and the brass weapon tore into the painting that we had placed on the table after removing the chain. The canvass ripped directly across the face and body of the portrait, knocking it to the floor.

My eyes focused on the table.

'Baker, over here,' I shouted. Baker lumbered over and together we picked up the table, one on either side. Harries was almost on to the Doctor as we staggered towards them, but he turned towards us as he caught sight of the movement. The heavy table hit Harries squarely in the chest. The momentum carried both him and us back towards the French windows. Harries was pushed inexorably out into the grounds, and Baker and I released the table as soon as he was over the threshold. The front two legs caught on the sill and the table cartwheeled its way after Harries.

While the Doctor recovered his breath and Hopkinson shut the windows again, Baker and I pushed all the furniture in the room over against them. After a few seconds we stood back, confident that Harries would take some time to smash his way through the barrier. Little if anything of the French windows was visible.

'Wait a second,' I said. 'If Harries is out there…' I didn't complete my train of thought. If I had, perhaps someone would have stopped me. I thought that if Harries was outside, then his sister would be as well – controlling his body. But I had not thought far enough along that track, so I crossed quietly to the door and said, 'Over here, quickly.'

I opened the door –

To find Catherine Harries directly in front of me with George Wallace's gun pointed straight at my face.

She fired.

Perhaps I moved slightly. Perhaps the weapon jumped in her hand. Revolvers are notoriously inaccurate and Catherine Harries was inexperienced in their use. Maybe killing a person with her own hands was far more difficult than using her brother's. I don't know. The period between seeing Catherine

Harries pointing a weapon at me that could easily take my head off and waking up with Hopkinson and the Doctor looming over me like mountains and the door securely locked is a blank in my mind. I cannot even remember the gun going off.

'How is he?' whispered Hopkinson. At least, I think he whispered. My mind seemed to be wrapped in layer upon layer of wool and my left shoulder ached like a rotting tooth.

'No lasting effects,' said the Doctor. His voice was louder. Did that mean he was closer, or was I coming back to consciousness? Or perhaps his voice was naturally louder than Hopkinson's. I tried to think back to times when I had previously heard them speaking together. I was sure I must have done, but I couldn't think when. Never mind. God, I was thirsty. Was I dreaming all this?

'Caught him in the shoulder,' the Doctor continued. I wondered if I had missed anything he had said. He scratched the side of his head and I saw his hands were red. Was that my blood? There seemed an awful lot of it.

'Bind it with this,' said Hopkinson, waving a handkerchief. 'It should cover the wound.'

They busied themselves with their task and as they did so I could feel myself drifting back to full consciousness.

'You're lucky, sir,' said Baker, bending over me. 'The bullet came out of the other side. Missed the shoulder bone, fortunately.'

'At least while they're besieging us they can't get at Susan, Kreiner and Simpson,' said Hopkinson looking towards the door. I became aware of a familiar hammering.

'Yes, but for how long?' I asked muzzily. 'They are just as trapped as we are.'

The Doctor, Baker and Hopkinson continued their conversation, but I lost interest and drifted in and out of consciousness. At some stage the hammering on the door stopped, but I don't know when. Time ceased to have any meaning for me.

Eventually, half an hour or half a day later, I came back into consciousness temporarily to hear Hopkinson ask, 'Haven't you got any idea what's happening out there, Sergeant?'

'There's some movement, sir,' came Baker's heavy voice, 'but I can't tell what it's all about. Nothing good, though, I'll be bound.'

'You surprise me,' muttered Hopkinson. I tried to say something, but all that came out was a croak. My throat was dry, and a dull ache had settled across my forehead like an iron band. Hopkinson reached for a decanter of water and poured out a glass. A layer of dust drifted across the surface. He raised it to my lips and I sipped, grateful for the coolness.

The three of them had raised me on to one of the couches that made up the barrier across the French windows while I had been unconscious. Now they helped me to sit up. My arm had been strapped across my chest with strips of material cut from the curtain. Ingenious, and probably the Doctor's idea. Underneath the rough bandages and Hopkinson's handkerchief there was a lot of dried blood. The shoulder and arm were numb, thank God, but the effort of sitting up caused little spots of fresh crimson to appear on the handkerchief, welling up from the wound below.

'Better than it looks, sir,' comforted Baker.

'She's still out there,' said Hopkinson.

'And presumably her brother is still outside the window?'

'Yes, just standing there.'

'Then there's only one chance, isn't there?' I said weakly. Hopkinson gave me a look that plainly said he thought I was delirious.

It was good old Baker who said, 'What's that then, sir?'

'The chimney.'

'The… Are you serious?' replied Hopkinson aghast.

The Doctor merely looked at me and smiled. 'Why didn't I think of that? If I remember correctly the study is next door, and the fireplace in the study is on this side of the room – the opposite side of that wall.'

I started to speak, but broke off into a fit of dry coughing. Hopkinson refilled the glass and replied for me.

'It's possible that the two fireplaces are connected,' he said, following my reasoning. 'They might share a chimney flu once they've started upwards.'

Baker finally got it. 'You mean you could climb from one room...'

'...into the other. Exactly.'

I felt well enough to continue, and said, 'Then you can get out through the study windows.'

'Me again?' said Hopkinson.

'Both of us, Mr Hopkinson,' the Doctor agreed. 'I'm used to being in tight squeezes.'

'Well, I can't manage with just one arm,' I said, 'and with all due respect I'm not sure Baker could get up the chimney too easily.'

Hopkinson considered briefly. 'All right, then. Give us a hand, will you, Sergeant?'

'Right-ho, sir. Do you want a light of some sort?'

'No, I think it'll be easier to climb without.'

While I remained propped upright on the couch, Baker, the Doctor and Hopkinson walked over to the chimney. The Doctor stepped carefully into the fireplace with his legs straddling the dead embers.

'When I am gone,' he proclaimed, 'think only this of me: that there is some corner of a British chimney that is forever Gally-free.' It was not a quotation I was entirely familiar with.

Within seconds he was gone.

Hopkinson peered upwards nervously.

'Awfully dark,' he said, more to himself than to us. 'Still, there's no time like the present.'

He too vanished upwards. For a moment or two there was the sound of scrabbling, and showers of soot flew out of the fireplace. Then there was nothing.

217

'Strange,' said Baker, peering up worriedly, 'I thought the Doctor was German, not Irish.'

'I'm beginning to wonder if he's real at all,' I muttered, but already the edges of my vision were turning grey. I was retreating down a soft hazy tunnel, and in my dreams I was back many years ago in John Hopkinson's office in London. I was standing there in my heavy police overcoat, kneading my hat in my hands. I had not wanted to come; it was demeaning, disgraceful…

'Forgive me for not standing…' he said. 'Fractured ankle; did it playing cricket. Plays up from time to time. Now, what can I do for you?'

I had not wanted to see him, I'd been expecting Gerald. He had been the family lawyer for years, handled all the arrangements when my parents died. Some sort of misunderstanding along the way…

'Well, you see…' I hummed and hawed, not knowing quite where to begin. How can you tell a perfect stranger that your wife has run off with another man, is living with him, sleeping with him? Cuckolded, isn't that what they call it?

The light shone from his glasses. Even then.

'It's a matter of some delicacy…'

'Of course. Perhaps you could tell me?'

So it all came out, the whole sordid story. My long hours at the Yard. My wife – bored, alone, lonely. Then the young artist with a double-barrelled name, filling her head with Mozart and romance. 'I still love you,' she said. But if she did, why couldn't she stay? 'It's not your fault, I'm to blame.' Then why did I feel so guilty? What had I done wrong?

Hopkinson was the model of solicitous behaviour, but underneath I could feel him squirming with embarrassment and distaste. He was obviously new at this job, perhaps as new as I was at the Yard. Thrown in at the deep end. God, I wish I hadn't come. I wish I wish I wish…

Hopkinson opened a drawer and pulled out a furry bundle. 'Could I offer you a rat?' he enquired. 'They're very good.'

The rat fixed me with its red eyes and I screamed.

And woke up again to the drawing room, the silence, and Baker.

THE ACCOUNT OF JOHN HOPKINSON (21)

The chimney was filthy, or so it seemed in the dark, claustrophobic passage up which I pushed myself, feet braced against the sides, my arms pulling my body upwards seemingly for ever. The blackness was physical, solid; lumps of soot disintegrated as my face touched them, showering invisible black dust into my straining eyes, rained down by the Doctor's scramblings ahead of me.

I could no longer tell whether my eyes were open or closed until the dry, clinging powder burst over them. It lined my face and my clothes, covering me in the darkness that had spawned it. I pushed on through, and felt it in my hair, my shoes, in the air I breathed – it *was* the air I breathed. I feared I should choke as the darkness scrabbled in my throat as I did in the brickwork. It caked my nostrils, grew tighter on my flinching skin and pressed against my clothes as my jacket tore on the ragged wall. I was grateful I had kept it on – that could have been my flesh tearing open – yet it hampered my freedom of movement.

Movement.

Yet it seemed that it was the chimney that was moving, trying to cough me out. But what I feared most was not that I should spend the rest of my miserable life crawling upwards towards a cross-shaft that had never existed, or that I should suffocate or be crushed slowly to death in this living blackness, but that I would have to cough – and that either Catherine Harries or the shattered remains of what had once been her brother would hear me, and be waiting in the study.

Nothing.

Ahead of me, the Doctor's movements were muffled by soot and distance. How far ahead of me was the man? And if I should get stuck, would he know? Would he come back to help me? Could he? I began to wish I had gone first, so that if I had been jammed I would at least have the benefit of someone following – someone who would know I was there, realise my predicament, push from behind.

My hand, reaching up and out for a hold to drag myself up a few feet further, not only failed to gain purchase, but failed to meet the wall at all. My weight was on the hand that had pushed through the wall and my body followed it through, and down. My first sudden thought was that I had indeed suffocated and that my spirit was leaving my body, becoming insubstantial and passing like the ghost it now was through solid bricks and mortar.

The thought was violently jolted out of me as my ribs, exposed under the outstretched arm, hit the ragged corner of the shaft that ran up and into the one that I had been climbing. I cursed silently (but nonetheless huskily) and wished I had had a spare hand to carry a lamp. For a second directions danced giddily and I had no idea which way I was facing, or where up and down were. However, just as I was deciding that the only way I could find out was by relaxing my grip and discovering which way I fell, I realised that my right arm was still lying along the floor of the gently sloping cross-shaft that met the chimney I was spread-eagled within. Indeed, my right arm and shoulder seemed to be supporting most of my weight. As the sensations of pain reached my consciousness, so did my instincts of position and geography.

As if to confirm my instincts, the Doctor's soft voice called back to me, 'Are you all right? Have you reached the turn yet?'

Just the sound of his voice was enough to renew my strength and confidence. 'Yes, I'm fine,' I whispered back. 'Right behind you.'

I had imagined in my naïveté that the descent would be much easier. Of course, it was not. If anything it was more hazardous still, with the force of gravity always in danger of becoming too helpful. It was certainly quicker to climb down but this merely helped the grazes to bite, and the bruises were deeper – caused as they were by a greater speed of impact on the gnarled and ugly brickwork.

My eventual arrival in the study fireplace, amid clouds of soot and a staccato rattle of dislodged masonry, would probably have aroused humour in any witness to this Nicholausian entrance. Fortunately the only witnesses to my indignity was the Doctor, and he was busied in the task of brushing the soot and indignity from his own figure. He shook his head, and clouds of black specks flew from his mass of hair. I picked myself up as quickly as I could, fighting back the bruises of pain and the need to cough out what I had swallowed of the chimney's innards.

There was a little light in the study, both from the moon outside the uncurtained windows and from the ajar door, and a faint glow from the remains of Harries's equipment, which still lay on the desk. Some residual energy of some sort, no doubt. But after my dark incarceration it was easily enough to enable me to see quite well. I followed the Doctor as we picked our way around the furniture, unable to read the pages of Stratford's notes that were scattered across the desk (now, I suspected, rather superseded by events), to the door.

The Doctor eased the door open a crack and peered out. For a moment he was frozen in position. Then he stepped aside and motioned for me to take his place.

My view of the hall was decidedly limited and I had no intention of opening the door any wider for fear it might creak. What I could see was Catherine Harries, her face set stiffly – almost like a death mask – and her hands as fixedly and unmovingly gripping the revolver that pointed at the drawing-room door. Suddenly her eyes flicked across towards my door and instinctively I stepped backwards, almost colliding with the Doctor as he stood silently behind me. But she could not have seen me; my soot-encrusted face was an advantage in that at least.

Although we had no need, and even less desire, to open the door, the window was a different matter. To escape from Banquo Manor we had to raise the sash, and I doubted that it had been opened since September's milder weather. It would certainly make some sound. We stood and silently considered this for a few moments and had all but resolved to risk the noise and hope to be away before Catherine or, God forbid, her dead brother could investigate, when help arrived.

I say help, for the noise from upstairs would easily have drowned any sounds we might have made in opening the window, but what it signified froze us to the spot for a moment and my heart went out to Simpson, to Kreiner and, especially, to Susan, trapped in the bedroom upstairs.

The noise was that of shattering wood, of splintering panels. Of a door being smashed open.

It seemed that I had stood motionless for ever, as the house was slowly ripped apart around me. But I can only have paused for a split second as the implications settled in my mind and galvanised my hands into action. The Doctor was already undoing the window catch and with my help the window opened easily and, as far as I could discern, soundlessly. My hurried exit was less smooth, my already torn jacket catching on a sharp edge of wood and tearing further as I followed the Doctor's enthusiastic dive through the opening space. But I had no fear of being heard – only for Susan's safety.

I staggered slightly as I hit the snow-covered path outside the window, and as I rebalanced the sound of the shot reached me. The Doctor was already staring upwards, his hand over his eyes as if to shield them from a nonexistent sun. I too looked up at the window high above.

The image that even now remains sharply printed on my

memory in crisp detail told the entire story of the fight for survival in the small room above. Again the universe seemed frozen for a moment until the explosion from the second barrel of the shotgun, closely followed by Simpson's cry echoing across the space between the upper window and myself. A cry of terror and pain mixed.

Ten yards away, the rope of sheets and blankets tied to the rail at the base of the casement reached almost to the level of my head. At the bottom of this rope stood Fitz Kreiner, his arms open, as if ready to catch something. Or someone. Above him, Susan was about halfway down, but she had stopped climbing and, like me, was staring upwards in the direction of Simpson's sudden cry. I tried to call out, to tell her to hurry, but my voice was as static as my body and no sound came. Susan began climbing down again, not because of my silent entreaty, but because of what she – and I – could see above.

I was running now, following the Doctor to join Kreiner as Susan continued her desperate journey.

And above her, Simpson was now framed in the light from the window. His back was to us, arcing over the sill as he tried desperately to find somewhere to escape from the monster in the room with him. He stumbled to one side, I guessed, as he tried to put weight on his broken leg. I wondered whether, realistically, he had ever had a chance of climbing down the rope of sheets. I wondered how Kreiner could have brought himself to abandon the man. But as I glanced at Kreiner's anxious upturned face I knew that he had been given no choice. This was their best shot. He was waiting to catch Simpson when, inevitably, his grip failed and he fell. He was there to break the man's fall. To save his life.

All this dawned on me in an instant. The instant it took for Simpson to turn towards us, desperation drawn across his face, then look back and scream again. Silhouetted, I saw the hands reach for him. I looked away as they pressed in on his face.

A moment later there was a scream. Not the frightened cry that we had heard before. This was a thing of complete and utter terror and pain. Despite myself, I looked upwards again, and saw Simpson's face contorted with the fear and the agony as he hurtled towards us. He was falling ever faster, his mouth seeming to widen as he approached, his arms flailing uselessly as he fell. But that was not the worst of it.

The worst of it, the nightmare-recurrent image that took away my breath and drained the blood from my face, was that he had no eyes. Empty, blood-seared sockets that stared accusingly, unblinking, at me as he crashed downwards.

I heard myself screaming now. A sound mixed in with Simpson's falling cadence, with Susan's shrieks, with the Doctor's shout for me to catch Simpson. Then the man's body collided with me, knocking me off my feet. The impact took my breath away, leaving it in a misty cloud above me as I fell. Simpson was across me, his dead weight pinning me to the frost-encrusted ground. I had no idea whether it was his desperate gasps I could hear and feel or my own. I didn't really care. I was on my back, staring up at the window, at the image framed there.

The broken, blackened face of Richard Harries stared unevenly down at us from the window, his own single remaining eye catching the moonlight and blazing as if it were again burning, melting, dripping like its twin from its socket. I thought at first that Susan was frantically slipping down the makeshift rope simply out of terror at the obscene picture above her framed by the open window. I did her an injustice: she might well have been terrified – I certainly was – but her hurry was for far more practical reasons.

Harries's skeletal and stripped hands were not clutching and working out of instinct or reflex. Susan was still some thirty feet above the ground. Above the unyielding, frozen gravel. Simpson was dead or dying I was sure. I knew what fate awaited Susan. Unless we could help her.

With sudden frantic strength I heaved Simpson's body off and dragged myself, gasping, to my feet. I staggered towards the Doctor and Kreiner, both of whom stood transfixed by the drama unfolding, unknotting, above them. From where I was, from the angled view I had, I could see that they were in the wrong place. The way the rope was swinging, the way she was leaning in her frantic scramble to safety. If – when – Susan fell, she would land perhaps ten feet from where the Doctor and Kreiner were standing.

I have heard it postulated that everyone has dreams that involve their trying – and failing – to run through what seems to be treacle or thick mud. I was not dreaming, but my progress did indeed seem so hampered. Harries had finished untying the sheets long before I was close to the point where I knew Susan must hit the ground.

Then she fell.

And as she fell I realised that I was running fast – faster than ever before. Running for her life. And she was falling as slowly as I seemed to be moving. An illusion, a speed relative to the adrenaline-enhanced working of my brain.

I reached the point below the window almost as Susan did. Harries watched, impassive, as she tumbled heavily into my outstretched arms, slowed – mercifully – by the sheets and her skirts. She was not heavy, but I was off balance and Susan was falling quickly. In short, I broke her fall but I failed to catch her and she collapsed, winded, on the edge of the lawn. I fell beside her, my ankle turning over and catching awkwardly on the stone-edged verge, unsoftened by the snow.

We lay there for a second, recovering the best we could. Kreiner and the Doctor were there at once, reaching out to help us. As Susan stood, I saw the pain in her face.

'Are you all right?' I asked

'Ankle,' she gasped. 'Can't seem to... When I put weight on it.' She took a few hesitant steps, limping badly.

'Let me see.' The Doctor knelt down beside her and she used his shoulder to support herself as he felt round the ankle. 'Not broken,' he said. 'But there's some swelling. A sprain, I would say.'

'A sprain?' Kreiner's concern seemed to me to be disproportionate to this immediate problem. I reckoned she was lucky to be alive. 'Doctor,' he went on urgently, 'if she can be hurt –'

The Doctor waved him to silence. 'I know, I know, Fitz.' He stood up, and Susan staggered slightly. I took her hand and she gripped it tightly. Warmly.

'We're not all as indestructible as perhaps we once were,' the Doctor was saying in a low voice to Kreiner.

'The Artron inhibitor?' he asked. Again his words meant nothing to me. I have made some slight study of forensics since the events I now recall, but I must confess that I am still no more enlightened as to their meaning.

The Doctor was nodding. 'It inhibits the block-transfer equations that make reconstitution and regeneration of the outer plasmic shell possible.' He looked across at the crumpled form of Simpson lying in the churned-up snow. 'And speaking of regeneration,' he went on, 'if you want a more extreme example...'

We were all following his gaze, so we all saw. We all saw Simpson move. Was that a groan of pain? I could not be sure, but certainly he moved his arm. A faint, almost pathetic gesture. At once the Doctor and Kreiner ran over to where he lay, leaving me to support Susan as she staggered after them.

The Doctor was already kneeling beside Simpson's broken form when we got there. 'Thank goodness,' he was saying. 'There is still time, you know. Still a chance. Just tell us where

227

you've hidden the inhibitor and you should be able to pull through. To regenerate.'

I assume he was trying to make the man feel better. It was obvious that Simpson was dying. I was surprised he still had any life left in him. His constitution must have been far, far stronger than it appeared. A trickle of blood ran from one of his empty eye sockets and dripped into the crystal snow.

Simpson, I think, in those last moments, was aware of it as well. Even though he was obviously delirious, obviously talking nonsense, he knew it was the end. 'You know I can't do that, Doctor,' he half murmured, half gasped. 'There's too much at stake here. More than just a life.'

'Several lives,' the Doctor corrected him. There was a tone of admonishment in his voice that seemed quite out of place in the circumstances. 'We're beyond games now, beyond debate, beyond the lies to get me arrested so you could carry on in peace.'

'You have to tell us,' Kreiner said, and his tone was even more severe than the Doctor's. 'Where the hell is it?' For a moment I thought he was about to reach down and haul the butler up by his lapels while he shouted at him. 'Tell us!'

There was a trace of a smile on Simpson's face as he stared blankly up at us. The pain, the shock of his sudden violent blindness must have somehow anaesthetised him to the fact he was dying. Or perhaps there is at that stage an acceptance, a calm, that overwhelms one. 'You work it out,' he croaked. I could hear the blood in his throat. 'You've read Borusa, just as I have.' I consider myself well read, but I had never – have never – heard of the author.

'Oh, big help.' Kreiner said. He stamped in the snow and slapped his hands together with cold and frustration.

'How did you find us?' the Doctor asked suddenly. 'And if you knew we'd be here, why just the one of you?'

I was neither following nor appreciating the conversation.

228

Under the circumstances. But I let it run its course. It was evident that it would of necessity be short-lived.

'We didn't know you would be here.' Simpson's voice was weakening, cracking. 'But we know where you have been.'

'Ah!' The Doctor's eyes widened. 'Quantum extrapolation.'

'With a probability matrix to prioritise the random choices.' I could hear the blood in his throat. He coughed, his whole body contorting with the effort. 'But even so there were several hundred times and places you might turn up.'

The Doctor seemed surprised. 'You covered them all? Then you must be spread pretty thin. One agent at each nexus point. Waiting and watching, scattered across the universe and down the years. On the off chance as it were.' He glanced up at Fitz. 'If nothing else, we've got them worried,' he said levelly.

'You too', Simpson croaked, 'have things to worry about.' There was a dry rasp from his throat that might have been a laugh. 'I have waited for you here for a hundred years. But I see that you don't have the luxury of much time.'

'See?' the Doctor said.

I had assumed it was an unfortunate figure of speech, like his mention of a hundred years. But Simpson went on: 'I see him leaving the room even now. Down the corridor. Towards the stairs. His tread is heavy, purposeful.'

Again, my feeling was that he was seeing all this in his imagination, in his mind's eye. But even so, we all turned and looked up at the window.

The window was now empty.

Harries was on his way down through the house. He was coming after us. How had Simpson known? Was it an informed guess?

'There is more to everything than meets the eye,' Simpson was saying. 'He is already at the half-landing.' Then, quieter, 'Away my little friend, away. Look to the others in the drawing room. And bring me your eyes.'

I do not know if I was more surprised at the way the delirium had transformed his character, the way the sarcastic façade of the butler had dropped away, or at his strange words. The Doctor, I saw, was frowning. He too, I was sure, felt the incongruity of it all.

'What's he talking about?' Kreiner demanded of the Doctor. 'How does he know? How can he "see"?'

The Doctor shook his head. 'I don't –' he began. Then suddenly he snapped his fingers, like a pistol shot. 'Of course. The rats.'

'What?' Were they both overtaken with delirium?

'Optic implants. Some sort of nano-cam with a direct linkage to his visual cortex. That's how he kept tabs on everyone. Especially us.'

The words made no sense to me, but I felt a shiver of fear nonetheless as I remembered the rats' eyes glinting at me in the darkness. Had Simpson released them from their cage for some reason? Had they really, and not merely in my imaginings, been watching me?

But, mercifully perhaps, before I had time to allow my imagination to roam more freely, Simpson gave a final gurgling choke of noise. His head jerked to one side allowing a last rivulet of crimson to splash from his empty eyes into the stained snow.

'Come on.' The Doctor was on his feet again, his whole body almost shaking with energy and impatience. 'Harries is coming. We can't hang around here.'

'Neither can we get very far,' I pointed out. 'Miss Seymour –'

'Miss Seymour can return to the house. She'll be safe there.'

'Are you sure?' Kreiner demanded.

The Doctor nodded. Harries will be after us. He doesn't know where we're going, but he'll need to stop us anyway.'

'Can't she just let us in?' Kreiner asked. The strain was

showing on his face. I wondered who he meant. Surely he couldn't want Catherine Harries to open the doors for us.

The Doctor sighed in answer. 'If she could, I'm sure she would have done by now,' he said brusquely. 'Aren't you?' They both looked at Susan, as if for an answer.

'I'm not sure I can make it to the house,' she said. Her face was ashen grey as she tried a few steps. She collapsed almost at once in the snow, her legs folding up under her so that her dress billowed out around her.

'Fitz, go with her,' the Doctor said. 'Look after her.' He lowered his voice, perhaps so that Susan should not hear. 'She can die just like you and me,' he said. 'And if that happens...'

'I'll go,' I offered immediately. The thought of bearing the responsibility for Susan's being injured or even killed probably affected me more than Kreiner.

'No, I need you,' the Doctor snapped back. Then he smiled suddenly, almost infectiously. 'Local knowledge.'

I wasn't sure whether this would be a help or not, but there was hardly time to argue. So I kept my peace as the Doctor quickly described to Kreiner and Susan how to climb through the chimney. 'Let Compassion go first,' he finished, 'and you can give her a push if she gets stuck or her ankle gives out.' It seemed both strange timing and manners to assign a nickname to Miss Seymour. But again, I held my tongue and Susan seemed to accept the name without comment or surprise. Silently I prayed that there was enough time for them to return to the house unseen.

We ran. Or at least the Doctor sprinted ahead of me while I tried to catch my breath. My own ankle was tired. I could feel my face contorted with the effort and the pain.

We did not look back until we had reached the cover of the first trees. We had to follow the path, but whichever way we went we left a trail of black footprints in the glistening moonstruck snow. They might be less obvious in the shade of the trees, but never difficult to follow. The Doctor reached the trees before I did and turned to pull me quickly after him. He stopped, arm outstretched towards me, his sparkling eyes resting well beyond me. I turned too, and in the moment before the Doctor dragged me forward again, my leg all but collapsing beneath me, I saw Harries's corpse silhouetted against the snow, lit from the Manor's open door, stalking inexorably after us across the lawn.

He was not moving as quickly as we were, but both of us knew that we would have to rest, would stagger and fall. Harries would not. We could hear the rasping as his lungs inhaled and expelled the cold air – out of habit rather than necessity, for the dead never tire – and we knew that he would catch us. He walked with his hands outstretched. He too knew what the outcome must be, and already his hands were hungry for our necks; already he reached out for us; already we were dead, like chickens that continue their panicked run as a reflex despite the loss of their heads. The Doctor gripped my shoulder, a gesture of reassurance and friendship. Then we staggered on, Harries's rough breathing drowned by our own desperate clawing for air – air that burned our throats, it was so cold and so thin.

THE REPORT OF INSPECTOR IAN STRATFORD (21)

Rats filled my dreams. Plump and scuttling, eager of eye and sharp of tooth, they hunted me through the corridors of my mind. And caught me. And ate me. But the pain of them biting into my unprotected skin was the pain of the pins and needles from lying in one position for too long. I stretched catlike on the couch to unknot my muscles, careful not to move my bandaged arm too far lest I turn the dull ache into the raging torrent of pain that I suspected was dammed up in the wound. Baker turned from his position near the window as he heard me.

'How do you feel, sir?' he asked gently.

'Absolutely terrible,' I replied, but the words came out wrong: muffled and unintelligible. My mouth was dry and musty, as if rats had nested there. Baker bent down and placed a surprisingly gentle hand on my forehead. It was dry and cold against my skin.

'You're running a bit of a temperature, sir. Ought to put a poultice on the wound, just to draw the fever out.'

'Old wives' tales, Sergeant?' I muttered.

'Oh no, sir. My aunt swears by poultices. She'll slap one on at the slightest opportunity.'

'Pity she's not here now, isn't it?'

'Oh I don't know, sir. We don't get on particularly well. How would you feel if *your* aunt was here?'

'I'm surprised she isn't already. She usually has an infallible nose for gossip and scandal –' I paused, my clouded mind finally unravelling what Baker had said. 'How did you know that my aunt and I don't get on?'

'Guesswork mostly, sir.' He smiled. 'And deductive training, of course. You haven't contacted your aunt since you've been here. Hardly the action of a concerned nephew, if you don't mind me saying so, sir.'

I sighed. 'No, I don't mind at all, Baker.' How to explain it to him: the family ties that bound my aunt and me together and the events that still stood between us? I felt I had to justify myself to Baker. He was crouched by my side, waiting for me to say something. Maybe it was my close brush with death, maybe something else entirely, but I felt as if I needed to tell Baker the truth. Too often in my time I had hidden behind my rank and what people expected of it. I wanted someone to know something about me before... well, in case anything happened. As well it might.

'She's the only family I have left,' I said finally. 'My parents died some time ago – my mother of pneumonia, my father soon afterwards of drink. The only person left in my family apart from me was my aunt.' I hesitated, reliving old events. Looking, still with some bitterness, at old scars.

'And?' Baker prompted quietly.

'There was a girl.'

Baker smiled. 'There always is,' he said.

'I wanted... We wanted to marry. My aunt forbade it. She was the executrix of my parents' will. It wasn't a lot of money, but...'

'I understand, sir.'

'My aunt had already paired me up in her mind with another girl. She introduced us, pushed us together at every opportunity, and eventually we fell in love. Deeply in love. And we married. I joined the police and we lived very happily together in a house of our own in London. Then I began to realise that my wife and I had very different ideas about what love and marriage actually meant. She is the sort of person who can love many people at once, not just her spouse. Oh, she was faithful to me – at first – but I couldn't understand her, couldn't cope with the fact that she loved so many people and just happened to be married to one of them. We argued... Oh, we argued...'

I could feel it welling up within me, a wave of sick coldness from the dark, scarred places that were the legacy of my brief marriage. An old, familiar feeling.

'We divorced… We had to. She had met someone else, someone younger than me. I couldn't hold her back. She went off with him for a while, then they split up and there was someone else; then I stopped asking.'

Baker's fatherly hand tightened on my arm.

'I blamed myself for a long while. Then I blamed my aunt. I can't stop visiting my aunt – she's all I've got left – but I can't forgive her.'

'And your wife?'

'Oh, I forgave her long ago.'

There was a long silence while Baker tried to think of something to say and I thought back to the happy days of the past. It was so long ago. So much had changed, and I had changed so much. I had some sort of flair in those days. I was a good policeman. Deferential, glad to be of use. Politic, cautious, meticulous. And now? Full of high sentence and a bit obtuse. At times, indeed, almost ridiculous.

'I thought I heard something earlier, sir,' broke in Baker. 'While you were asleep. It seemed to come from upstairs.'

'What was it?'

'I'm not sure, sir. I thought at the time that it might have been a scream, but thinking about it I'm not so sure.'

'Susan!'

'No sir, not Miss Seymour. It was too deep, whatever it was. I think it might have been Simpson.'

Simpson. The eternal footman. Was he dead? Had his quiet snickering at the pretensions of his masters finally ceased? There was no way to tell, stuck there, trapped there, in the drawing room. I felt as if Baker and I were standing at the still point of a vast conspiracy which wheeled and revolved about us. The dance went on, but we were not dancing.

My train of thought was derailed by a scrabbling within the walls. Something was moving within them, sensing us, surrounding us. With the remnants of my nightmare still clinging to my mind, I attempted to get to my feet, knowing beyond any possibility of doubt that a stream of rats was about to descend from the chimney and devour us. Baker attempted to restrain me with one hand while fumbling for some impromptu weapon with the other.

A fine haze of soot fell into the fireplace.

'Sir, I think we ought to get you to the door.'

The haze became a trickle…

'But isn't Catherine Harries still outside?'

A cascade…

'Even so, sir –'

A deluge…

'Baker, we're staying where we are!'

And suddenly, too fast to properly comprehend, two black, powdery bodies fell into the grate. Bodies that coughed and thrashed around, spraying soot across the room. Bodies that eventually opened startlingly white eyes and stared at us with relief.

'That heaven for that,' Fitz Kreiner said. 'I was worried we were going to end up in Harries's lap.'

'It's just like *The Water Babies*,' Susan Seymour said, exhilarated. Even covered in soot, she was striking.

Baker crossed the room and helped Miss Seymour to her feet, while Fitz used George Wallace's precious upholstered chairs to haul himself upright. Amid the joy of knowing they were still alive, I still felt a stab of pain when I thought about Wallace and his wife. I had not known them for long, but they seemed decent sorts. The kind of people that make England what it is. They did not deserve the ignominy of what happened to them.

'Ian, you're hurt!' Susan exclaimed, and she limped across the room to my side, in obvious pain.

I managed to murmur words that I have always imagined myself saying, although not under the circumstances in which I actually said them. 'Oh, it's only a flesh wound. But what's happened to your foot?'

Fitz quickly brought us up to date with what had transpired outside – the abortive escape attempt, the death of Simpson, the decision by the Doctor and Hopkinson to distract Harries's attention while Fitz and Miss Seymour re-entered the house.

While Baker checked Miss Seymour's dressing, Fitz crossed to the door and made as if to open it.

'No!' I shouted.

He paused. 'But if Richard Harries is chasing the Doctor –'

'His sister?'

'But surely she'll be occupied in controlling her brother's body.'

I shook my head. 'I think it's more complicated than that. She seems to be able to control him and herself at the same time. If what she says is true, if her brother's mind is sharing her brain, then there's no knowing what they might be able to –'

The lights flickered.

Baker crossed quickly to one of the electrical appliances that lit the room, now flickering in intensity and causing our shadows to tremble. He turned with a hapless expression on his face. 'I don't think there's anything I can do, sir. I'm not familiar with these electrical contraptions.'

'They must be powered from somewhere.'

'Down in the cellar. I remember when Wallace had it installed. It runs on coal, I think.'

'Damn! The fuel must have run out. It's not just here, then. The lights are going out all over Banquo Manor.' I glanced around and caught sight of the remaining oil lamp on the mantelpiece. 'Light that,' I said. 'Quickly. If Catherine thinks she's got us at a disadvantage, heaven alone knows what she will do.'

As Baker went about the task I pounded the couch with my good arm. Why did we have to be so helpless?

The lights gave a final flicker and went out, leaving us in the dark until Baker could light the lamp.

The wood was our enemy. We crashed through the icy branches that clawed at our flesh, our clothes. Our eyes. We slipped and stumbled over the frozen ground – hoping that we still followed the path. I limped on, the pain spreading up my leg, meeting the cold spreading down and exaggerated by the freezing air which we fought to breathe.

The cold air, almost physical, clawed at out hands, our faces. Our fingers were dead, our ears spiders' webs of pain, our faces burned with the ice and snow that whipped at them.

My jacket was in tatters; my ankle felt as though a red-hot knife had been plunged into it; and then savagely twisted. I could feel the tears clinging frostily to my cheeks, slowing in their traces as they froze to my face. We crashed on through the icicled branches, across the ice-encrusted snow knowing that at any moment one or both of us would collapse and be unable to go on. The cold sapped our confidence as the effort drained our energy. Only our will to survive and the necessity of keeping warm spurred us on. But too slowly.

Behind us, Harries moved effortlessly. Closer. The snow powdered and froze beneath his dread feet as it melted beneath ours. Icicles exploded as his head met them, showering his ripped face with their shattered remains, cold and dead as he; unmelting. Closer.

Perhaps it was nerves, perhaps the anxiety that I would die without understanding why or how, but I felt compelled to talk. My voice was ragged and broken between my gasps for breath. By contrast, the Doctor's responses were measured and unhurried. How much effort that actually took on his part I can only guess, but the effect on my own confidence and demeanour was positive.

'So why', I gasped, 'did you pretend to be dead?'

'Oh, a foolish notion,' he replied. 'I went for a walk in the grounds, thinking, working some things out in my mind, when I realised I was being followed. I knew why of course, but I didn't know who by. Fortunately, by the time my follower got close I was at the top of the hill, looking out over the grotto. I guessed his intention and so I took my coat off and stuffed it with sticks. Then I threw it over the edge. By the time it came to rest on the ground below, it looked pretty convincing.' He grinned at me suddenly.

I sniffed. 'More luck than judgement, I'd say.'

The grin was wiped abruptly from his face. 'There's no such thing as luck, Mr Hopkinson. Those of us who fight on the side of good often find that the universe smiles on their wilder schemes. It's what's kept me alive so far.' His boyish smile returned. 'My attacker came upon me in the dark; we struggled, and I pretended to fall over the edge. In truth I hid myself just beneath the overhang, where the grotto was intended to be. My attacker assumed I was dead and went on his merry way. I still didn't get a good look at him, despite the sheer ingenuity of my plan, but as we now know it was Simpson.'

'Simpson?' I gasped, as much out of incredulity as shortness of breath.

'Of course.' He seemed surprised that I needed to ask. 'Watch that branch there, won't you? So having been apparently removed from the board I decided I would do better to stay put and play dead for a while. Had to do without my coat before I could borrow a new one from Sir George's room – which is where you found me – but no pain, no gain, as they say.'

'The gain being?' I enquired.

'Well, it took me out of the picture and allowed me to snoop about a bit.'

'Trying to identify your attacker – the murderer, you thought?'

'What? Oh, no. Something much more important than that.'

'More important.'

'Mmm,' he agreed lightly. 'Still haven't found it, though. And I wasn't being as clever as I thought anyway. But then I didn't know about the rats.'

By now I had decided that he was rambling, saying anything to keep the conversation going and me distracted from the real and ever-closer danger that was stalking after us.

'Simpson probably knew about Harries for a while. Through the rats. Maybe it was even an intentional side effect, something he let happen to smoke me out as it were. Who knows?'

'Who indeed?' I gasped. As I spoke, I stumbled. Behind me, as I fell, I saw Harries stepping inexorably forward; closer. He pushed on through the glistening darkness. Closer. I pulled myself up again and staggered after the Doctor.

'So, what is it between you and Simpson?' I asked. Better to talk. Even nonsense.

'Oh, nothing personal.' He held back a tree branch to allow me to pass. When he let go it showered snow into Harries's path. The Doctor stared at the approaching figure for a brief moment. 'Doesn't give up, does he?' He shook his head as if slightly annoyed at the inconvenience, as if he had better and more urgent things to be doing. 'In a strange way,' he said, 'it's about love. Love of independence and personal responsibility on the one hand; love of form and structure on the other. And, in Simpson's case, I suspect a more personal attachment as well. Romana is as beautiful now as she ever was, and there aren't many of us who would spend a hundred years on a mission for the sake of duty.'

'Not that it matters now,' I grumbled, perplexed.

He seemed genuinely annoyed at the sentiment. 'Oh, it matters now more than ever. And increasingly by the moment.'

I did not reply. I had no breath.

The trees parted for Harries as they hemmed us in. He was closing on us, yet he did not hurry, did not quicken his pace. He did not have to. And as we slowed we became increasingly aware of the apparition at our backs, the moonlight reflecting upwards from the snow, picking out the pale bone of his partially blackened skull beneath the unthawed snow as he lurched after us. Closer. Only his eyes – or what was left of them – failed ever to catch the snow-shroud light. The black of his mind, of his intent, seemed to thrive in the holes that were his eyes. Was it out of some perverse sense of envy that he had gouged out Simpson's eyes? I wondered. My own stung with the cold and the implied threat as I blinked at the blackness of the night. And the blackness grew ever larger as he loomed closer.

Closer.

The Doctor slipped and fell, dragging me down with him into a sudden soft snow bank. We floundered for a moment and lost each other. A hand lifted me and I smiled a thank-you – I could not have risen without help. Then the Doctor surfaced in front of me, his sodden hair clung with snow, and his face filled with anxiety and warning. With sudden energy I lunged forward, towards him, feeling the corpse's dead hand tearing at my shoulder as I moved, dragged.

Harries too stumbled at the edge of the path, into the deceptive white pool, almost pulling me with him as he fell, tearing my tattered jacket from my back and ripping the muscle in my left shoulder. I ran, or rather staggered, waded, stumbled through the deep snow, hurling myself back up on to the path, catching up with the Doctor. I turned to see Richard Harries pull his carcass towards us out of the snow, the bone protruding from the broken ends of his fingers where the dead, rotting flesh had torn away as I pulled free. His speed was unimpaired.

He would catch us again. Soon...

Suddenly it was much harder to stand up, and for a second I could not discern why.

'We're here!' shouted the Doctor with something akin to triumph. I peered into the gloom, against the snow being blown from the ground into my face.

Ahead of us – thirty yards (twenty?) – stood a small building, a shed. For a moment I was puzzled, then I realised where we were – the increased wind meant it was a clearing, and the wooden structure in front of us told us where.

'Come on,' he called into the wind, and we battled towards the small building, the sound of our pursuer's approach reaching us above the howl of the wind... 'Just a small wooden shed full of tools and so on,' a voice whispered in my ear – and I realised that it was an echo of my own. I also realised that this had been where the Doctor had been aiming for all along. The scene, bizarrely, of his own earlier 'death'.

The near side had no door, just a small window set at eye level – my eye level – in the wooden planking. The Doctor shouted to me to find a stone or a piece of wood to break the window, then he peered through, wiping away the snow and ice. I joined him, but of course I could see nothing save a reflection of myself – and Richard Harries lumbering into the glassy clearing behind us.

'A stone, quickly!' the Doctor repeated, shouting into the wind.

I turned sharply as the wind rocked the horror thirty (twenty?) yards away. The torn flesh of his shattered face seemed to peel away under the pressure and his insane, dead smile widened as he lurched onward again, barely slowed by the gale.

Protruding from the snow a few feet away was a pile of stones. Materials for constructing the grotto, I realised. I snatched one up, staggering under its weight. I raised it in both hands and battered at the window, smashing it at once and, predictably, slicing open the back of my hand with the falling glass. The blood froze along the cut – from fear as much as from the cold. I reached inside the dark hole of the window, framed with glittering triangles which tore at my right arm and shoulder, and for a moment I felt I was reaching into the blackened pit that was Harries's eye socket – the remains of the splintered iris reflecting and distorting my intrusion.

Harries was halfway to us now.

The Doctor was beside me as I reached in, hopping from one foot to the other in impatience. At last, my hand closed around a wooden stave, and I pulled upwards and out. A pickaxe. Now at least we had some chance.

Ten yards.

The handle was through the opening.

Eight yards.

But the head of the pickaxe smashed into the frame. It was too wide to fit through the window.

Seven yards.

I pulled again and twisted, hoping to wrench the iron head through the diagonal and at an angle to the sill.

It jammed halfway, preventing me from reaching inside again, and impossible to pull through.

Five yards.

With a jarring push I managed to dislodge it...

...and the pickaxe fell back inside the shed.

Harries's clenched, iced fingers were ten feet from my face. I reached back into the shed with one arm and pushed the Doctor sideways with the other.

He almost fell, but he seemed to realise my meaning and half staggered, half ran along the side of the shed and round towards the front.

I ducked away as Harries's arms lunged at me, barely aware that I was holding a shovel – I could feel nothing, my hands were so cold.

Harries took a short step backwards, the shovel's head

catching his arm – by chance rather than design – as I staggered after the Doctor. Harries paused, watching, then he started after us.

The Doctor was working on the padlock on the shed door with some sort of metal instrument. I shouted at him to stand away, that we hadn't time for that. He seemed irritated by my interruption but nevertheless he stood aside and I swung the shovel. I shattered the padlock on the second blow, pulling open the door, and we fell inside.

I knew at once that this was a mistake – we were trapped in the shed, and there was no way to secure the door. Harries would be here in a moment, in the shed, with us. None of the tools I could see, mainly pickaxes and shovels, would stop the nightmare outside, or even slow it much. But the Doctor was immediately preoccupied with an innocuous-looking pile of wooden boxes in the far corner.

'Don't just stand there, give me a hand,' he demanded, and I was too frightened, too cold, too helpless to argue. I got the shovel's blade under the lid of the top box and levered it up. At that moment the first loud crash came from the door as Harries tried to pull it open over the blowing snow. He lacked the strength of raw desperation that the Doctor and I had had, but it would not take him longer than a few seconds to widen the gap enough to enter.

It took only one second to rip the lid from the box, and the Doctor snatched a handful of the small cylinders from inside while I thanked God that George's workmen had not yet used them to excavate his proposed artificial cave.

The Doctor knew at the same instant I did that we had no means of igniting the dynamite, and at the same moment the door was savagely ripped fully open, revealing Harries silhouetted against the snow.

The light was behind him. We could see the figure clearly against the white, but Harries could not see us huddled in the dark, far corner. Even his eye, it seemed, needed a moment to adjust to the change in light. He stepped forward, his arms outstretched, feeling, clutching.

The Doctor crept closer. Close beside him, I could see the intent concentration clearly on his face. And if it was that clear...

Harries saw us as I pushed the Doctor towards the white opening. The Doctor tumbled past and Harries turned partially to see what was happening. I seized the moment and shouldered the cadaver at full tilt, wishing as my side struck his back that I had had the sense to use my undamaged shoulder. Harries was still turning – off balance – and he staggered sideways, tripping over the pickaxe, which had skidded across the floor when I pushed it back through the window. I continued my charge and narrowly missed the door frame, collapsing in the snow as the Doctor struggled to push the door shut.

We both knew that there was no hope of reaching the village, and without discussion we stumbled back the way we had come, towards the house, pausing only to allow me to relieve the Doctor of some of his cargo. He was stuffing dynamite into his pockets and I mimicked his actions. The wind was behind us now and we were almost swept along to the deceptive shelter of the trees.

As we plunged back into the woodland I saw Harries's dead face watching us through the shattered window of the shed, framed by the splintered glass. After a second his splintered face was gone and I knew – we both knew – that he was still following us, chasing us for as far as we could go, with all the unyielding, untiring determination of death.

Like a leaf drifting downstream I drifted in and out of consciousness, and my dreams were populated by people I thought long forgotten, and others I would rather not have remembered. Places and times far distant from each other shared space in my mind. For a while I relived the last scene with my wife. I was making a fool of myself, begging her to leave her lover and come back to me. She in turn was regretful but implacable. And in the corner of our London parlour sat my aunt, although her gout had always prevented her from leaving Three Sisters.

'It'll end in tears,' she kept repeating like a budgerigar, 'it'll end in tears…' And so it did. I ran out into the street with the tears streaming down my face. Somehow the street outside my house was the street outside Great Scotland Yard, although I lived many miles away. The building had been stripped of its frontage, and the offices behind were revealed like a stack of little boxes furnished with filing cabinets and flimsy desks. The road was littered with dead bodies, either whole or in pieces, and rats scuttled to and fro through the human wreckage. For a while I wandered along the pavement looking for someone, although I didn't know who. I suspect I was looking for my own body. I never found it. Instead I wandered across the road to a nearby public house.

'Good for business,' said the barman.

'What is?'

'The bomb blast. Good for business, There's nothing like wholesale slaughter to pull in the crowds.'

I looked closer, and saw with little surprise that the barman was Chief Inspector Driscoll. He placed a foaming tankard of porter on the bar before me. 'Drink up, laddie. It's good for your health.'

'Whose bomb was it?' I asked.

'Anarchists. Anarchists and radicals. Anarchists, radicals and the Irish. Anarchists, radicals…' He seemed content to list the perpetrators to eternity, so I got up and made my leave. My attention was caught by the mirror above the bar. Beneath the fly-specked glass I could make out my own image; but there was something strange about it. My face was white and waxen, almost as if…

I raised my hands to my face. The skin was warm and clammy, and seemed oddly loose in my hands. I felt further. There was a ridge of flesh beneath my ears. I wriggled my fingers underneath and pulled

My face came away in my hands. It was a soft fleshy mask and I stared down at it in skin-crawling disgust as I turned it over in my hands. Then I raised my eyes to the mirror again.

A skull looked back at me with dull empty holes for eyes. My skull. The skull beneath the skin. I had peeled my own face off.

I awoke screaming, struggling, clawing my way out of nightmare.

Fitz and Baker broke off from talking. 'Don't worry, sir,' said Baker. 'I'm still here.'

'What's the time?'

'Don't rightly know, sir. Past midnight at any rate. Well past midnight.'

'Any movement?'

'Difficult to say. I think Professor Harries went off after Mr Hopkinson and the Doctor. Miss Harries spends most of her time in the hall making sure that nobody can escape from here. Then again, any time I consider going to the window I can hear her moving around outside. Or it might be Harries himself. That's the problem, sir. There's no way of telling.'

'And Sus– Miss Seymour?'

'Resting, sir. Her ankle took a hell of a bang falling from that window. How are you feeling, sir?'

'I think I'm all right now. I feel rather weak, but the fever

247

appears to have passed off.' Indeed my head felt much clearer than it had for some time. My shoulder ached and my stomach still churned but I felt that the periods of unconsciousness had ceased. I made an effort to stand up.

'Are you sure that's wise, sir?'

'I'll have to get up sometime, Baker. Better now than in an emergency.'

'All the same, sir...'

'You're not my aunt, Baker.'

'For which I am sure she and I are truly grateful, sir.'

I walked unsteadily over to the door. My stomach lurched a couple of times but decided to remain where it was. There was an odd sort of tingling in my joints but I felt considerably better. I put my ear against the door.

'Hmm. Can't hear anything.' Quietly I unlocked it.

'No!' Kreiner was horrified. 'You can't –'

'We have to be sure,' I whispered. 'For all we know both Catherine and her brother might have headed off in pursuit of Hopkinson.' Carefully I eased the door open...

And slammed it shut as Catherine Harries fired. The bullet embedded itself harmlessly in the teak. I rapidly locked the door.

'Well, at least we know,' I muttered.

Trying to get my joints and muscles working again, I wandered about the room. Most of the furniture was piled up against the French windows, with deep scuff marks in the carpet attesting to the haste with which the barricade had been built. The only thing that was not being used to block out our captors was the portrait that had originally hung opposite the fireplace, but that now rested on its side by the wall.

I crossed over to the windows. I could just see through a gap in the barricade to an unobscured pane of glass. A faint breeze blew through the gap between the two sides of the window. 'Must be near dawn,' I muttered. 'You know the area, Baker. How long would it take the Doctor and Mr Hopkinson to get to the village and back again – assuming that's where they're headed?'

'Not more than an hour or so each way, sir. After all, Mr Hopkinson does know the area as well. What do you think he'll do when he gets to the village?'

'I don't know, Baker. If I were him, what would I do?' I mused for a moment. 'I think I would use the telephone in your office to call for help, then round up every able-bodied man in the village and come back here. That shouldn't take more than an hour. So, three hours. Four at the outside, from his leaving to help arriving.'

'It's been about that long already,' Kreiner pointed out.

'Hmm.'

The time stretched on while I stared out of the French windows on to the snowbound landscape. The waiting is always the worst part. Where were they? I imagined myself out there with them, running through the forest, breathless, cold and scared. What if Hopkinson's ankle had suddenly given out, leaving him unable to move? What if the Doctor, pausing to help, had been caught by Richard Harries and ripped, limb from limb?

Shadows were moving on the edge of the light cast from the drawing-room window. For a moment I thought Harries was out there, balefully watching us with his one good eye. I realised that the movement was too fast, too panicked. With shocking suddenness John Hopkinson stumbled into the circle of light. The hope that was born within me died as the figures of our rescuers behind him became the elegant form of the Doctor closely chased by Richard Harries. Baker and I frantically began pulling the barricade apart with as little finesse as we had used in putting it together. Something ripped in my shoulder in a flare of fiery agony and I collapsed back on to the chaise longue, leaving Baker to complete the gap.

Our last hopes of rescue staggered into the room, exhausted and defeated.

'Hi,' Kreiner said with misplaced jocularity. 'Good day at the office?'

As soon as Baker had pulled enough weight away from the doors for us to force them open a fraction, we squeezed ourselves into the drawing room. The Doctor went first, easily negotiating the narrow aperture. I pushed after him, all too conscious of Harries's figure looming out of the blackness behind. I jammed for a moment in the doors and then, with brute force and panic to help me, I was through. And so was Harries's arm, reaching – clutching – after me.

Baker slammed the battered remains of the French windows shut, throwing his considerable weight against the wooden frame. I turned to help him as Fitz Kreiner and the Doctor pushed some of the furniture dislodged from the barricade back into the heap in front of the opening.

Harries's twisted arm still clawed at us from the gap; and he was slowly forcing the aperture wider despite our efforts. We pushed harder and Stratford attempted to raise himself from the chaise longue to help us, his injured arm hampering him and the pain showing in his brows as the strain did in ours. Susan, collapsed in a chair beside him, awoke with a scream.

Stratford had just managed to raise himself and was just pushing himself to his feet with his good arm when the windows finally gave way. Caught between our combined efforts to close them and Harries's inhuman attempt to force his way in, the inner frames finally caved inwards at us, glass exploding across the room as if fired from a cannon as the wood bowed and splintered. And through the shower of crystal shards stepped Harries, driving a path through the furniture and shattered wood, his snow-crusted feet crushing the fragments of glass as he trod.

We saw him enter through the snowstorm of glass as it crashed on past us, whipping at our clothes and cutting our skin. Susan covered her face with her hands and Baker stepped back under the impact, his cheek ripped open by a flying sliver of ice. Kreiner ducked. Only the Doctor stood his ground, erect and purposeful – defiant – as the glass crashed round him but seemed not to touch him. The glass was ice-cold as it hit me, lashed at me, as if gloating over Harries's arrival, and instinctively I covered my eyes and turned away. In a second the blizzard was over.

But Harries was inside the room and the only other escape was past his sister.

Harries stopped in front of the remains of the windows. Waiting, cutting off our escape. The Doctor slowly, carefully, pulled several of the sticks of dynamite from his jacket pocket and passed them over to Baker beside him. The back of Baker's hand was pressed to his torn cheek with the blood squeezing out from behind it.

'Where in buggery did you get that?' Kreiner demanded.

'Never underestimate the local village shop,' the Doctor said.

Baker's comment was more practical. 'We'd have to position it before we could set it off,' he pointed out in a husky whisper. Stratford joined us, a defiant group dwarfed by our own fear rather than by the figure standing motionless between us and escape. Between us and life.

'If we use the fuse, he'll have as much time as us to get out of the way.' At least his wound had not clouded Stratford's precise mind.

'Unless we tie it on to him,' Kreiner offered

'I doubt we can count on his co-operation,' the Doctor said.

Suddenly Harries was moving again, as if switched on, or woken by our low voices, knocking the Chippendale chair beside him across the room. He had not been a large man, but the chair crashed into the wall and splintered with a crack.

At the same moment there was a far louder crack from behind us and we whirled round as the lock on the door exploded and the wounded wood swung open to allow Catherine Harries, her revolver still smoking, to step into the room opposite her brother. Twin mirrors – with us trapped between the glass.

'So, what happens now?' the Doctor asked Catherine, and again I was surprised at the calmness and ease of his voice.

'What are you going to do with us?' I asked, as much to dispel the deathly silence that had followed the storm of noise as because I wanted an answer.

She turned her pale wide eyes from her brother and fixed them on me. 'I am not going to do anything with you,' she said quietly.

'What do you mean?' asked Kreiner.

She turned quickly on him: 'It's Richard you've harmed. He will take our revenge. We'll kill you, won't we, Richard?' And Richard Harries stepped towards us as if in answer.

'We?' Susan's voice shook, her bottom lip trembling against her teeth.

'Oh yes. We are one now. Our minds, our bodies have the same thought – the same instinct. To kill you.'

'All of us?' The Doctor remained the calmest of us.

I could see the perspiration on Stratford's brow, though Sergeant Baker seemed to have found depths of character and strength that eluded the rest of us. 'Even Miss Seymour?' he asked levelly.

'Especially Miss Seymour.'

'Oh bugger,' breathed Kreiner beside me. I appreciated the sentiment, though not the vocabulary.

Catherine turned to her brother, her brow creased, and her voice quieter again now – quieter, but tense with suppressed emotion. 'She was going to take you away from me.' Her anguish lasted only a moment, then her voice regained its vigour, its confident madness: 'Kill her, Richard – kill her at once!'

And then she smiled. And it was somehow beautiful as well as terrible.

Harries took a lurching step forward, his arms stretched out at us, and Susan stepped back. The Doctor immediately moved between them, although he must have known he could never stop the grotesque form that moved slowly over towards Susan.

'No, Harries. Think what you are doing,' he pleaded uselessly. 'Don't let her use you.'

'Think?' laughed Catherine behind me. 'His mind is mine.'

Harries brushed the Doctor easily aside and reached out for Susan as he stumbled and fell back.

'Richard – no… Please.' She was not actually crying, but her cheeks were studded with tears. 'Richard…'

He hesitated. A second – no more; but he hesitated. I could see from the Doctor's expression as he struggled to his feet again that this was the opening he had been looking for.

'That's it. Struggle against her mind,' he shouted. 'This is Susan – remember Susan. You were going to marry her.'

Harries took another step towards Susan.

'You loved her!'

He stopped again, and half turned towards where the Doctor stood, defiant, then to his sister as if for help. Finally he looked into Susan Seymour's eyes, and saw his confusion reflected in her fear and desperation, and his torn flesh in her irises. Harries stopped.

'Don't listen.' Catherine was desperate, as if she sensed his dilemma would give way in Susan's favour. Perhaps she did. 'You must kill them. For me.' Harries stood immobile still. 'For you. For us!' She was all but screaming at him now.

Harries lurched forward a fraction, leaning over Susan. His arms stretched out ready to strangle, to embrace. But still he held back.

'Kill her!' And this time it was a scream. But Harries made no move to obey his sister. Susan backed away another step – hardly any distance at all, but it was enough. I moved to bar Harries's way again, as oblivious as the others to the more immediate threat. If Harries was paralysed with emotional confusion, his sister was galvanised by it. Susan was closer to her now and Catherine stepped quickly forward, reversed the revolver she held and made to hit Susan hard across the head with the butt. I leaped towards her, managing to knock her aside, but the blow still glanced off Susan's skull, making her stagger under the impact.

My immediate reaction was to see to Susan. But before I could reach her, Harries shoved me aside. He followed through the action, bringing his arms up once more and reaching out for her soft white neck, his confusion resolved and his instincts again in control. His fingers closed on Susan's flesh as Baker and the Doctor both launched themselves at Harries, dragging him back and away from Susan, who sank choking to the floor. I pulled her clear of the struggle. She was unconscious, but her eyelids flickered with life. Stratford eased himself aside while Kreiner helped me rest Susan's body on the chaise longue.

I glanced up, meaning to thank Kreiner for his help. But he was no longer there. He was rushing to help Baker, as the Doctor was hurled aside.

The sergeant was losing his battle against Harries, who had closed a hand on Baker's throat. Kreiner hurled himself on Harries, driving him back. But still the creature kept its bloodied hands round Baker's throat despite Kreiner's efforts to prise them away. It took me a moment to work out why Baker was fighting one-handed, and before any of the rest of us could move to help him Catherine recovered herself and brought her revolver up to cover us.

She had recovered her breath, although her eyes streamed with the effort as she searched for a clear shot at the men who grappled with her brother's corpse. It seemed she could not bring herself to risk shooting her brother, no matter that he would not feel the bullet. At last, as Kreiner struggled to distract Harries, Baker managed to slip the two sticks of dynamite he held into Harries's jacket pocket. With Kreiner's help he was able almost to break free of the dead grip before Catherine shot him.

The bullet caught Baker in the back as he pulled clear of Harries, exposed. The force of the shot knocked him back at the living corpse just as a second bullet – the twin of the first – cracked into the back of his head and the burly sergeant crashed to the floor, sliding down Harries's blackened form, his uniform as bloodied and torn as his head. Kreiner leaped aside, diving behind an armchair as Catherine's arm swung round to cover him too.

The attack seemed to have brought Harries completely under Catherine's influence again after his earlier hesitation and he turned to face us, his sister watching, smiling. Kreiner was for the moment forgotten. Stratford and Susan were on the chaise longue, and Catherine ignored them too. For the moment. The Doctor and I moved backwards as Harries advanced until I could feel the mantel shelf pressed coldly against my shoulder blades. There was nowhere left to go, except up the chimney again, and then Harries would merely reach up and pull us back down into the fireplace.

The Doctor turned away, searching the wall for impossible escape.

'Hopkinson,' he hissed and I turned to follow his gaze along the mantelpiece. To escape – perhaps.

Harries was still several paces away as I realised what the Doctor had meant. I reached out slowly, hoping not to alarm Catherine into shooting. After an age, a step of Harries's in fact, my fingers closed on the warm base of the oil lamp, and with as fast and fluid a motion as I could achieve I gripped and hurled it.

The lamp shattered on Harries's chest, oil spilling down his body. Catherine watched horrified, petrified, as the pool of flame spread and ran down towards the jacket pocket. Harries himself seemed not to notice the fire and lurched closer to us, his body enveloped by the yellow tongues, the remains of his mouth and hair blurring until everything was scarlet hot. His stained clothes burned easily away from his ripped torso despite the snow. The remaining skin on his face crawled away from the fire, curling back from the glistening bone beneath, the flames bubbling into his mouth and nose and eyes.

There was a sizzle as the fuse caught, followed by a deafening roar as the dynamite exploded, hurling us back against the fireplace and rocking Catherine back on her heels. Harries's right arm, complete up to the elbow, landed at her feet. It was the only recognisable part of him left intact apart from the head.

Catherine screamed, in anger as much as in fear or surprise, and the skull of her long-dead brother came to rest against the piled furniture at the window, flames licking out of the sockets that had contained his eyes, and melted flesh rolling like tears down the stripped cheekbones. Then the fire died and the skull toppled on to its side.

Baker's death will always be with me. Time after time it replays itself in my mind, as constant and as faithful as Baker was himself. I torture myself with the thought that his death could have been avoided. If I had done *this*, if *that* had happened, then Baker might still be alive. But somewhere deep inside myself I believe that everything that happened to us was ordained by something that took no account of our free will. His death was a function of his life. If Baker had not done what he did he would still be alive, but if he had not done what he did he would not have been Baker. I can honestly say that Baker was one of the bravest and most unselfish men I have ever met. All through the affair he displayed both his rock-solid common sense and a disregard for his own life in the face of danger.

It was these things that brought him down, of course. Only he out of all of us was clear-headed enough to remember the dynamite during the struggle against Richard Harries. Only he was foolhardy enough to try using it. His reward was quick in coming. Two bullets, enough not only to kill him but also to render him unrecognisable when I turned him over. Oh yes, I owed him that much. Despite the gun in Catherine Harries's hand I crawled over to the sergeant's sprawled body. Everything had happened so quickly that I could not be sure he was dead. The raw mask of muscle and bone that stared up at me made me look away in disgust, but in my mind it is always his honest, sweating face I see when I turn the body over.

It was a long time after his death that I realised that I did not know Baker's first name. It would have been easy to check through the police records, but I never tried. I had thought of him for so long as just 'Baker' that anything else would have seemed an intrusion. There was so much about him that I did not know. It didn't matter. I had the measure of the man.

I wondered as I sat there, crouched over Baker's body, how

Catherine would react. The shock of finally killing someone herself rather than using her brother to do the dirty work might have been disturbing. When I looked up I saw that her thoughts were on something else entirely. Catherine Harries's gaze was fixed upon the remnants of her brother's head by the French windows. Tears streamed unheeded down her cheeks as the tongues of flame licked around the skull, blackening and cracking the bone until it looked as though it had been roughly hewn out of oak. While Susan lay unconscious on the chaise longue, Hopkinson, Catherine and I watched the flames die down and the smoke issuing from the eye sockets thin out and vanish in the pale of the approaching dawn.

Catherine's gaze moved from the skull and travelled round the room, where the small pieces of her brother lay charred and lifeless. Eventually her wandering eyes fastened upon the arm that lay at her feet, by some ghastly chance the only complete segment of Richard Harries that existed. A sob broke through her self-control.

'What have you done?' she whispered. 'Oh my God, what have you done?' The gun wavered in her hands, the gun that had snuffed out Baker's life. I could see Hopkinson and the Doctor tensing, ready to leap for it and bring Catherine down. Unfortunately she could feel it too. The gun swung up to cover them, then wavered unsteadily between Hopkinson, the Doctor, Fitz and me.

'You'll pay for this,' she spat.

'For what?' asked the Doctor in a reasonable voice.

'For killing my brother. For killing the only person I ever loved.'

'Sergeant Baker destroyed him, Catherine. And you've already killed Baker.'

'But you would have tried,' she whispered. 'You all wanted him dead. You hated him: all of you. Hated him enough to kill him.'

'That's not true,' said the Doctor calmly. I could see what he was trying to do. Catherine Harries was too overwrought to be expected to act rationally. He was trying to calm her down by talking slowly and reasonably and attempting to engage her in a discussion. Now that she didn't have her brother as a blunt instrument to carry out her desires it was possible that we could talk her into handing over the gun.

Barely possible…

'You were jealous of Richard,' she hissed. 'All of you. You couldn't match his intelligence so you destroyed him.' The fire of madness burned in her eyes.

'He destroyed himself,' I said. 'His experiment went wrong. You're overwrought, Catherine. Put the gun down and we can talk about this reasonably. What do you say?'

'You're a fool, Inspector, if you think I'll give you the chance to disarm me. You think I'm mad? No, for the first time I know what reality is.' She glanced over at the Doctor, who was leaning casually against the fireplace. 'You were right when you guessed that contact had been made between Richard and me. But you didn't know, you couldn't know, how beautiful it was.'

'You might be surprised,' the Doctor said.

'We were in total communion. I was Richard and he was me. We knew each other in the most intimate way possible. He took me out of myself and showed me an entirely new way of looking at things.' Her eyes transfixed me, pleading with me. 'You can't understand, Inspector, with your world of reports and eyewitness statements and files. Nor you, John, with your cross-examinations, your trials and your verdicts. You both think you can pin down the truth like a butterfly and say, "There it is. In front of me, the truth." You can never understand.'

The gun wavered as Catherine punctuated her statements with gestures from her left hand. 'No one person can look at things objectively, but with Richard's eyes I saw two sides of everything. And it was as if until then things had just been made of card. Nothing had any depth until Richard and I shared our minds. Then it all sprang into sharp relief. Oh, you can't understand – I knew. I knew the truth about everything!'

The Doctor glanced over at me. 'Always grateful for a rough analogy,' he muttered, then turned to Catherine.

'Was it worth it?' he asked. 'Look around you. Your brother is scattered all about the room, and five other people are dead due to this obsessive quest for reality. You and Richard systematically blackmailed and murdered your way through your friends to finance his experiments and to protect his name. Was it really worth it?'

Catherine bowed her head and then looked up at Hopkinson. 'Have you ever wondered if human beings have some sort of self-destructive urge?' she asked, apparently at a tangent to the conversation. 'Why do people go on drinking too much, or taking drugs, or hurting themselves emotionally? Even falling in love is hurtful, but everybody does it. According to Richard there's something in everybody that needs pleasing for a short time, the shorter the time and the more intense the pleasure, the better. And this thing in people doesn't care about what happens eventually. Richard used to say it had no sense of *time*, only of the *now*.'

'Everything in moderation,' the Doctor said.

Catherine surprised us all by turning what we assumed was some insane rambling back to the conversation again. 'That's what Richard had, do you see? The shortest, the most intense gratification he could possibly have. And it didn't matter what happened to him after that. He didn't care. So the answer is yes, Doctor. It was worth it. We would do it again, if we could go back and choose.'

That is when I think we all realised there was no hope. Catherine Harries, like her brother before her, was completely and utterly mad. They could both discard the feelings and the lives of the people who had perished in their lunatic quest for an untouchable, indescribable concept they couldn't even define. Quite, quite mad.

Slowly, under cover of pretending to adjust my sling, I glanced at Susan on the chaise longue. A look from her frightened eyes told me all I needed to know; she was awake and had heard most of the conversation. She knew that her only hope was to keep quiet.

Catherine had not noticed my glance: she was too busy trying to screw up the courage to shoot us in cold blood. Baker had been easy: he had attacked her brother. Hopkinson and I were just waiting. That was what all Catherine's talking was for. To get herself into a state where she could gun us down.

Fitz straightened up from behind the chair, steeling himself for a sudden leap at Catherine. I tensed as well, ready to support him, but a warning glance from the Doctor caused him to subside. I did not know what the Doctor was planning, but I had to assume it was better than Kreiner's suicidal attack.

'We were perfect,' Catherine was saying to the Doctor, 'Richard and I, perfect. Then his head was turned.' Bitterness wormed its way into her voice. 'He met her and she took him away from me.'

The gun gestured towards Susan, and Catherine suddenly realised that she was awake. I could see Hopkinson tense, ready to protect Susan if necessary.

'You took him away from me,' Catherine repeated, her voice harder and glittering now. She had found the key, the emotion that would allow her to kill us – all of us. That key was jealousy. 'He said he loved you, but he didn't – he couldn't. He only loved me.'

'No,' said Susan, standing up from the chaise longue. Her voice was strong and calm, and I felt very proud of her. 'He did love me, and I loved him and it was a pure love, not the twisted unhealthy feeling that you held for him.'

'No!' screamed Catherine. 'It's not true.'

'Remember how he hesitated – how he wouldn't kill me?' Susan said. Her dark hair seemed to have become a shimmering red in the pale light 'He loved me too much. Even dead, he still loved me.'

'It's true,' said Hopkinson, joining the attack. 'He turned on you when you ordered him to kill Susan.'

'He loved her more than he loved you,' I said, just loud enough for her to hear.

We were closing from three sides, Hopkinson, the Doctor and I. Catherine did not know which way to turn. The gun wavered between the three of us, crossing Susan each time it oscillated. We were playing a very dangerous game – one that we lost as Catherine Harries snapped. The gun unerringly came to rest pointed at Susan's stomach. Catherine screamed an unintelligible stream of words as her finger tensed on the trigger.

She took a step backwards as she prepared to fire. The movement brought her foot into contact with the severed arm. As Catherine's foot touched the dead fingers, the white bone and bloody tendons that were all that remained of the hand fastened vicelike on her ankle. A reflex. She looked disbelievingly down at her brother's dismembered arm and screamed and screamed and screamed. Then an explosion tore the air as she blasted chunks of flesh and clothing from the arm with Wallace's gun.

Hopkinson and I both leaped at Catherine Harries. She swung the gun, catching me on the shoulder. I fell, almost fainting with the pain, to the carpet. Looking up I could see Hopkinson grappling with Catherine in a wild dance of death while the Doctor attempted to wrest the gun from her hand. Fitz had crossed the room and flung himself in front of Susan, protecting her with his body.

Then there was a single shot.

For a long moment the three of them stood there. Catherine

looked up at Hopkinson's eyes; he gazed down at her face. The Doctor's gaze was fixed on her, and the expression on his face was tragic. Then she stepped back. There was blood on Hopkinson's shirt, his jacket, his hands. Catherine held the crimson-splattered gun. She looked down at the spreading stain on her dress. I don't know who was more surprised at her wound – Catherine or Hopkinson. Only the Doctor seemed to have been expecting it.

She fell to the ground like a floating leaf. The Doctor bent down over her body. After a while he looked over at me and shook his head.

'He tried to save her…' murmured Catherine, staring up at the ceiling, or beyond. 'He wanted to save her.'

'No,' the Doctor said reassuringly, 'he was trying to save you from yourself.'

Catherine's face seemed to glow. 'Yes,' she said, 'he did love me. He did love me after all.'

Something went out of Catherine Harries then. Nothing changed in her gaze, her position or her expression, but we all knew that she died after she said those words.

THE ACCOUNT OF JOHN HOPKINSON (24)

Susan was still very shaky and she clung to my shoulder for support. I put my arm around her waist to help her stand. Did she respond? I wanted to think so, but then I have always been incurably romantic.

'We wanted to stop her,' I murmured, looking down again at Catherine's inert form, as much to myself as to Stratford or Susan. 'She tried to kill us all.' Susan held my arm tighter.

'It was she who pulled the trigger,' the Doctor said quietly just behind us.

'I know,' Susan whispered, not wanting Stratford to hear.

Ian Stratford straightened up from his brief examination of Catherine Harries's body, the blood from her side seeping and sinking into the carpet. 'She committed suicide after killing the others,' he said briskly. 'Her brother's death in a tragic accident unhinged her.'

'Is that what you will say in your report?' Kreiner asked him.

'Yes. It's about all I can say really.'

'Yes,' I agreed. 'Thank you.'

I looked down at Catherine again – so still, so pale, so peaceful. And the charred mess of her brother.

'This dead butcher and his fiendlike queen,' the Doctor declaimed to the room at large. 'Who, as 'tis thought, by self and violent hands Took off her life...' Then suddenly, in another of those swings of mood with which I was becoming familiar, he was serious again. 'Right,' he announced, 'let's hope we still have time.'

'Time?' Stratford asked.

'Before they get here. Before we lose her completely. Before whatever cancellation field she's able to project folds up and disappears.' He spoke as if we should all understand what he was saying. But Stratford and I stared blankly at one another and Susan shook her head in plain and evident incredulity.

Only Kreiner seemed to grasp the meaning of the Doctor's urgency, or perhaps he was humouring the man. 'Where do we start?' he asked.

'Where does a butler spend his time?' the Doctor countered.

'In the butler's pantry,' Stratford immediately responded.

The Doctor clicked his fingers. 'Exactly. No time to lose, then.' And he was off.

Kreiner followed him immediately. The rest of us – Susan, Stratford and I – exchanged another confused look, and then set off after them.

The Doctor and Kreiner were already rummaging through the bits and pieces on the wide shelf when we joined them.

'I wouldn't have thought he'd leave it unlocked,' Fitz was saying.

'No Artron energy for the timonics,' the Doctor muttered to himself as he leafed through a pile of outstanding bills and invoices. Neither of them seemed to notice us crowded into the doorway. So partly to draw their attention and partly to escape the crush, I went and lifted the bottle of port that I had been holding when Simpson had found me trespassing in his domain before. I didn't care whether it was crusted or not, I was going to drink it.

Kreiner was looking about himself now, his eyes searching high and low for... something. 'You know, Doctor,' he said, 'this place is bigger inside than out.' He said it as if this was a significant discovery.

I laughed at his naïveté. 'Of course it is,' I told him. 'All butlers' pantries are like that.'

'Mmm,' the Doctor said. He did not sound convinced. Then he saw me holding the bottle and his whole attitude changed. 'Ancillary generator, of course!' he declared and fairly leaped across the room. 'May I?' He lifted the bottle carefully from my grip without waiting for an answer.

'Oh, be my guest,' I said as I watched him pull the cork.

'It'll be quantum-field generation or some such non-Artron source,' he said. The cork emerged from the bottle with a pop and the Doctor swung round to survey the room.

We all looked round. Nobody said anything for several moments. I cleared my throat. It seemed to me that several objects I had previously seen in the room were no longer there. But I put this down to my memory of my last visit and being somewhat tired. 'What are you looking for?' I asked.

'If we knew, we could help,' Susan offered. She still looked pale and I was irritated to see that she and Stratford seemed to be supporting each other in the doorway.

'You don't know?' the Doctor asked. He was worried now.

She shook her head and gave a short, high, nervous laugh. 'I really have no idea.'

The Doctor's mouth worked soundlessly for a few seconds. 'I don't know what to say,' he eventually managed.

'Bugger?' suggested Kreiner.

'Could be,' the Doctor agreed. 'Could be.' He shook his head. 'I thought, I really thought... Never mind,' he decided. 'Must have its own power source.'

My mind floated back to the weird conversation between the Doctor and the dying Simpson. 'Something Simpson hid from you?' I asked.

'Indeed.'

'Well, if it isn't in here...' I looked round again. 'I'm afraid I haven't read any... what was his name?'

The Doctor's palm slapped into his forehead. 'Of course. Where would you hide a tree?'

I stared at him.

'In a wood,' Stratford said from behind me.

'Or a forest. Exactly.' The Doctor was wandering round the small room again now. Was it my imagination or was it even smaller now than it had been when we came in. Somehow we all seemed to be standing closer together. 'The trouble is,' the Doctor said, 'we don't really know what the tree looks like.'

'Can we make an educated guess?' Kreiner asked. 'Meaning can *you*?'

'Something that wouldn't look out of place in the period,' the Doctor said. He tapped his chin with his index finger as he considered. 'Wouldn't want to use up a lot of its limited power by altering the form too much. A sophisticated electrical component of some sort perhaps?'

'Nothing like that here,' Kreiner said.

'Except Harries's equipment,' Stratford offered. 'It's in the study.'

'That's right,' I agreed. 'I could see one of the valves glowing still when we were sneaking out earlier. I suppose –' But I got no further. The Doctor and Kreiner had both pushed past me and were already out of the door.

'Is it just me,' Stratford asked slowly, 'or are we missing something important?' There was a bang as the study door was slammed.

'I think if anyone's missing something important...' I began. But again I stopped. Susan suddenly gave a shriek of pain and collapsed to the floor.

'What is it? What's wrong?' Stratford immediately helped her up and out of the small room back into the corridor. I joined them and together we guided her to the dining room and sat her on a chair by the table. As we went, I realised she was no longer limping.

When she looked up, the change in the woman was startling. She seemed to have recovered her strength. Her eyes were shining and bright, deep whirlpools of experience.

'Are you all right?' I asked her, concerned more than I care to recall.

She tilted her head slightly to one side as she replied, as if amused by the question. 'Obviously,' she said.

'Ah, there you are.' The Doctor strode into the room, Kreiner close on his heels. He too looked at Susan. 'Feeling yourself again, I trust?' He held the shattered remains of a valve, and tapped the metal base against his palm as he spoke. Several shards of smoky glass still clung to it.

'You could say that, yes,' Susan replied. Her voice seemed harsh suddenly.

'Excellent.' The Doctor clapped his hands together in delight.

'Can we leave, then?' Kreiner asked wearily. I got the impression the weariness was part of an act.

'Better ask Comp– er, the young lady,' the Doctor told him. Then he turned to me and Stratford. 'It's been such fun,' he said. 'A delight. In parts.' He grasped my hand, then Stratford's. 'We live and learn,' he said. 'If we're lucky, that is. Now, I hope you won't think us rude, but perhaps you'd be kind enough to wait outside just for a moment.'

'I beg your pardon?' Stratford said. I was too surprised to say anything.

'I'm sorry I can't explain,' the Doctor said gently, as if to children. 'But if you could give the three of us a minute or two. Please.'

He ushered us out of the room. I caught sight of Susan's face as she watched us leave. If she had given the slightest hint of anxiety or suspicion I would have objected, but she seemed calm and relaxed. And after all, where could they go?

'What's all that about?' Stratford wondered as we stepped out into the corridor.

My reply was drowned out by the noise. I have never heard anything like it. A rasping, throaty cacophony of sound that seemed to be in competition with its own echo as it built and built and then simply faded away.

Stratford and I did not hesitate. We ran back into the room. The Doctor and Herr Kreiner were gone. Impossibly, they

268

were no longer in the room. I even looked under the table. Susan was sitting where we had left her, but her expression was one of wide-eyed surprise. She looked from Stratford to me and back again.

'Where have they gone?' Stratford demanded.

She shook her head in confusion. 'My memory,' she gasped.

'Amnesia? The shock perhaps?' I said.

'It's not unusual,' Stratford told her gently.

'No, no,' she said. 'You don't understand. I haven't lost my memory. It's...' She struggled towards the right word. 'It's changed. I remember such strange things. Things that I know are impossible. Have never happened. Could never have happened.' She got unsteadily to her feet, and took a limping step towards us, wary of her bad ankle.

'Where did they go?' Stratford asked again. 'Do you know that?'

'Oh yes,' she said quietly. 'That I do know.' She looked at me, smiling weakly. 'In my dreams. But I must never tell.'

I let Susan take my hand and she led me shakily into the hall, Stratford following behind us. I could sense Susan looking up at me and I returned her faint, sad smile, squeezing her waist slightly. We waited as Stratford closed the door, and then followed him out towards the pale light of dawn.

THE REPORT OF INSPECTOR IAN STRATFORD (24)

I felt sad and alone when we walked out of Banquo Manor. Hopkinson and Susan stood hand in hand, basking in the light of the dawn sun. All I knew was if I turned round I would see my shadow stretching back into the house. It was difficult to believe that it was over. It was harder to believe that it had ever happened.

Even now, as I reread these words in the comfort and distance that hindsight affords, I find it difficult to pin down my motives for writing this account – an account longer and more detailed than required by Chief Inspector Driscoll. Publication is out of the question, but I must have had some reason. I think deep down that Catherine may have been right. I do need there to be a truth. A single, simple reality that does not change depending on which person is viewing the matter. This account, as far as I am able to see it, is the truth.

I returned to the detail of police work fit in body, if not in mind. That should have been the end of it, but now I hear that I am being considered for a new post – the head of a special Scotland Yard squad set up to deal with incidents that transcend the normal and enter the realms of horror. I may protest that the last thing I need is to be reminded of what happened to me, but it will do no good. I have experience of these things now. My sanity is as nothing compared with my usefulness to the police force.

Such is the legacy of Banquo Manor.

I remember asking John Hopkinson if he thought he had changed as a result of our experiences.

He thought for a moment, then took his glasses off. 'Yes, I believe so,' he replied. 'Before I went to the Manor I was incurably romantic. My dreams were always better than reality, and I hated reality for not living up to my expectations. What we went through brought me down to earth. It made me adopt a more realistic outlook. What about you?'

'I've always been a pragmatist,' I said after a moment. 'I always believed that if a thing couldn't be proved or demonstrated then it didn't exist. If Banquo Manor – if the presence of the Doctor – taught me anything it taught me that there is room for unreality as well as reality in the world. Some things can't be proven, only accepted.'

'More things in Heaven and Earth…' said Hopkinson, laughing.

'Wrong play,' I muttered, and we moved on to more comfortable subjects.

I seem to have got ahead of myself, an easy thing to do when I cannot tear my mind away from the events of those few days. The three of us left the Manor, as I have said. Somehow I could not face standing in the dawn light with Hopkinson and Susan. It seemed too much like an intrusion. I turned and walked off, around the corner of the house. I doubt whether they even saw me go.

For a while I wandered around the outside of Banquo Manor, committing its bizarre façade, its strange, non-Euclidean angles, to my memory. The house was as much a character in the drama as Richard Harries, Sergeant Baker or Simpson (whether he was merely the butler or, as the Doctor had seemed to imply, something much more besides). I could not imagine the same events occurring elsewhere.

Talking of Simpson, I came at last to the area beneath John Hopkinson's room, where Susan Seymour had sprained her ankle during their ill-fated escape attempt and where Simpson had fallen, blinded, to his death. There was no sign of his body. Somehow, I was not surprised. During the previous thirty-six hours I had been exposed to two corpses that had come back to life – Richard Harries's and the Doctor's – and seen two people disappear from a small room without leaving through the door. How could I have expected the mystery to end there? I refused to speculate on whether Richard Harries or his sister had removed the body for their own macabre purposes,

271

whether Simpson himself had crawled away to die again in the woods or whether this Romana character who seemed so important to the Doctor and to Simpson had come to repatriate the corpse. I knew I would never know the true answer.

I re-entered the house through the kitchen. Like a ghost, I moved through its many rooms, but my footsteps were drawn back to the scene of the final confrontation between us all. Baker lay flat on his back where I had turned him, staring at the ceiling with his ruined face. Catherine Harries lay curled on her side. She looked so calm that she might have been asleep. Only the pool of blood soaking into the carpet gave her away. And there, over by the windows, lay the last intact piece of Richard Harries: his burned and pitted skull. I stared at it for a long moment –

And felt myself go numb with horror as something moved inside. My skin began to crawl as if it had taken on a life of its own. I could not tear my eyes away. There, within the shadowed oval of the eye socket, something moved.

A brown furry snout peered blindly from the hole. Two tiny red eyes appeared, gazing inquisitively around the room. Finally a pair of pink forepaws clutched at the lower rim.

Behind the skull something flicked into sight. It was a fat, pink tail moving restlessly from side to side. Its owner appeared from around the other side of the skull. It was a rat, the mate of the one inside the cranial cavity.

Richard Harries's rats had found a new home at last – within the cage of his skull.

Closure

Finale: 1968

'In my dreams, sometimes, I am still her.' Susan Seymour had slumped back and was staring at the dimly distant ceiling. There was a cobweb in the corner. The spider was long dead.

The tap-tap scratching was a background now, a counterpoint to her memories as she talked. The figure beside the bed was absolute stillness as he read and listened. When he had finished reading, he still listened.

'It was strange when she left me. A wrench. In every sense. I felt her torn from me, as if a part of myself had gone. Not just some tenant within my head, my body. A joint owner. Sister, perhaps.' Her voice was weak and dry from the talking. From the memories. 'They'll bring the tea soon, won't they? I could feel them within me. I could see them. The Doctor standing at my centre, working his hands over the controls. Familiar, but strange.'

The figure's head snapped up. 'You see him?' the throaty rasp demanded.

'In my mind's eye.'

'What is he doing? Do you know? Can you see?'

She squinted at the distant ceiling, tried to untangle the blurred, hazy web. 'He is setting the…' Her head rolled slightly on the pillow. 'Randomiser? Is that it?'

The figure was leaning over her now. Rancid breath hot against her dry face. 'What is the setting? Can you see the setting?'

'I… I'm not sure. Let me concentrate…' She looked him in the face. In the empty spaces where his eyes should be. 'Is it important?'

'Without the seed,' he croaked, 'their destination, their route through the vortex, is indeed random. Unknown and unknowable. We can use temporal quantum theory to predict their possible destinations. We can narrow the options to the most likely with a probability-projection matrix. But that still leaves thousands. Too many to intercept them.'

His clawlike hand gripped her shoulder. 'Think!' he hissed. 'Think! An interception must be precise. Not like scattering agents across the most probable quantum locations. Not like waiting for one of a thousand to signal his success.' His grip relaxed slightly. 'If you can tell me the random seed setting the Doctor used when he left you, then I will not yet have failed.' He stepped away from the bed. 'The years, the waiting, the pain. They will not have been for nothing. If…'

A sigh from the bed. Slowly, almost painfully, she exhaled long and slow.

'You know it.'

'Yes,' she breathed. Then, hesitantly, 'It is for the best. Isn't it?'

'Everything is for the best,' he assured her. 'In time.'

He dropped the manuscripts back into the drawer of the cabinet. There was a deadness in the sound of their landing, a finality in the drawer sliding home. But her attention was on neither. Her eyes were fixed, watching the movement on the top of the cabinet, as she told him what he wanted to know.

'Thank you,' he breathed when she was done. He leaned forward slightly, and she pressed her head back into the pillow, afraid for one terrible moment that he was about to kiss her.

But he was leaning towards the cabinet. Cuthbert Simpson held out his hands for the rats, and they scuttled into his open palms, their claws clicking on the surface of the cabinet in their skidding hurry, segmented tails curling and twitching as they nestled in. He straightened up, placing each of the creatures in a pocket of his torn jacket.

One of them peered over the top of the pocket, its nose testing the air as its eyes showed him the way to the door.

He paused in the doorway, once again framed in the amber

light from outside. Susan Seymour could just make out his movement as he pulled something from inside his jacket. It looked like a pack of cards. Except that they were square. He seemed to be lining them up along their edges, forming them into a shape. A box. She knew instinctively, as if from some memory or knowledge that was not her own, what he was doing. What it meant.

'It is all for the best,' she whispered to herself as she let her eyes close and the dreams take over once again.

Simpson stepped out into the corridor. He felt no elation, no satisfaction at the completion of his task. Others could worry about the morality and the consequences: he had only to live with them. As the door clicked shut behind him, the plain three-inch cube that rested on his open palm coughed and wheezed and disappeared. His task was complete, at last. At long last. He could go home now. If they – if she – would have him. He started down the corridor.

It was the last thing he never did.

About the Authors

Over the past ten years Andy Lane's writing career has flitted erratically between TV tie-in novels, TV novelisations, short stories, scripts, non-fiction books and, tragically, trading cards. He hopes to write something using his own characters one day.

Over the past ten years Justin Richards's writing career has flitted erratically between magazine articles, technical manuals and help text, short stories, scripts, non-fiction books and, happily, no trading cards whatsoever. He hopes to write something that really makes a lot of money one day.

PRESENTING

DOCTOR WHO

ALL-NEW AUDIO DRAMAS

Big Finish Productions is proud to present all-new *Doctor Who* adventures on audio!

Featuring original music and sound-effects, these full-cast plays are available on double cassette in high street stores, and on limited-edition double CD from all good specialist stores, or via mail order.

Available from June 2000
THE SPECTRE OF LANYON MOOR

A four-part story by Nicholas Pegg.
Starring **Colin Baker** as the Doctor
and **Maggie Stables** as Dr Evelyn Smythe.

*In a desolate Cornish landscape littered with relics of prehistoric man,
the Doctor and Evelyn uncover a catalogue of mysteries.*

*What is the secret of the fogou? Can the moor be haunted by a demonic host of imps?
And what is Brigadier Lethbridge-Stewart doing in Pengriffen?
Teaming up with his friend, the Doctor realises that an ancient conflict
is nearing its conclusion – and Lanyon Moor is set to be the final battleground.*

If you wish to order the CD version, please photocopy this form or provide all the details on paper. Delivery within 28 days of release.
Send to: PO Box 1127, Maidenhead, Berkshire. SL6 3LN.
Big Finish Hotline 01628 828283.

Please send me [ ] copies of *The Spectre of Lanyon Moor*
each @ £13.99 (£15.50 non-UK orders) Prices inclusive of postage and packing.
Payment can be accepted by credit card or by personal cheques, payable to Big Finish Productions Ltd.
Name...
Address...
....
Postcode...
VISA/Mastercardnumber ....
Expiry date...
Signature..

Other stories featuring the Sixth Doctor still available include:

WHISPERS OF TERROR   THE MARIAN CONSPIRACY

For more details visit our website at
http://www.doctorwho.co.uk

THE MONTHLY TELEPRESS
The official BBC Doctor Who books e-newsletter

News – competitions – interviews – and more!

Subscribe today at
http://www.onelist.com/group/Telepress